Also by Nero Blanc . . .

A CROSSWORDER'S HOLIDAY
Five short mystery tales for a long winter's night with
crosswords included . . . plus a bonus recipe!

A CROSSWORD TO DIE FOR

NERO BLANC

BERKLEY PRIME CRIME, NEW YORK

This is a work of fiction. Names, characters, places, and incidents either are the product of the author's imagination or are used fictitiously, and any resemblance to actual persons, living or dead, business establishments, events, or locales is entirely coincidental.

A CROSSWORD TO DIE FOR

A Berkley Prime Crime Book / published by arrangement with the authors

PRINTING HISTORY
Berkley Prime Crime trade paperback edition / July 2002
Berkley Prime Crime mass-market edition / June 2003

ISBN: 0-425-19075-7

A Letter from Nero Blanc

Dear Reader,

Who is Nero Blanc? Many of you have asked us this question.

We chose the *nom de plume* because of its crossword connection: *nero* being black in Italian, and *blanc* being white in French. The words are also favorites with many puzzle constructors.

Writing the Nero Blanc series is a dream come true for us. Like our protagonists, Belle and Rosco, we find working together a true pleasure. We love the surprises that arise when creating mystery novels, and hope you do, too.

And we always enjoy hearing from you! We invite you to send your messages through our web site, www.crosswordmysteries.com, where you'll find information about other Nero Blanc books as well as original puzzles.

Happy solving and sleuthing,
Cordelia and Steve
AKA
Nero Blanc

Every man is as Heaven made him,
and sometimes a great deal worse.

—Cervantes

CHAPTER

1

"Oh, yes, ma'am . . . On this train? Are you kidding? I've seen just about everything that can come down the tracks . . . No pun intended . . ." John Markoe turned his hefty frame sideways, allowing a lanky and large-footed teenager in a Celtics' tank top to pass. The narrow center aisle of the Amtrak car hadn't been designed for people of John's girth, and the act of twisting his body sideways had little effect on how much space he consumed.

"Yes, ma'am," he continued after the teen had squeezed by, "I've been a conductor on this Northeast Corridor run for twenty-three years now, and nothing surprises me anymore. Back in 'ninety-seven a woman gave birth to triplets . . . Just after we pulled out of New Haven. We had to clear the club car for her. Lucky we had a doctor on board or I guess I would've had to do the honors myself—"

"I think I read about that in the newspaper . . ." the woman chimed in. Her hair was dyed an aggressive ebony color, and her journey had been spent in detailing her life story to all and sundry until she'd worn out every ear around her. The conductor was her final target, but he was proving as voluble as she:

". . . I make it a habit to read both the local paper and the Boston—"

"Yes, ma'am . . . Big news. Right on election day, too—"

The woman opened her mouth, but the conductor continued without pausing for breath:

"Stole the headlines in the Boston papers right out from under the pres-eee-dent-eee-lect." John Markoe wheezed slightly. "But it's something crazy on nearly every run. There's always some freeloader trying to get a complimentary ride; you know, beat the fare by complaining about this or that? Or trying to hide in the can . . . And, of course, we get the pickpockets and the weirdies. But if you've been working for this line as long as I have, you develop a nose for them, a kind of sixth sense . . . Oh, yes, and an engine slammed into a pickup truck once, and a cow another time . . . That was about fifteen years ago. No cows around these parts anymore . . . Winter it was when that particular event took place. Remember when we had three major blizzards in as many years? Ninety-three inches in total?"

The slowing of the engine returned John's thoughts to the job at hand. He checked his watch. "Yes in-deed-dee, right on time . . . Early, actually . . . Yes, ma'am, nothing surprises me anymore."

"Is this Boston already?" the woman asked. "I'm visiting my son up there, you know. He's a doc—" She was about to say more, but again John curtailed her speech.

"Oh, no, ma'am. This next station stop will be Newcastle,

Massachusetts. Boston won't be for another thirty minutes or so, so you can relax."

"I've never visited Newcastle, but I've heard that the city is quite a—"

"A pleasure to be of service, ma'am." John Markoe turned to face the front of the train, raised his voice, and barked to the carload of passengers, "Newcastle! Newcastle! Our next station stop will be Newcastle, Massachusetts. This way out, please!"

He strolled along the aisle, pulling Newcastle ticket stubs from the metal clips that adorned the overhead luggage racks, all the while announcing: "Please use the rear door out, folks. The front door will not open at this station stop. I repeat: The front door will not open at this station."

The train began chugging to a crawl, allowing passengers on the harbor-front side of the cars a sweeping view of the river and distant bay that led down into the Atlantic Ocean. Fishing boats, oceangoing tugs, and pleasure craft bobbed in water now suddenly grown dark and squally while the sky was turning equally black and ominous with rain.

A smattering of warning drops flung themselves against the windows as passengers waiting to detrain began grabbing bags, suitcases, children, and attaché cases as they rushed to avoid what seemed an imminent deluge.

"Take your time, folks! Take your time! No one's going to leave without you!"

Those still seated on the station side of the track watched the massive brick edifice loom into view. Designed by H. H. Richardson, the master of midnineteenth-century baroque-revival architecture, the hulking station house had the peculiar distinction of affording shelter only to southbound passengers. Those disembarking on the northbound, shore-ward lane had to stand beside the track and wait until every rail car departed for Boston before crossing to the twin-turreted and multidormered building. Rain and snow—neither one a rarity in New England—often made the transition to the dry comfort of the interior waiting room a trial.

"This way out, folks! Taxis are across the platform at the station. Seating areas across the platform." John opened the coach's sliding door and lowered the metal steps to meet the wooden platform. A group of fifteen or twenty passengers, luggage in hand, waited anxiously to board. The wind had begun whipping around them, forcing several to lunge for summer hats, and several more to brace themselves against the sudden blasts.

"Please stand back, folks," John ordered in his stentorian tone. "Let's let the arrivals off, shall we? No one's going any-where without you!"

The sky was now inky, and those gathered to entrain so tightly clustered that the new arrivals could hardly fight their way down onto the platform.

"Folks! Folks! A little elbowroom . . . ! Let the passengers through! Boston! Boston! Plenty of seats to your right."

Boarding finished, the conductor lugged his weighty body back up the steps, waved to the engineer, and shut the sliding door. Within a minute the train was rolling again, and the rain already driving at the hurrying metal and glass. Those seated nearest the windows drew back reflexively as if the storm were capable of entering the carriage. Overhead read-ing lights flickered on, and a sudden sizzle of lightning rent the sky.

"Oh my," said the chatty lady to the group in general. "I hope we all brought umbrellas."

Positioning himself at the rear of the car, John pulled his punch from his belt and called out the familiar, "Tickets. Tickets, please. The next station stop will be Back Bay Boston. Boston, Massachusetts, next station stop. All doors open in Boston . . . Tickets, please."

He worked his way down the aisle, removing Boston-bound stubs from the overhead as he inspected and punched the tickets of the passengers who had boarded in Newcastle.

About halfway down the car, the conductor spotted a man sleeping unconcernedly, his head resting against the window, and his sports jacket carefully folded into a square pillow shape. John glanced at the metal clip on the luggage rack above the peaceful figure but found no ticket stub—meaning one of two things: someone had taken it by mistake, or more likely, the passenger had intended to detrain in Newcastle and missed the stop altogether.

The conductor bent across the aisle seat. "Sir? We've passed Newcastle, sir—"

The man didn't stir.

"Sir," John repeated in a louder voice, "we've passed Newcastle. If you intended to detrain there, you'll need to get off in Boston and take the next southbound train."

Still, the man refused to awaken, and John was reluctant to nudge him. Passengers roused from a deep sleep often made irritable riders. He bent down closer to the man's ear.

"Sir . . . ? We've passed Newcastle."

This had no effect. After a minute, John opted to give the man's shoulder a slight nudge. "Sir?"

Again, there was no reaction so John tried with more vigor. His efforts caused the passenger's head to roll to one side while his torso slumped forward and slammed onto the open tray table in front of him.

"Sir?" The conductor sat beside the man. "Sir? Are you all right . . . ?" He placed his hand on the man's wrist and checked for a pulse. Nothing. He moved to a vein in the man's neck.

"Dammit!" John pulled his walkie-talkie from his belt, and radioed the other conductor. "Herb, this is John, do you read me?"

A gravelly "Go ahead" crackled through the receiver.

"Herb, I think we've got a heart attack victim on Car Three."

"Oh, boy . . . Do you need some CPR up there?"

"No . . . This guy's a goner."

CHAPTER

2

Annabella Graham raced into the parking lot just in time to see the last car of Amtrak's Boston-bound train disappear down the track. She squinted her gray eyes in exasperation as she grabbed up her purse. *Of course, Amtrak would have to be on time for once!* she thought. And not only on time; by her watch it was positively early. She cursed herself for not arriving sooner even as she imagined the cutting critique she'd receive from her father: *The daughter who had failed to "achieve" her "potential" has failed again.*

Belle jumped out of her car, slammed the door, inadvertently locking her key in the ignition while, simultaneously, a vast zigzag of lightning slashed across the late afternoon sky. Thunder barreled and crashed in its wake; the air filled with wind-whipped water; and the river beyond the asphalt-covered parking lot churned itself into an angry dirt-black indicating a storm heading in from the Atlantic Ocean. Belle turned and ran for the station, but by the time she'd reached the passengers clustered beneath the protective awning on the southbound platform, she was drenched through. And her father was nowhere in sight.

She took a breath and sighed. It went without saying that Theodore A. Graham, former professor of anthropology at Princeton University, would have been one of the first travelers to detrain. He'd probably been gauging the storm's approach, velocity, and estimated moment of impact since the train had departed New Haven, Connecticut. Naturally, he'd now be anticipating his daughter's arrival while comfortably ensconced within the brick building's comforting walls. Let those who were unprepared, whose brains were scattered, and whose thinking was muzzy brave the elements! Dr. Graham would stay high and dry and very much in control.

Belle worked her way through the crowd, murmuring a diffident but edgy "Excuse me . . ." with nearly every step. Her tan sandals squelched with water, a new Indian-print skirt clung dismally to her calves, while tendrils of soaking blond hair sent frigid droplets down her neck. The bride of three months' time wasn't about to make a great impression on a father she hadn't seen in nearly a year. She tried to affix an enthusiastic smile, then pulled open the heavy door that led to the inside waiting area.

There, another throng of damp, disgruntled passengers shuffled to and fro. The storm's onslaught had delayed the southbound train and marooned many would-be travelers while the crowd whose journey had recently concluded were now encamped in the waiting room sitting out the worst of the rain before venturing outside to the parking lot or the taxi stand. The station house was packed.

Belle attempted a brighter smile and strode into its midst,

working her way toward the seating area near the building's west entrance.

No Theodore Graham tarried there, either.

She suppressed a grimace, and a sudden fit of pique. *Thanks a heap, Dad!* her brain began carping. *Another no-show! I suppose you missed your connecting train in New York . . . Or else we'll get a call from Florida tonight with an excuse about mixing up the days . . . or a back spasm that kept you in bed . . . and you're sorry you didn't phone sooner, but the doctor put you on pain medication and you plum forgot you had a date in New England . . .*

She shut her eyes tight; tears of sorrow and anger welled beneath her lids. *If my father doesn't want to visit; if he never chooses to meet my new husband; if the idea of Rosco's casualness—or his less than Ivy League education—annoys Father's finicky sense of perfection, then he didn't have to plan this trip!*

Belle yanked open the terminal doors and hurried to her car, unaware until she was thrusting her hand into her purse that her key was still in the ignition and the doors of the vehicle were locked. "Oh . . . oh . . . Honestly!" She clenched her teeth in frustration at her own disorganization.

Thoroughly chilled now despite the returning summer heat, she dragged herself back through the rain to the waiting room, where she considered her options. She could phone Rosco and explain her predicament—he'd definitely have another set of keys—or she could seek help from a stranger. Neither choice made her feel remotely capable or wise, but she decided upon the second alternative, wondering even as she went looking for a maintenance man to jimmy open her car window why it was so much more embarrassing to admit personal defeat to an unknown person than to someone you loved.

Brad was the name of her rescuer. He'd been in Newcastle only a couple of months, and was juggling two jobs in order to save enough money for college. He seemed like a nice kid—albeit one who was remarkably adept at gaining access to locked vehicles. Belle gave him a ten-dollar tip, which he greeted with an effusive: "Thanks, lady . . . ma'am . . . I mean it! Thanks a lot."

Belle tried for another smile, but found herself too cross or depressed or just plain aggravated to be successful.

Rosco was waiting on the porch as she pulled into the small drive of their home in Captain's Walk, an area that had once been the purview of eighteenth-century seafarers and that now housed three growing families, several "empty nesters," and another young couple like themselves who appreciated the eclectic mixture of historical integrity and quirky modernity. Her husband was wearing a brand-new shirt, pressed chinos, and shoes with socks—a true mark of his unease and awe at finally meeting his illustrious father-in-law. Belle found herself wondering how long he'd been waiting in this fashionable pose, and grinned despite her cranky humor. *Rosco in socks! Who would have thought it?* The gesture—and his entire outfit—filled her with a comfortable sense of belonging.

Beside him sat Kit, their "found" mongrel puppy. The two created a picture that was almost too good to be true: a charming New England town home, interior lights flickering through ancient windowpanes to illuminate an exterior wicker settee, an old-fashioned letter box, and porch floorboards painted a soothing, time-worn gray. Even the rain now seemed pleasant and serene: a happy injunction to stay inside.

"Where's your father?" Rosco called out while Belle hurried up the walkway.

"He either missed his connection in New York, or else he's still in Florida . . . I take it he didn't phone—"

"No one called . . . Not even my client . . . Surprise, surprise. But I should have known better than to sit around waiting for him to beam in."

Kit ran down the front steps to meet her mistress.

"Hi, Kitty . . . Ready for your supper?"

Rosco scrutinized his drenched wife as she ascended the stairs to the porch. "A wild guess . . . You locked your keys in your car again, didn't you?" His tone barely hid an amused and loving chuckle.

Belle stamped her wet feet, ran a hand through her dripping hair, then ruffled the dog's soft, brown ears. "I might have . . ."

Rosco squelched another urge to chortle. "I don't see why you refuse to keep a second set in your purse—"

Irritation at herself and the situation made her voice turn snappish. "But I'd only lose those, too, Rosco! You know I would! And pretty soon, the entire city would be awash in misplaced keys . . . No, what I need to do is start concentrating on one thing at a time . . . You know, finishing a task before beginning another. Keeping a schedule and writing things down . . . Learning how to be organized—"

This time Rosco laughed in earnest. "I hope you're not serious about that resolution."

"I am. Absolutely!"

His smile grew. "I tell you what, why don't you dry off,

call down to Florida, find out where your dad is, and then I'll take you out for dinner."

Belle gazed at him. "I still don't know why Father didn't bother to call. I mean, how difficult is that?"

"I'm sure he'll have an explanation."

She shook her head. "He was the one who suggested this visit . . . in order to 'atone for a lack of attendance at the May nuptials' . . . It's not that I was urging him to travel up North—"

"Belle . . . sweetheart . . . Families, what can I say? You're always telling *me* not to get bent out of shape by *my* loony relatives. Look how often *they* change plans in midstream."

She was silent a moment, then sighed again, although this time it was a sound of release. "Anything exciting happen while I was gone?"

"A bunch of crossword puzzle submissions were hand-delivered from your office at the *Crier*. I put the envelope on your desk."

Belle's expression turned rueful. "Sometimes, I wish I'd never started this project. Who knew that compiling a cross-word collection could be such an exercise in weirdness? You've seen some of those submissions, Rosco . . . Not that the major-ity of them aren't interesting and well constructed—"

He put his arms around her. "My suggestion is that you take the evening off, leave this newest envelope unopened, and I take you to dinner."

Belle looked up at him. "The Athena?"

"Why not? It's cheaper than going to Greece."

"Which you promise we're going to do someday—?"

Rosco put his hand on his heart. "Which I swear, on all my ancestors' heads, we will do someday . . . Even if it means I have to get on a boat again."

Nestled close, Belle sighed happily again. "I kind of hate to admit this, but I'm glad my father didn't show up tonight—"

"You're only putting off the inevitable, you know."

Her mouth puckered into a playful smile. "I know. Call me rash. Call me heedless. It's been done before."

CHAPTER

3

Al Lever, Newcastle's chief homicide detective, lit a cigarette, inhaled deeply, and placed his feet on his desktop. His open jacket slid to the sides of his broad chest, revealing a .38-caliber revolver attached to his belt on the right side and his gold shield equally secured to the left. A paunch that had formed long before the onset of middle age sent rolls of flesh cascading over both official objects while Al leaned back in his chair and then smiled. It was the expression of a man who has at last found peace.

Lever positively lived for moments like this: the long, lazy afternoons of mid-August, the sky still light at six-thirty—despite the few lingering clouds produced by the recent summer storm. He lived for the quiet of a station house that had no pressing police business other than a minor fender bender involving some tourists from Idaho. He reveled in a world in which the usual cacophony of noises—the "Lieutenant! Call on line three!" or "Jones has those prints you ordered," or

"They just brought that Harper character in for questioning, Al," or "Meeting in the ward room in ten"—were gloriously absent.

And this blissful experience of summer calm was why he hadn't left the station at the end of his shift. In his book, this kind of solitude was as good as it gets, and he'd been savoring it for a full half hour. That and his precious cigarettes—items his wife had banned from their house two months ago. For Al Lever, times like these were like being alone on a mountaintop in Montana (except that he'd never again be physically fit enough to hike a Montana mountain), and he was enjoying it for what it was: the ultimate P and Q.

He took another pull from his cigarette and watched the smoke turn green as it drifted toward the fluorescent light fixture on the ceiling. Then the smoke became a bluish-brown as it floated out the open window while a horn up on Sixth Street honked. The noise was subdued, almost apologetic.

The lieutenant let out a second happy sigh, but before he could raise his cigarette to his lips, his serenity was shattered by two loud taps on the glass-paneled door that separated his office from the world beyond. The taps were followed by Hal Davis, a soon-to-be-retired detective assigned to Newcastle's robbery division. Davis eased the door open.

"Sorry to bother you, Al, but I figured you'd still be here . . . There's a call on line three. A Boston detective by the name of Tanner. I think you ought to take it."

"Homicide?"

"Nah . . . At least, I don't think so. Tanner doesn't think so."

Lever tried to smile again. This time the expression looked like a grimace. "Why me, then? I don't know any Tanner. Besides, I was on my way out of here." Al stubbed his smoke out in an ashtray overflowing with butts. He made no motion to reach for the phone.

After a small silence, Davis said, "I think you should take this one, Al."

"Argh, something tells me this is going to ruin a perfectly good evening." Lever picked up the receiver, punched line three, and grumbled, "Homicide, Lever here."

"This is Sid Tanner, Lieutenant. I'm up in Boston . . . Back Bay. We had an Amtrak train pull in a little while ago with a stiff on board."

"So . . . ?" Al said this in a tone that made it clear he had no desire to get involved. As far as he was concerned, Boston's business was Boston's business, and they could keep it right there. Tanner didn't respond, so Al followed it with, "Was it a homicide?" and immediately wished he'd kept his mouth shut.

"I don't think so. Our ME's on-site prelim seems to indicate heart attack. At this time, we have no autopsy scheduled . . . I don't like cutting stiffs apart unless I smell a rat. And nothing looks out of place. Next of kin would have to order an autopsy at this point."

"So why call me? I'm homicide, in case no one informed you. And what's this got to do with Newcastle PD in the first place?"

"Look, Lieutenant, I don't know why your buddy put you on the phone, but I don't need a runaround here. I'm just trying to find out where this stiff belongs, okay? Because he sure as hell doesn't belong in Boston."

"What makes you think I want him?"

"You gonna help me with this or not, Lieutenant?"

Lever coughed a typical smoker's cough and muttered his all-purpose excuse, which was: "Allergies . . . allergies . . .

When do you get a break from this damn pollen count?"
Then he straightened up and returned to the phone conversation. "What have you got?"

"We didn't find any ticket on this guy, so we don't know
for sure where he was supposed to get off, or where he got on,
for that matter. But the conductor, a John Markoe, is almost
positive the guy was on board when he started his shift in
New York City, and held a ticket for Newcastle. So, I'm starting with what I got from the conductor. Markoe seems like
the kind of guy who remembers a lot more than he needs to.
He sure as hell talks more than he needs to."

"No ticket stubs on the body?"

"No. But Markoe says he probably collected it just before
they arrived in Newcastle, or possibly some other passenger
took it by mistake when they went off to the café car or
something."

"You didn't find any receipt, either?"

"Nah, but people don't always hold on to them. If it's not a
business trip, they usually toss 'em."

"Why Newcastle? Why not Providence? New London?
New Haven?"

"A possibility, but I'm working my way down the coast,
Lieutenant, and you're the first stop south—"

"Right. You got a name for this clown?"

"Yeah, Theodore A. Graham."

"Huh . . . ? What . . . ?" Lever stuttered. He dropped his
feet off the desk, sat straight in his chair, and wrote the name
down on a slip of paper. "Graham? You're certain about
that?"

"Credit cards in the wallet. And the photo on the driver's
license matches up."

"An old guy?"

"Sixty-eight, according to the license."

"Don't tell me . . . It's a Florida license."

"Yeah . . . ? Where'd you get that?"

"Unlucky guess." Lever said this almost to himself.

"You know the guy?"

Again, Al stuttered. "Well, yeah . . . Or no, not *know* him. I mean I've never met him, but I was Best Man at his daughter's wedding. He never made it up from Florida for the event . . . That was in May of this year. I'm sure his name was Theodore, though. He's the father of Annabella Graham— Belle Graham, the crossword puzzle editor at one of our local newspapers, *The Evening Crier*. She never mentioned to me he was on his way north."

"And she's a friend of yours?"

"You could say that. She married a guy who used to be with the department here. My partner, in fact. He's a PI now. Rosco Polycrates."

"Hey, look, Lieutenant, I'm sorry about this." A tone of "fellow-cop" compassion had filtered into Tanner's voice. All of a sudden the *stiff* was family. "I mean, I didn't figure the deceased to be a family friend. I guess that's why Detective Davis wanted you to get on the line . . . Look, how do you want to handle this . . . I mean Graham's body . . . You tell me. I have no problem holding it for a day or two."

Lever sighed again. Any hint of contentment was long gone. "I appreciate the offer. I'm gonna have to drive out to his daughter's house and break this news personally. I can't do it over the phone . . . It could take me a few hours to get back to you. What's your number up there?"

Lever scratched Tanner's name and number down on the slip of paper next to *Theodore A. Graham*, signed off, and dropped the receiver back into its cradle. Hearing the clank,

Detective Davis stepped back into the office.

"So, it *was* Belle's father, I take it?" he asked as he pulled a chair up to Lever's desk.

Lever only nodded.

"Yeah, I figured," Davis continued. "That's why I thought you ought to get it from the horse's mouth rather than from me." Davis reached across the desk, removed a cigarette from Lever's pack, and lit it. "Look, Al, why don't you call Polycrates. Get him down here, brief him, and let him tell Belle. Hell, he never met the old man either, right? How broken up is he gonna be?"

"Mr. Sensitive."

"Who? Polycrates?"

"No, you, Davis. And I was being facetious, in case it went over that thick head of yours. I'm not going to pull a stunt like that on Rosco. He's my best friend, for pete's sake."

"Hey, suit yourself, Al. I'm just trying to make it easier on you. I could care less about Polycrates. As far as I'm concerned, it was a banner day when 'Dud-Lee-Do-Right' left the department."

"Any other comments you'd like to share?"

"No."

"Good. Then get out of here."

"Jeez . . . Talk about sensitive."

CHAPTER

4

The funeral arrangements were made hastily. Belle was conscious of a bizarre sense of disconnect; and despite—or perhaps because of—Rosco's tender concern, she was more deeply aware of her own disturbing dearth of emotion. *My father's dead,* she reminded herself over and over again. *He died of a heart attack . . . alone on a train.* But the words had a hollow ring that rendered them nearly meaningless. When her mother had died, there had been tears; now there were none.

Almost, and she loathed to admit this, she felt a sense of relief. Relief that she and her father no longer were forced to play out the complex roles of uncommunicative parent and child. Relief that she no longer need suffer guilt from her lack of filial devotion—or "measure up" to an ideal she'd never attain. Relief to finally shake off the past, to stand on her own feet and face the world guided by principles she herself had devised. However, the sensation of release had a way of hauling her back full circle into guilty confusion.

In typical Belle fashion, she decided to ignore (and perhaps evade) her jumbled thoughts by instead placing her total concentration on the many large and small activities that surround a burial.

First off: the involvement—or lack thereof—of Sara Crane Briephs. Newcastle's dowager empress and self-appointed mentor to both Belle and Rosco had wanted to give a luncheon following the service, had *insisted* upon giving a luncheon; and Sara, as everyone knew, had rarely lost a battle of wills in her eighty-plus years. But Belle had been firm on the issue of a post-service reception. She loved Sara; she considered her a surrogate mother and grandmother rolled into one. However, Belle also realized that Sara needed parameters on occasion. And this was one of those times.

"No," Belle had stated over tea at White Caps, Sara's ancestral home. "Father wouldn't have wanted all that hoopla. He didn't want it when Mother died . . . He said we should celebrate life, not death."

"This isn't a celebration, Belle dear. Rather, it's a means of comforting the grieving."

Belle had put down her gold-rimmed porcelain cup and regarded the indomitable old lady. "I don't know where his former Princeton crowd has dispersed to now, Sara. Besides, I never really knew his acquaintances there . . . Father and Mother didn't move to New Jersey until after I'd gone to college."

"Well, colleagues from his previous positions then?"

Belle shook her head. "Father had a peripatetic career. The longest amount of time he spent anywhere was in Ohio when I was little . . . When he and Mother accepted new positions in Iowa, they simply moved on. Friendships were never a focus of their lives . . . Nor was maintaining contact with distant relatives. My parents were happiest in a little cocoon that included only two people." Belle paused. "As for me, I don't require comforting, because I'm not grieving."

"You will, dear."

Belle had hunched her shoulders and stared down into her teacup. "My father and I weren't close, Sara . . ."

Her hostess had inclined her proud head, her perfectly sculpted white hair exuding an aura of omnipotence while her blue eyes had gazed at the younger woman. "I'll do anything you wish, my dear."

"No luncheon, then. And no reception. We'll have a brief funeral service . . . nothing extraneous . . . In fact, the fewer in attendance, the better."

"People will wish to pay their respects, dear . . . Rosco's family . . . Albert . . ."

Belle had stared silently out the window while Sara had continued to regard her.

"No luncheon. I agree . . . But, Belle, know that experiences of loss may appear in supposedly unrelated forms. Anger can be one. Or a feeling of betrayal. Hollowness, seeming callowness—"

"I don't feel anything, Sara . . ."

"So you think, Belle dear. So you think."

"I don't."

Sara had finally nodded at Belle's still averted face. "More tea, dear? A cup of hot tea is such a boon when our souls are troubled."

Al Lever was the first guest to arrive at the Putnam Funeral Home on upper Winthrop Drive. The day was hot and muggy, and the mortuary reception room and chapel cooled to the point of chilliness, creating a odd division between the worlds of the living and those in the limbo of mourning. Al clothed in a black dress suit was another dichotomy. He'd always been a man whose idea of formal attire was a poplin windbreaker. Belle watched him walk in from the glare of outdoors, and smiled at his obvious care and consideration. A faint whiff of mothballs moved forward with him.

"Condolences, Belle." Lever shifted back and forth on heavy feet. "Hiya, Rosco. Sorry about all this." He gestured loosely and frowned as if hoping to find someone—even himself—to blame.

"Al." Rosco shook his former partner's hand while Belle also extended her fingers. "Thanks for coming."

Lever's brow wrinkled again. "Tough losing your dad like that . . ."

Beyond the trio, bouquets of white roses and lilies, all from Sara Briephs's extensive gardens, created a startlingly festive air, as if the occasion were a social gathering or the awarding of a much-vaunted award for sportsmanship.

"Place looks nice," Al added, staring from vase to vase and then off into the quiescent chapel. "Real nice . . ."

"You're a good friend, Al," Belle said. "I can't tell you how much I appreciate everything you've done—"

"All in the line of duty . . ." Then after a long pause, "Hey, what are buddies for?"

"I meant it when I said you didn't need to put in an appearance here."

Lever attempted to laugh off the suggestion. "Mrs. B. would have had my hide if I hadn't showed; you know that." Then he added a serious: "At least, your dad went quick. I mean, there wasn't illness involved . . . you know . . . long-

term suffering . . . that kind of thing . . ." Lever looked at
Rosco for a hint on how to proceed, and then back at Belle.

"That's true," was her brief answer.

"And on his way to visit his daughter . . . He must have
died a happy man." Al tried to smile. Belle did, too. But
again, she found she had no appropriate response.

It was at that moment that the extended Polycrates clan
blew in: Rosco's authoritarian older sisters and their meeker
spouses; Danny, his younger brother who would always
remain the "kid" of his generation; Helen, the quintessential
Greek-American matriarch; and assorted young offspring, all
of whom proceeded to push each other, giggle, and release a
stream of *Did nots!* and *I'm telling Moms!* To say they were a
boisterous bunch was an understatement. To say that an only
child like Belle sometimes found this energetic brand of inti-
macy disconcerting was also an understatement.

"Belle, *darling.* I'm so, *so sorry!*" This was Cleo speaking,
Helen's eldest, and already in line to receive her mother's
mantle. Cleo was addicted to high drama both in life and
speech. "*Nicky!* Tell your auntie Belle how *sorry* you are that
her *father* passed away." She propelled her eight-year-old son
forward, but instead of mouthing the words his mother
wished, Nick blurted out an excited: "Can we see him? Your
dad, I mean? Like, dead and everything."

Both Cleo and her sister Ariadne gasped. Cleo reached a
many-jeweled hand to steer her offending child away, but
Belle bent down to the little boy.

"Sorry, Nicky. You can't see him."

"I can act like a zombie," he replied. "Wanna watch?"

This time Cleo had her way. Nick was propelled toward his
cousins while his six-year-old sister approached. Effie had once
been Belle's nemesis; she was now her biggest fan although it

was sometimes difficult for the child to reconcile her idol wor-shipping with her own sense of superiority. *I'm a fairy princess and you're not* was written all over the little girl's face.

"Are you sad, Aunt Belle?"

"Not really, Effie. My father had a good long life."

"You should be sad, though."

Belle smiled gently. "So, I've been told. I guess I am a lit-tle bit."

Effie pondered the words and tone. Her scrutiny of Belle intensified. "Mom wanted to have a party for you at our house. She says people should have parties after *tragedies* like these."

"I've been told that, too."

"Then how come you didn't listen?"

Belle gazed at her new niece. "Sometimes, we have to pay attention to what our own hearts tell us to do. Rather than listening to other people."

Effie's eyes grew huge. "Don't tell that to Mom. She'd make you count backwards from ten."

"I won't."

Effie continued to regard her aunt. "What does it feel like to die, Aunt Belle?"

"I don't know."

"Nick screams a lot when he's playing soldiers and pre-tends he's being killed."

By now, Rosco joined in. He also bent down to Effie's level. "I've heard your brother."

"Mom says it's 'enough to wake the dead.' Did your dad do that? On the train? Yell and everything?"

Belle found herself smiling gravely again. The notion of her father calling attention to himself—or even calling out in pain—was so astounding she could scarcely picture it. "My father never once raised his voice, Effie. Not in his entire life."

"Then he's not like *my* dad." With that decisive statement, the little girl marched off to join her cousins and brother.

After Effie came Sara, making her stately way forward. Following Sara was Martha, the head waitress from Lawson's, Newcastle's all-purpose coffee shop/gossip mill and decades-old institution. Belle considered the two women now standing almost side by side. They were so different in background, but so similar in intent. Sara was a New England WASP through and through. Martha, thirty years younger, had created her own heritage, but she bore it as royally as Sara's.

Martha never appeared without her blond, beehive hairdo well-shellacked, without undergarments that creaked with every turn, or fingernails painted a vivid American Beauty pink. She'd chosen the era and "look" she most preferred, and stuck with it through thick and thin. Belle was almost surprised to notice Martha had relinquished her flamingo-colored uniform for the occasion—and more surprised to see she was weeping softly. She was not a woman Belle had imagined knew how to cry.

"It reminds me of when my own dad went . . ." Martha pulled a gauzy handkerchief from her purse. Belle noted it was edged in a delicate rose-hued lace; the small gesture of gentility and femininity made her feel a sudden stab of sorrow. Where had the handkerchief come from? she wondered. Had it been a gift from some long-vanished beau? An impulse purchase to "complement" her Lawson's uniform? Or had she inherited it? A present her "dad" had given her mother?

"You're really kind to come today, Martha."

"It's important for friends to stay together in times like

these . . . When Mother went . . . and then my dad, I don't know what I would have done without the support of the folks at Lawson's . . ."

Belle found herself grasping Martha's hand in sympathy.

"You're going to miss him, Belle. You'll never get over missing him."

Belle bowed her head. What could she say?

"Never," Martha repeated. "Your parents are your parents as long as you draw breath."

Vicariously, Belle felt her heart constrict.

CHAPTER

5

Belle flinched as she exited Fort Lauderdale's airport. Not one piece of the picture seemed pleasant or inviting: the blindingly bright blue sky, the sun searing down on the concrete divider that cordoned off the mammoth parking facility, the humid air that billowed upward carrying the smell of diesel fuel, and wave after wave of scorching heat. *Welcome to Florida in August,* she thought. The weather wasn't going to make sorting through her father's effects any easier.

Dutifully she followed the directional signs to the shuttle bus that would transport her to the rental car company. A queue of chatty businesspeople mingling with a group of beaming tourists were already waiting at the stop; their obvious enthusiasm for the bright skies and swaying palm trees made her feel even more isolated and despondent. She climbed aboard in silence while her fellow travelers bounded up the steps in a rush of enthusiastic conversation.

Belle sank into a seat and stared through the windows as

the shuttle skirted through the airport, entered a six-lane highway, turned, then turned again and again while a glut of highway signs zipped past. Miami. Everglades City. Coral Springs. Routes 595, 75, 95. How she was going to return her rental, or even relocate the airport, seemed impossible to imagine. Even under the best of circumstances, Belle's navigational skills were no match for a Ponce de Leon or de Soto. She began to sorely wish she could have flown directly into Fort Myers on the west coast, but those flights had been booked— at least the ones allowing her to use frequent flyer points. Now, she was left to traverse the breadth of the state on her own recognizance. CROSSWORD QUEEN QUITS COURSE: CAR CRASHES IN EVERGLADES. Belle could almost see the headline.

She squared her shoulders in a facsimile of bravery and derring-do, exited the bus, handed her driver's license to the rental clerk, mumbled when presented with a plethora of automotive choices, and finally tossed her small suitcase into the trunk of a small, red, four-door *car.* Rosco would have recognized the make and been able to discuss its various merits; Belle wouldn't have remembered the manufacturer or model even if it were printed on the steering wheel.

Strapped into her seat belt, she gazed intently at the map provided by the rental company, then eased out of the parking lot—and made her first wrong turn. She did a 180 at a gas station that seemed located specifically for the purpose of aiding lost tourists, retraced her steps, and eventually found Route 595, where an exit sign indicating HIATUS ROAD arrested her attention. She smiled for the first time since stepping onto Floridian soil, although the expression wasn't happy.

Hiatus, she thought. *An interruption . . . a missing part . . .* It was at times like these that she missed her favorite possession: her multivolumed *Oxford English Dictionary,* the fabled

O.E.D. Her brain began spinning its own lexical connections. *A cleft is also a chasm, a gulf, a rift between two areas once attached.* Belle frowned, then willfully turned off her thoughts.

Soon 595 became Route 75, the flat and knife-straight highway officially called the Everglades Parkway but which every local referred to as "Alligator Alley." The idea that there actually might be alligators dragging their thick bodies across the macadam or sunning themselves at the side of the road produced a second and easier smile. In spite of her mission, she found herself beginning to relax. Just then she caught sight of an enormous bird stretching brown-black wings above a barren and leafless tree; a few feet farther along, a white-plumed egret stood gimlet-eyed in the swamp grass swelling around the cypress roots. Nearby perched a heron whose breast was as blue as cobalt.

"Miccosukee, Immokalee . . ." Belle mouthed the strange place names as she drove, peering at the wilds beyond Alligator Alley in the hopes of glimpsing human habitation. But as far as the eye could see, there was nothing but inhospitable swampland. She twisted on the radio dial, only to hear a wailing rendition of "Dust in the Wind" invade her air-conditioned pod.

She flipped off the radio before the deejay could blitz her senses with additional ominous selections, then continued in determined silence. *Why did Father choose to live here?* she asked herself again. *What emotional climate was he trying to find—or escape? An apartment in the Keys last year, then this recent move to Sanibel . . .* Belle couldn't remember all the spots her father had inhabited during the years since her mother had died. She only knew that the sojourns had been brief, and that when he'd relocated—as he'd done from Marathon less than half a year ago—she'd been totally surprised.

Finally, just east of Naples, the highway turned northward, and she found herself connecting to Route 867 and heading southwest toward Punta Rassa and Sanibel Island. As she began to traverse the causeway connecting the island to the mainland, a brown pelican floated into view, drifting at an unconcerned eye level with the steady stream of bridge traffic. Then another pelican appeared. And another and another and another: all five loafing lazily through the languid air until one of the group suddenly plunged out of formation and dove beak-first toward the water.

Belle uttered a pleased "Yikes!" dispensed with the "climate control system," and rolled down the window. At that point a sudden revelation hit her. *Of course,* she realized, *that's why Father decided to move here. It was because of his pet project on the ancient Olmec civilization. This is the Gulf of Mexico, the same body of water that carried the Olmecs' canoes as they embarked from La Venta or Veracruz. Maybe Father imagined he could see beyond the modern cruise lines and tankers and cargo containers into the distant past. Maybe he was trying to find a connection between the east coast of Mexico and the western half of Florida.*

Belle studied the scene, trying to see it as he might have, but her brief inspiration began to evaporate so she maneuvered onto Periwinkle Way instead, carefully following directions faxed from the real estate agent as she passed Dixie Beach Boulevard and Casa Ybel, before making a right onto Palm Ridge. From there, she counted street numbers aloud until she found what she assumed was her father's low-standing condo complex.

Belle turned off the ignition and sat staring through the plantings of bougainvillea and hibiscus. She sincerely wished she hadn't been so pigheaded in refusing Rosco's offer to accompany her. Sorting through her father's possessions wasn't going to be fun.

She drew in a weary breath, climbed out of the car, and started inspecting the grouped buildings, reasoning that 11B would probably be on the second floor, and most likely in the back overlooking the neighboring wildlife refuge. She was right—a hollow victory.

Belle climbed the concrete exterior stairs, extracting her father's key ring as she did so. It was simpler to concentrate on a commonplace object than consider the fact that the last time her father had trod these steps he was very much alive and on his way to Massachusetts. Alive and about to visit a daughter who hadn't particularly wished to see him.

She drew in another long, reflective breath, then walked the length of the outside corridor while gazing away toward the facing buildings, the date palms clustered in the center "square," the Bermuda grass now sere and brown with summer's heat. "No time like the present," she finally muttered as she turned toward 11B and slid the key into the lock.

Belle attempted to twist the key clockwise but couldn't. She frowned and opted for counterclockwise. The lock's inner mechanism clicked easily, but the door refused to open. She grasped the knob and shoved. No go. She pushed harder. Nothing. She stared at the painted metal face. The door merely gazed silently back. She tried the key again, this time rolling it slowly clockwise, then again gripped the knob.

The lock dropped open and the door gave way. It had never been locked.

A sudden fear overtook her. *Had her fastidious father truly left his home unprotected? Or had someone entered the place in his absence: a maintenance person, a member of a cleaning agency—and had that employee forgotten to lock the door upon finishing their task? Or was it possible her father was the victim of a theft? And could that criminal be lurking inside the apartment now?*

Belle stood, motionless and quiet. Sweat made the knob slip in her hand. She was tempted to back away, find the building's supervisor, and report the incident, but stubbornness and mounting irritation kept her feet pinned in place. *Damn it!* she thought. *My father's dead, and someone has either carelessly left his apartment unlocked, or else a lowlife has decided this is the optimal time to break in and rob the place.* Anger at this unfair treatment propelled her forward. She grasped the knob in slick fingers and threw her weight against the door.

What she saw waiting in the entry was a young woman. Her hair was black and cut so short it looked like a swimmer's racing cap while her enormous dark eyes glistened with a mixture of anger and fright.

"I've notified Security," the woman rasped out. "They'll be here in a second, so don't try anything funny."

CHAPTER

6

"And you are?" Belle's teeth and knuckles were clenched, her voice aggressive.

"Stay right where you are, sister," was the black-haired woman's rapid reply. "Security's on its way." Then she added a fierce: "Why were you trying to break into Ted's apartment? There's nothing here worth stealing."

"Ted?" Belle stammered. "Ted?"

But her surprised query went unanswered, because at that moment "Security" arrived in the form of a twenty-something bodybuilder whose ultratanned face and arms belied the fact that guarding residences was his sole vocation. "Do we have a problem here?"

Belle noted with dismay that he was armed with more than a walkie-talkie. His right hand maintained a firm grasp on a jet black pistol that rested in the holster on his hip—itching like "Billy the Kid" to go for the quick-draw.

"I have no idea who this woman is—" Belle began.

"I caught her trying to break in—" was the equally aggrieved reply.

"I was not breaking in! I was only—"

Static squawked over the guard's receiver, silencing both antagonists. The guard yanked it from his belt, and held it to his mouth. "Negative . . . Female . . ." He looked at Belle critically. "Mid-thirties . . . blond . . . average height. Yeah . . . Possible forced entry . . . No . . . Nothing I can't handle . . . No visible weapon—"

"I did *not* break in," Belle reiterated while brandishing her set of keys. "I have—"

The security guard removed his hand from his pistol and raised it like a traffic cop. "Hold on, lady." Then he returned to his radio, "Subject claims legitimate access. Has keys she states belong to occupant. Did 11B leave vacation directives or any sublet notifications?"

Before the walkie-talkie could bleat further instructions, the woman with the black hair started to retreat into the apartment. As she did, she affixed Belle with a baleful stare. "Thank you, Officer. Ted will be very happy you—"

"No!" Belle exploded. "No, he won't be! He won't be *happy* . . . 'Ted' won't even learn of this situation! Because 'Ted'—Theodore Graham, my father—is dead." She took a deep breath, tried to calm herself, then focused an outraged expression on the other woman. "He passed away last week."

The woman turned slowly toward her. "Ted . . ." she mumbled. "Ted is . . . ?" Finally she added a shocked: "You're . . . Are you Annabella?"

"Of course, I'm Annabella! And who, may I ask, are you?" Belle fought her desire to use stiffer language, but a ferocious scowl made up for the lack of tougher speech.

It was "Security" who answered. "Deborah Hurley. Professor Graham's assistant. She's the only one *I* recognize here."

Belle stared. "My father didn't have an assistant."

"I've been here for almost three months, lady, and Ms. Hurley's been around near as long as I have," shot back the guard. "You're the one I've never seen before."

The woman named Deborah looked at Belle with pained and horrified eyes. "What . . . ? What happened . . . ? When Ted left here, he was fine, in fact—"

"He died on the train. A heart attack." Belle ground out the words. Frustration, latent grief, and the sudden appearance of a person like "Deborah" combined to make her tone less than kind. "The conductor found him slumped over and—"

"That's some swell attitude," the guard offered. "You want this *Annabella* person escorted off the premises, Ms. Hurley?"

"Are you really Ted's daughter?" Deborah began while Belle found tears inexplicably filling her eyes.

"Why would I claim to be someone I wasn't?"

"Easy, now . . . Easy . . ." said the guard. He made a step as if to separate the women, but Deborah Hurley ignored him.

"Ted can't be dead," she said. "He can't be . . . He was . . . He was . . ."

"My father never told me he'd hired an assistant," was Belle's equally distressed response.

L eft alone, at long last, in her father's apartment, Belle stared about in utter bewilderment. Her brain seemed to be echoing and pinging as if sloshing full of seawater. First, there was the discovery of a person so familiar and comfortable with her difficult parent as to refer to him as "Ted."

Then, there was the equally unpleasant sensation that not a single piece of furniture in the two-bedroom condo looked remotely familiar. Her father had moved from Marathon Key to Sanibel Island, and had apparently decided to refurnish his life. Or else someone had done it for him. And the evidence pointed to *Mrs.* Hurley—as the guard had helpfully revealed her marital status to be.

Belle sank down on a sea green couch covered with a flowery chintz throw and an armful of matching pillows. She regarded the ultrafeminine decorating scheme with dismay. The Dr. Graham she'd known had held no truck with such "boudoir-appropriate blandishments"; and they made Deborah Hurley's status as "assistant" seem even more specious and peculiar.

"Besides, she must be several years younger than I am," Belle found herself muttering. She shook her head; her brain clanged louder. Then she realized it wasn't Deborah's age that bothered her, but the fact that she'd never known of the woman's existence. *Why didn't my father tell me?* her thoughts demanded—to which another part of her mind replied with an equally insistent: *Why didn't you ask? Why didn't you bother to visit?*

Belle stood and walked to the kitchen, purposefully ignoring the spreading view of blue lagoon and tranquil air. Another group of pelicans hovered in the distant sky; she averted her eyes and instead set the tea kettle on the stove. At least, the stainless steel container was a familiar sight, as were the teacups: the remnants of her great-grandmother's Blue Willow pattern and the only visible evidence that her father had once had previous attachments—and an existence prior to Sanibel and *Mrs.* Deborah Hurley. Belle stared at the aged blue and white china; again, she felt tears swimming into her eyes.

The kettle boiled. She carried her tea past the dining area, past the screened veranda, past her father's bedroom, and into the shuttered room he'd obviously used as a study. She hoped his collection of books and scholarly pamphlets and treatises might provide solace—or at least familiar surroundings in which to begin to gather her thoughts.

But again, she was surprised. As she switched on a lamp, what arrested her glance was not her father's beloved books but a grouping of photographs that nearly covered the wall above the desk. They were pictures Belle hadn't seen before: her parents in their youthful prime, then her father alone in middle age surrounded by academic types draped in university robes or accoutered in somber jackets and ties. And then there were a number of him as an older man in the company of people whose backgrounds and livelihoods were impossible to discern.

In one photo her father looked as if he'd been deep-sea fishing. He was standing shirtless and uncharacteristically tanned and fit in the back of a large power boat. In another, he sat at an open-air restaurant dotted with palm trees; several empty beer bottles littered a stained tablecloth while the backdrop was a blur as if a large number of people were dancing. The shadow of the photographer lay across the table while her father gazed up in apprehension, his expression the dismayed scowl of a man who's been caught where he shouldn't be.

Belle drew back and dropped her eyes as if she'd glimpsed some unsavory part of her father's life, then she returned to her perusal of the portrait gallery. Among the entire collection, there was not one picture of Theodore A. Graham's only child; the framed photo Belle had sent of Rosco and herself on their wedding day was nowhere visible.

A knock at the front door disturbed whatever unhappy thoughts this discovery might invoke. Belle stifled an impatient groan, crossed the living room, and opened the door to find Deborah on the threshold. She looked as if she'd been crying hard.

"Can I come in . . . Belle?"

Reluctantly, Belle stood to one side. She knew she should attempt to be gracious and consoling, but thoughtfulness wasn't in the cards at the moment. Instead, her tone turned irritable. "You wouldn't know where my father put a picture taken on my wedding day, would you?"

Deborah shook her head, drew in a quavering breath, then added a sorrowful: "Ted could be a pretty secretive person . . . I mean, there were lots and lots of things I didn't know . . . But I do remember him saying you were married . . ."

Belle raised her eyebrows. She was tempted to utter a snide and probably withering comment, but counted to ten, opting for a more subtle: "Well, I gather there's a good deal of information that wasn't shared with me, either."

Deborah walked to the couch, automatically replacing a ruffle-edged pillow Belle had tossed aside. "I can't believe he's gone . . ."

"He is." The words were more unkind than Belle had intended.

"I mean, Ted was so . . . so vital, and . . . and energetic and everything . . ."

Belle found herself gritting her teeth. "Just what did you do for my father, Deborah? If you don't mind my asking—"

"Please . . . call me Debbie . . . That's what your . . . I mean, that's what everyone calls me . . ."

"Okay. Debbie." Belle struggled to maintain a civil tone. "And what precisely was it my father hired you to do?"

"Oh, this and that . . . answer letters, you know . . . stuff like that . . ." *Debbie* sniffled and drew in another grief-filled breath while Belle's heart hardened. "And I helped research that paper he was writing—"

"Ah, yes . . . Father's monograph on the Olmec civilization." Belle didn't believe a word she was hearing. Her spine grew straighter, her jaw tighter.

"That's why your dad hired me . . . On account of my research capabilities . . . He said I was real good at digging up facts. When I was at Rutgers, you know up in New Jersey—"

"You met my father back in New Jersey?" Surprise made Belle's voice turn even more brittle. "When he was a professor at Princeton?"

"No. No. Of course not, silly! I was just a little kid when he was up there doing his teacher thing. Ted and I met down here. After Mike was transferred T-A-D from the Bayonne facility—"

"Mike? T-A-D?"

Debbie Hurley tilted her head to one side and studied Belle. "My husband. Mike Hurley. T-A-D: Temporary Assigned Duty." Then she changed the subject, adjusting her demeanor to simulate a chatty, hostess mode. "This view's really fabulous, isn't it? I mean, Ted just loved to stare out the windows or hunker down on the veranda out there. I'd catch him goofing off almost every day . . ."

The idea of her disciplined father "goofing off" or gazing vacantly into space was as troubling as the nickname "Ted"— and nearly as upsetting as his hiring a "research assistant" whose grasp of language was so slovenly and imprecise. Professor Graham had never been a charitable soul—especially when it came to educational standards.

"But I guess that was on account of the birds—"

"The birds?"

"Yeah . . . You know . . . 'Cause he liked counting all the birds . . . He had those huge binoculars of his with him all the time—"

"My father was a bird-watcher?" Here was another piece of information that didn't jibe with the parent Belle remembered. In fact, in her recollection, he'd been the very opposite—"neophyte ornithologists" was the term he'd employed to dismiss those whose hobby was "birding."

"Oh, big time! I mean, that's why he kept that notebook with him every living second . . . Like, you know, to count the anhingas and turkey vultures and bald eagles and stuff. I swear, he never went anywhere without it . . . I mean, he even packed it when he went off to see you. Said the migratory ospreys would be—"

"It wasn't among his effects." Belle's tone remained perplexed and flat.

"One of those cardboard-covered composition books? You know, the kind school kids use . . . with the sort of black and white marbly cover? 'A Murder of Crows,' that's what he wrote on the outside—"

"What?"

"You know, like a name for a bunch of critters: a 'siege of cranes,' a 'rafter of turkeys'—"

"Yes, I'm aware of those phrases—"

"Well, Ted told me neat stuff like that . . . a 'cast of hawks,' a 'skein of geese,' and other stuff . . . He knew everything about 'ornithology.' That's when you study—"

"I know what it is." Belle could only stare at her father's assistant. *Migratory ospreys,* she thought, *anhingas, turkey vultures: Who was this man Debbie knew as Ted?* After a long and silent moment, Belle produced a baffled: "The notebook wasn't in the suitcase the police returned to me."

Debbie shrugged. "Hey, no biggie . . . Maybe the cops swiped it or it fell out of his bag . . . Like I said, he only used it to—"

Belle stiffened. "Members of Massachusetts police forces are not in the habit of stealing possessions from the dead—or from anyone else. Especially composition books."

Debbie's sad face finally brightened. "Oh, golly! Sorry about that! I should have my head examined. You married an ex-cop! Ted did tell me that. I can see why you'd be sensitive on the subject."

When Deborah Hurley had finally babbled her way off into the sunset, Belle returned to the kitchen and made herself another cup of tea. She wasn't hungry in the slightest—not even for the deviled eggs that were her favorite treat. She knew that reasonable people ate meals at regular hours, and that her body was probably experiencing extreme deprivation. But reasoning was of little use today; Belle's psyche felt too battered to handle the cheery world of welcoming restaurants and friendly waitresses.

Instead, she opted to take her chances on what she could scrounge in her father's kitchen. She opened a cabinet, spied a lone can of celery soup, and began hunting down a can opener, pulling open drawers that contained a few paper napkins, a set of flatware that looked brand-new, a few mismatched knives—or nothing. Both her father and her mother had lacked any interest in the domestic sciences.

Belle shook her head. "No wonder I can't cook," she muttered under her breath.

Finally, she unearthed the target of her quest. It was in the drawer of a side table in the dining area. Beside the opener, carefully wrapped in tissue paper, was an object she recognized as a picture frame. Belle picked it up and began to unwrap it, imagining she'd found her missing wedding photo, but discovered, instead, a very different memory.

It was a crossword puzzle she'd created for a long past Father's Day: an homage to famous Princetonians—Dr. Theodore A. Graham among them. She'd conceived the gift cryptic as an amusing diversion, something to be enjoyed and then tossed away. Instead, the man who'd been so disparaging of her choice of work, who'd been so sparing with compliments, who'd been so *unknowable* and aloof, had not only saved it, but framed it.

Across

1. Cheer from 48-Across
4. Cleverness
7. Yours and mine
10. "To__is human"
13. Burton co-star in "Look Back in Anger"
14. Fuss
15. Simian
16. "__for Two"
17. Famous class of 1965 Senator
19. Famous class of 1939 dropout
21. Begat
22. Lamenter
23. Pride of 48-Across
29. Born
30. Cupid
31. Prickleback
32. Part of UCLA
34. Picasso's homeland
37. My Dad!
41. Spoiler
42. Pinch
43. Col. sports grp.
44. JFK arrivals
45. __alai
48. Orange and Black Cats
54. Composer Edward
55. Mr. Lanza
56. Famous class of 1932 Actor
59. Famous class of 1771 President
61. Fate
62. Get a gander
63. R-V man?
64. Superlative ending
65. "__or no?"
66. Aves.
67. Gosh
68. __Hoo

Down

1. Roasts
2. Show up
3. Court call
4. "Coming Home" writer Salt
5. Chemical suffix
6. Diversion
7. Woodier
8. Whomp
9. Library option
10. Summer in Salses
11. Mr. Buttons
12. Mr. Charles
18. Calendar abbr.
20. Gun grp.
22. Title for 37-Across
24. Courage
25. Arab chieftain
26. Wife of Jacob
27. Ms. Horne
28. Put-down
32. Army bed
33. Summer cooler
34. Discharge
35. 34-Across Mrs.
36. Bud
37. Snare
38. Rime
39. Needle case
40. Env. letters
44. Washington and Virginia
45. See 49-Down
46. Melodic
47. Gets it
49. With 45-Down, home to 48-Across
50. Teacher's pets?
51. Shore bird
52. Gambler's lament

FATHER'S DAY

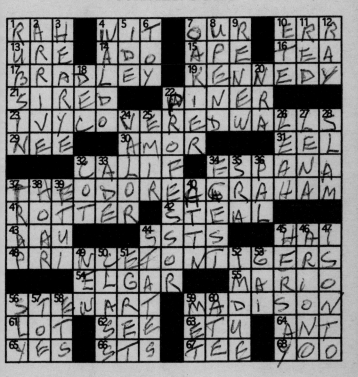

R	A	H		M	I	T		O	U	R		E	R	R
R	E			A	D	O		A	P	E		T	E	A
B	R	A	D	L	E	Y		K	E	N	N	E	D	Y
S	I	R	E	D			D	I	N	E	R			
T	Y	C	O	V	E	R	E	D	W	A	L	L	S	
N	E	E		A	M	O	R				E	E	L	
		C	A	L	I	F		E	S	P	A	N	A	
T	H	E	O	D	O	R	E		G	R	A	H	A	M
R	O	T	T	E	R		S	T	E	A	L			
A	U				S	T	S				H	A	I	
P	R	I	N	C	E	T	O	N	T	I	G	E	R	S
		E	L	G	A	R			M	A	R	I	O	
S	T	E	U	A	R	T		M	A	D	I	S	O	N
L	O	T		S	E	E		E	T	U		A	N	T
Y	E	S		S	T	S		T	E	E		O	O	O

53. Godard's "Le__Savoir"
56. Fox feature
57. One of ten
58. Aliens; abbr.
59. NYC arena
60. Dined

CHAPTER

7

Waking the next morning, Belle experienced a jolt of confusion as to her locale. She'd slept on the office couch—a foldaway she hadn't bothered to transform into its bed position; and she realized before she'd even lifted her head from the pillow that she was in alien territory. As her eyelids popped open, she found herself staring at her father's rogues' gallery of photos, and cognizance swiftly returned. She was on Sanibel Island for the first time in her life; she was there to pack up her father's books and papers, and place the apartment on the market.

She sat up; the day spreading before her seemed suddenly endless, and she wished once again that she hadn't been so pigheaded about performing this task alone. Rosco would not only have been a help, he would have been an enormous comfort. He would have put his arms around her when she needed a hug, interjecting humor and patience—a quality she often lacked. Above all, he would have told her he loved her, and that things were going to be just "peachy."

But then Belle felt herself bristling at the notion of requiring support. A frown furrowed her brow. She was a person with a major independent streak. "Okie-dokie," she muttered aloud. "Up and at 'em."

She showered, dressed, put on water for tea, wondered why there wasn't so much as a cereal box in the cupboards, then drifted into the dining area as she waited for the kettle to boil. There, on the table where she'd left it, was the framed crossword puzzle.

She smiled and picked it up, feeling a small sense of pride at her work: Her father's name in full at 37-Across; his title PROFESSOR at 22-Down; and at 19-Across, the last name of a man better known as a Harvard grad. That John F. Kennedy had been enrolled in the Princeton class of 1939, and had left for health reasons, was a piece of trivia she'd been inordinately pleased to discover.

Belle murmured a couple of the answers she considered among her more arcane and clever—"Mary URE at 13-Across; STU for 63-Across: *R-V man?*"—before returning to the tea kettle. Then she finally raised her eyes and took in the breadth of the apartment's stunning view. An enormous bird with chocolate brown wings swooped past; all at once—and not happily—she remembered Deborah Hurley's insistence that "Ted" had been an inveterate bird-watcher.

Belle grimaced; the expression grew steadily more irritable as she became aware of someone pounding on the door. She banged her cup down on the kitchen counter and strode through the living room. She didn't feel like entertaining her father's "research assistant" again.

"Yes, Debbie. What is it?" Belle uttered the cranky words before the door was fully open.

But instead of Deborah Hurley, Belle found a man in his later middle age. He had graying hair that hadn't seen a barber in some time, a barrely physique suggesting physical strength but also a total disinterest in anything remotely athletic, and skin so deeply tanned it looked cured like leather. He wore a T-shirt dotted with rust and paint stains, shorts that had probably once been blue canvas, and rubber flip-flops whose thongs were the color of grape jelly.

"Who are you?" His terse speech matched his appearance. This was clearly a man who didn't believe in standing on ceremony.

"If you're looking for Debbie, she's not here. I'm Dr. Graham's daughter, Annabella . . . Belle. And you are?"

Instead of responding to her question, the man regarded her curiously. Belle thought she noted a fleeting twinkle in his eye—almost as if he were happy to see her. But the expression vanished so rapidly, she decided she'd been mistaken.

"Ted around?"

"No . . . No, he's not." Belle hesitated; she intuited that this man and her father had been more than passing acquaintances, and she wasn't sure how to break the difficult news. "You're . . . you're a friend of my father's?"

"You might say that." The man rocked on his flip-flops; they made a scrunching noise on the concrete passageway: a combination of rubber and small shards of stone or shell.

"And your name is?" Belle put out her hand.

The man shook her hand for the briefest of seconds, then resumed his hesitant silence as if wondering whether or not to relinquish his identity. "Folks call me Woody."

"Well . . . Woody . . . I'm down here because my father . . . because my father died on his way up North to visit me . . ."

Woody didn't utter a sound, but the sudden stillness of his body told Belle he found the news very disturbing. She searched his face, and watched an emotion too fleeting to successfully categorize pass over it. *Anger?* she wondered. Or *betrayal?* Then she remembered what Sara had said about grief assuming various guises.

"My . . . Father was on the train—"

"Anybody with him?" The question was abrupt, suspicious. A scowl matched the tone.

"No . . . Well, other passengers, of course . . . But no one he knew, or we would have learned of Father's death the moment it occurred. A conductor discovered—" Belle stopped herself. There was no need to burden this man with the grim details. "Apparently heart attacks can happen like that."

"Your father was healthy as an ox."

"I'm sure he looked that way, but he complained that his back was often—"

Woody snorted. "The back? Huh, just didn't like to do what he didn't *want* to do . . ."

Belle didn't respond. Supposedly, the "bad back" had kept "Ted" Graham from attending her wedding. Finally, she said, "Would you like to come in for a minute? I'm sure my news can't be easy to accept—"

"Ahh, no . . . No time." Woody began backing away.

"But I'm sure Father would have wanted you to—"

"Maybe I'll see you around." Woody glanced at his watch, but the move seemed overly presentational. "Gotta run."

"Is there somewhere I can reach you . . . ? I mean, perhaps

you can tell me other people I should contact. I'm afraid I don't know who Father—"

"I'm late . . . I'll be in touch."

"But I—"

Woody was gone before Belle had time to protest further. She walked to the corridor railing and looked down into the condo complex. There was not a trace of the man. Not a sound of footsteps, not a car door opening or engine starting. Belle closed her eyes. *Why did she find the discovery of strangers in her father's life so disturbing? What had she expected? Even if her father had discussed his relationship to Woody and Debbie, even if he'd described them in meticulous detail, why would she imagine those two people could feel the remotest connection to, or concern for her?*

B elle had finally succumbed to hunger and gone off for a midmorning feast. Scrambled eggs, and cinnamon toast, and grapefruit juice, and extra-crispy hash brown potatoes, and coffee—not tea—drenched with cream: She did nothing halfway. Cholesterol-hell, Rosco said of her eating habits. And he was right.

Climbing the stairs to her father's apartment, she encountered Debbie Hurley on her way back down. "I put the mail on Ted's desk like always," she sang out.

Belle stopped. This wasn't a situation she'd anticipated. Nor was it one she appreciated. "You were in my father's apartment?"

Debbie gave her a look that plainly stated: *Dub!* then continued in a chirpy tone. "I mean, it makes him not feel so, like *gone,* you know?"

"Look, Debbie . . . I think we have to do things differently from now on—"

"Oh, yeah, I know . . . I mean, there isn't so much work for me anymore . . ."

Belle drew in a breath. "None, actually."

Debbie's face fell. She opened her mouth, but didn't speak.

"I'm going to be selling my father's condo. In fact, I've already contacted a realtor. In order for the place to be shown, I need to pack up his books and papers and ship them up North. The rest of the furnishings—"

"But what about his project on the Olmec civilization?" Debbie seemed stricken at the idea of forsaking "Ted's" final opus.

"I'm afraid it will have to be shelved. I'll see that his extant research is delivered to Princeton. That's the last university he worked for. If someone there chooses to continue what Father began or make use of the information—"

Debbie Hurley's lips compressed. She looked as if she was going to begin crying again; and Belle found herself gripping the banister as if it were capable of transmitting emotional as well as physical support.

"I'll also see that you get two weeks' severance—"

"It's not the money—"

Belle's jaw tightened automatically. "No, I didn't think so . . ."

"I mean, he was your dad! You must know how crazy everyone was about him!"

"Well, no, I didn't," was Belle's unhappy reply. "I'm sorry, Debbie, but you must realize by now that my father and I weren't close." Belle paused. There seemed nothing more to say. As an afterthought, she added, "Oh, by the way, Woody stopped by. I had to break the news to him . . . It seemed to upset him quite a bit although he clearly didn't feel like talking . . . at least not to me. If there are other friends or acquaintances I should contact, I'd like to have a list of—"

But Debbie Hurley's goggle-eyed stare stopped Belle's speech. "Woody? Ted didn't know anyone named Woody."

CHAPTER

8

Belle closed the apartment door behind her, leaning heavily against it as she tried to make sense of Debbie's statement and those that had followed. "Ted" hadn't known anyone named Woody—of that Debbie had been adamant. And yet this Woody person had stood on the doorstep, looking for all the world like a man who'd suddenly discovered he'd lost his dearest friend.

But what had he actually said? Belle tried to reconstruct their brief conversation. As she thought, she unconsciously slid the chain lock in place, then stepped back and regarded this paranoid piece of handiwork. *What was she worried about? Debbie Hurley sneaking in? Or the reappearance of a man who might—or might not—have been a close friend of her father's?*

I've got to get Debbie's set of keys, Belle told herself, but made no move to seek out her father's assistant. Instead, she walked slowly into the office as she tried to recall her conversation with the man in the tattered blue shorts.

Maybe Debbie's wrong, she reasoned. *After all, she isn't necessarily an authority on Father's life; she's only known him for a few brief months.* Then Belle remembered that she herself had supplied the term "friend"—not Woody; and that although he'd definitely hinted at a long-standing association with her father, his primary concern had seemed to be whether "Ted" had been accompanied by someone when he'd died. In fact, reflecting on the scene, what Belle most recalled was the man's sense of prickly anger—almost as if he'd expected to hear the news.

While Belle thought, she began opening file cabinet drawers in preparation for packing her father's effects, but the volume of paperwork all at once seemed more than she wanted to tackle. Instead, she decided to begin with the photos. She knew she'd feel a good deal more comfortable with the gazes of those unknown faces stashed safely out of sight.

She found a box and started pulling pictures off the wall. The snapshots and portraits of her parents she would save, and the ones whose backdrops were obviously academic. But when she came to the photo of her father as a fisherman, and the one taken in the mystery restaurant, she paused. *What's the point in keeping those?* She laid the restaurant snapshot on the desk, then reached for the picture of the boat. Something was taped to its back. Belle turned over the frame, found an envelope, cut it free, and turned it face up. In her father's old-fashioned script the word "Woody" appeared as plain as day.

A cry of triumph rang through her brain: *Miss know-it-all's not as smart as she thinks she is!* Then the obvious secrecy of her father's behavior turned puzzling. Belle slit open the envelope. Inside was a purchase paper—a receipt for a 42-foot Hatteras fishing boat. The paper was dated four years earlier, and Theodore A. Graham was listed as the boat's new owner. The yacht broker was Sunny Day Boats of Sanibel.

"Lemme think now . . . It was three . . . no, four years ago . . . Yeah, that's right . . . four and change . . . 'cause it must have been March. The weather was gorgeous. Real nice. Mellow, you know . . . before the heat starts to build . . ." The owner of Sunny Day Boats graced Belle with a broad, untroubled smile, then leaned back in a well-padded swivel chair while she almost simultaneously leaned forward. She yearned to interrupt him and hurry along the process, but forced herself to bide her time. "Jimbo" Case was clearly a man accustomed to a slower rhythm in conversation as well as in life. "I tell ya . . . The Gulf in March is darned near perfection itself . . . I take that back. It *is* perfection."

"So my father paid you in cash?"

Case nodded slowly. "I mean, how's that for a salesman's dream? Dr. Graham and Woody were the easiest customers I ever did see."

A puzzled frown creased Belle's forehead as she pushed the official papers across the yacht broker's desk top. "My father is the only name listed, Mr. Case."

"Jimbo, please! Call me Jimbo, or Big Jim, if you'd prefer. Some folks have a fondness for one way of speaking; some another . . . I've been Jimbo near as long as I've been on this earth, and Big Jim, well . . . you can imagine how long that nickname's tagged around after me . . ." He held up two large hands and allowed himself a low, good-natured chuckle that rolled across his ample belly. "I never was no puny kid . . . So . . . Now, none of that Mr. Case business. I know you people up North go in for the formality bit, but it makes folks down here downright uncomfortable—"

"Jimbo . . . My father's name—"

"Good girl!" Case grinned again and peered at the form. "You're right as rain, little lady. Theodore Graham appears to be the sole owner. However, I distinctly recall Woody's part of the transaction. Heck, he was the guy who tooled around in that pretty little Hatteras. Not your dad. I don't recall ever seeing Dr. Graham at the helm . . ." Case's previously serene brow also creased. "Come to think on it, I don't believe he spent a whole heap of time aboard, either . . . So, you know what I'm thinking, little lady? I'm thinking your daddy bought the boat . . . I mean he was a professor, an upstanding member of society, and all that . . ."

Belle nodded. *As opposed to Woody?* she wanted to interject but didn't.

". . . So he buys the boat, and Woody pays him back . . . Or some such scheme . . . 'Cause otherwise why would Woody be beboppin' around in the Hatteras without your dad? I mean, everyone around about here *assumes* that boat belongs to Woody . . . And I've got to admit, before you came waltzin' in here, I'd plumb forgot the whole transaction . . . Except the cash part." He beamed again, the expression benign and smug. "That was sweet."

"You wouldn't happen to know Woody's last name, would you?"

The happy smile turned thoughtful. "Come to think on it, no . . . Woody's just Woody . . . like I'm Jimbo . . . Last names don't always stick with us boat crowd. Woody must be short for something . . . Woodson, Woodburn . . . Heck, I'd call myself Woody, too, if I was stuck with a mouthful like that . . ." Jimbo let out a small harumph and said, "Heck, maybe he plays the clarinet, and somebody made a joke . . ."

A thousand additional questions peppered Belle's brain, but she'd begun to intuit that Big Jim Case was not the man to answer them. She returned the purchase papers to her purse, then stood, a polite smile affixed to her face. "You wouldn't happen to know where the boat is moored, Mr. . . . Jimbo?"

The sunny expression returned to Case's wide face. "There you go, little lady. You're getting the hang of it . . ." He stood, extended his hand, and shook Belle's while exuding the steady charm of a person adept at selling things. "Sure, I know where she's moored. She's at the Anchorage Marina . . . A nice setup. A real class act." Then his eyes and mouth turned genuinely sad. "Sorry about your dad, little lady. I'm sure he'll be powerful missed . . ."

Belle produced another falsely hearty smile. "Thank you . . . Jimbo." Then she turned toward the door.

"Aren't you forgetting something, little lady?"

"I put the bill of sale back in my purse—"

"Like, maybe the name of the boat? The Anchorage is a real big facility. Hunting up a no-name Hatteras is gonna be tough."

Belle nodded and smiled again. By now she recognized how this game was played. "You wouldn't happen to remember it, would you?"

"Why, sure I do! It's *Wooden Shoe* . . . Like in the kiddies' poem . . . 'sailed off in a wooden shoe' . . ."

Belle finished the line in her head: *"into a sea of blue."*

* * *

The Anchorage was a marina, resort, and upscale shopping complex rolled into one: a miniuniverse of verdantly landscaped walkways, tile-roofed buildings, and palm trees threading their spiky leaves against an azure sky. Oversized terra-cotta pots of pink and coral geraniums clustered at every turning; thatched gazebos invited sitting, and bike stands stood at the ready, sporting not racing machines but giant three-wheelers for relaxed and leisurely pedaling. Belle studied the scene; she couldn't imagine her father comfortable in such a Sybarite's paradise, but then she hadn't pictured her father as a yacht owner, either.

A teenaged attendant in khaki shorts and a blue polo shirt emblazoned with white scroll letters announcing *The Anchorage* was busy sweeping a single fallen geranium leaf into a pristine metal canister. When Belle asked directions to the marina, he looked at her as if she'd lost her marbles.

"You mean, by the water?" he asked.

Belle didn't retort that marinas—given the origin of the appellation—were always on the water. After all, she was the one who'd asked the stupid question. She hurried down the walkway toward the shore.

But there, as Big Jim Case had suggested, a sea of large— and larger—boats greeted her: hundreds upon hundreds, so it seemed. Where *Wooden Shoe* floated among them, Belle didn't have a clue.

She found the marina office, where another remarkably easygoing and unrepentantly male greeted her. "Hey there, young lady."

"I'm looking for *Wooden Shoe*—"

"Woody's boat?"

"Mmmm." Belle nodded.

"You just missed him, pretty lady. Sorry to say."

Belle pasted on what she imagined resembled a disappointed but hopeful smile. "I'll be on the island another day or two, so I can stop by—"

"Oh, you won't find him coming back by then . . . When ole Woody heads out, he's gone a couple of weeks or more . . . sometimes upward of a month or two. The man's what they call a free spirit—"

"Was his friend Ted usually on those trips?"

"Who?"

"Ted Graham . . . Theodore Graham . . . Did he ordinarily accompany Woody—"

"You mean, ship out with him?"

Belle nodded again.

"With Woody?"

Belle felt as though she'd been trapped in an endless game of twenty questions. "That's right."

"I never heard of anyone named Ted Graham . . . But I'll tell you right now, Woody never takes anyone on that boat of his. Oh, an occasional fishing buddy for a day, but never for an extended stay . . . Like I said, he's a free spirit . . . Goes where the breezes flow."

Belle considered the information. "You wouldn't happen to know his full name, would you?"

The man studied her, his expression suddenly less friendly. "Sure I do," he answered, although the information wasn't forthcoming.

"I guess I should fess up," Belle admitted. "Woody and my dad are old friends . . . army buddies, in fact . . . if it *is* the same Woody . . . Ted Graham was . . . *is* another pal . . . Anyway, since I was passing through Sanibel, I thought I should say 'Hi.' Dad would be furious if I didn't . . . In fact . . . in fact, he gave me some personal papers to pass

along should I happen to run into him . . ." Even as she spun
out the story, she realized it had a major hole. If she knew the
name of the boat, why wouldn't she also know the true identity of its owner? Belle's smile grew brighter and broader in
the hopes her interrogator wouldn't notice the flaws. And she
was in luck.

"Horace Llewellen, of course. Least that's what's printed on
the Hatteras's Coast Guard documentation. But I'll betcha he
doesn't let your dad or this Ted Graham character ever call
him Horace."

Belle grinned. "I guess not . . . So, you'll tell Woody I was
asking for him?"

"When—and if—I see him."

"When you see him, of course . . . Nothing urgent . . . But
I do want to pass along the information from my dad." Belle
produced a business card from her purse. "He can contact me
here."

The man took the card, peered at it, and cocked his head to
one side. "Crossword puzzle editor, huh?"

"That's right."

"In Massachusetts . . ."

"Yup." Belle felt her smile muscles growing weary.

"You should move down here, pretty lady. I read somewhere that Sarasota County—that's north of here—is the
crossword capital of the country . . . maybe even the world."

"Is that so?" Belle considered this reply less than stellar,
but it was all she seemed able to muster.

"You have to be pretty brainy to do those things,
don'tcha?"

"Well, it takes a certain—"

"Me? I can't even remember that rule about 'i' and 'e' and
'c.' But I know P-O-S-H: Port out, starboard home." He

tucked Belle's card in his wallet. "I'll be sure to tell ole Woody to give you a jingle . . . but it may be some time."

Strolling back through the marina toward her car, Belle experienced a combination of relief and dissatisfaction. Jim Case's breezy assumption that her father had purchased Wooden Shoe and then transferred the title to a friend who lacked a retired professor's stable financial history seemed not only reasonable but a foregone conclusion—which made Horace Llewellen merely another unsolved mystery in the larger unknown that had been her father's existence.

Belle considered how little she knew of the Theodore Graham who'd bought boats and formed friendships—and who'd also apparently inspired a good deal of fond admiration. She sighed, and as she sighed, her eyes strayed to the ground, causing her to run almost square into a man hurrying along the marina walk toward her.

"Excuse me, miss."

"Oh!" Belle jumped. What she saw as she glanced up was a dark suit, a starched white shirt, a hat shaped like a fedora held formally in one hand. In the near distance behind the man's back idled a motor yacht of voluptuous size and sparkle. It looked newly minted, and its crew, busy attaching docking lines, looked freshly equipped, too.

"Excuse me, miss," this impeccably accoutered specimen repeated. "I have just come from Europe—directly."

Belle turned around, imagining he was addressing someone else. No one was nearby, and it dawned on her that he'd mistaken her for someone else. But before she could rectify the situation, he continued. "I have been gone a good while. Can you tell me the name of the bartender in this establishment?"

Belle stared at the suit, at the hat, at leather shoes so polished their reflection stung the eye. "I'm sorry. I've never been here before . . . But you might inquire at the marina office . . . or in the restaurant . . ."

It was only after she returned to her father's apartment that she considered how odd the exchange had been. And what an unfamiliar accent the man had had. *It wasn't Western European,* she thought. *Maybe from the East? A Slavic language perhaps? Or Israeli? Or maybe Russian or Ukrainian with an overlay of British schooling?* The only certainty was that it seemed entirely too exotic to encounter in a quintessentially American resort like the Anchorage on Sanibel.

Belle continued sorting through books and belongings as she pondered this newest curiosity. Gradually she became aware of a voice talking into a phone next door. Angry and insistent words stabbed their way through the open veranda door. Belle walked outside; the voice hissed and growled in the air, but its owner was invisible behind the dividing wall that separated one veranda from another. *"Nyet,"* she heard, and then a string of loud sounds whose meaning she couldn't remotely fathom.

"Excuse me?" she called. "Do you mind not shouting so much?"

The voice fell abruptly silent, so quiescent, in fact, that Belle almost believed she'd imagined the noise.

"Thanks!" she sang out, but there was no response. She shrugged her shoulders and returned to the task of packing her father's possessions. A Russian neighbor, a multimillion-dollar yacht whose owner was clearly an international tycoon. Obviously, she'd been vastly mistaken about what life as a Florida retiree entailed.

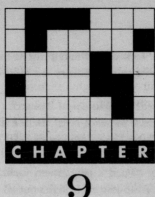

CHAPTER

9

"I don't know, Belle . . . That sounds like a pickup line. And a pretty clever one, to boot." Rosco chuckled as he spoke. "Did the guy happen to invite you aboard his floating palace? Or did he just use the 'I'm new in town, and you look like a woman who knows her way around, so what's the name of the bartender' routine?"

"Very funny . . ." Belle couldn't help joining in Rosco's amusement, however; she laughed as she gazed through the windshield at the serious-looking edifices of granite and steel lining the Massachusetts highway. *Palm trees are for swizzle sticks,* their dour demeanors seemed to say. She chortled again. "It did strike me as a strange—"

"Tommy Lipton had a nice yacht, too."

"Who?"

Maneuvering his aging and beloved Jeep into the Sumner Tunnel and away from Boston's Logan Airport, Rosco glanced sideways at Belle. He loved it when he discovered information she lacked—although not as much as he loved her. "The late nineteenth-century tea king—and confirmed ladies' man—"

"I'm impressed! Mr. Historical Research . . . I never know what you'll surprise me with next." Belle's laughter grew. "Is that what you think I was doing in Florida? Being wooed by international business tycoons?"

"Old Tommy owned a gargantuan yacht, too; not many gents were invited to join their ladies out on the briny."

Belle chuckled again, then moved close, and leaned her head on his shoulder. "The bizarre facts you can pull out of your hat . . . I missed you, Rosco—"

"I should have gone down there with you, Belle."

"To protect me from handsome yachtsmen?"

"You never said the guy was handsome! How handsome?"

"Nothing compared to you . . . Anyway he was wearing socks, and shoes—with laces . . . Definitely not your style. Or mine." She sighed contentedly while Rosco continued in a more serious vein.

"I should have been there to help sort through your dad's stuff . . . all those memories."

"There were no memories, Rosco. That's what felt so weird . . . None connected to me, at any rate; aside from the crossword Father had framed." Belle paused. "That was a nice find . . . odd, but nice . . . and rather sad, too . . ." She remained silent a moment, then continued talking. "I told you I tried to toss out a number of the photos—at least, the ones whose subjects I didn't recognize, but I found I couldn't do it . . . I don't know, I guess I'll end up storing them in the attic until I'm ninety-five . . . And I didn't take time to sort his papers. I simply stuffed them in boxes, along with his financial material. Then I lugged them to the local Global

Delivery office and sent them hurrying north. I was told the shipment might even beat me home."

"I should have been there," Rosco repeated.

"I'm a big girl. I'll tell you when I'm in trouble."

"That's exactly what bothers me."

Belle squeezed his arm. "Which means you don't trust me to know when I'm getting into difficult terrain—"

"Which means you don't have to pretend to be brave . . . I know it was tough encountering this Deborah person, and tough just being in your dad's apartment."

Belle didn't answer; after a moment Rosco continued. "So, what happens to *Mrs.* Hurley now?"

"I gave her two weeks' severance pay, got Father's keys back—which wasn't as easy as it sounds. She wanted us to 'stay in touch,' but . . ."

Rosco gave Belle's knee a gentle pat. After another pause, she resumed her tale. ". . . aside from waiting for the realtor to find a buyer for Father's condo, the only unfinished business is reconnecting with this Woody character—Horace Llewellen. I assume he'll want to obtain the purchase papers to *Wooden Shoe.*"

"Not having any papers doesn't seemed to have slowed him down for the last four years. Maybe the yacht broker was right in suggesting that Woody and your dad completed another type of transfer transaction. It's easy enough for me to check that with the Coast Guard and the state of Florida. Certainly seems simpler than chasing Woody down."

"Mmmm . . ." Belle nodded as Rosco sped down Route 93, following the signs for THE CAPE. "I hadn't considered that possibility. I guess that's why Woody didn't mention the boat when he stopped by . . . Unless he was too shocked by Father's death to think clearly."

"My supposition—without ever having met your dad—is that he was too fastidious a person to leave loose ends behind."

"He didn't know he was going to die, Rosco."

"That's true . . . But I don't imagine he would have been comfortable with someone other than himself piloting an expensive boat—without having previously relinquished all claims to ownership. For one thing, there's a matter of insurance: in particular, liability insurance. If anyone sustained a serious injury—"

Belle interrupted. "You're right. I never considered that. Father was definitely not a casual person. So, I guess I've seen the last of Mr. Horace Llewellen . . ." She turned pensive, and her spine sagged as though in regret, then straightened again as she returned the memory to the unknown and mysterious past where it belonged. "How's your new case going?" she finally said.

"A mess," was Rosco's tight-lipped reply. "How I ever got into investigating maritime fraud is beyond me. I don't even like boats."

Belle smiled at him. "Except this Mr. *Tommy* Lipton's . . . and the one we were married on."

Rosco raised his eyebrows but didn't speak.

"You didn't turn remotely green, and you know it! In fact, I think you secretly loved being at sea . . . Starting today, I'm going to begin angling for a vacation on a cruise ship. The Caribbean . . . the Mediterranean—"

"It sounds to me as though you missed your chance for foreign travel when you were in Sanibel—"

"With you, dopey!" Belle laughed again while Rosco's tone grew serious again.

"I should have gone to Florida with you, Belle . . ."

"It's okay, Rosco. It is. But you can fly down with me when we sell the apartment, how's that?"

"I missed you, that's all."

"I missed you, too," was her peaceful response.

The phone was ringing as Belle stepped through their front door. Simultaneously, Kit started in on her signature combination bark-and-joy-filled whimper, and a Global Delivery truck pulled into the drive. Belle reached for the phone while tousling Kit's velvety brown ears; and Rosco stepped back outside to receive the shipment from Florida. When he returned, he saw Belle rolling her eyes while mouthing "Sara" and continuing to stroke the delighted Kit.

"No, the flight wasn't delayed, Sara. It was just that the traffic—well, you know Boston—I don't think they're ever going to finish that darn roadway . . . Of course, he picked me up in his Jeep . . . No, it's a good car, Sara, it is . . . I know. I know . . . But Rosco wouldn't drive it if he didn't believe . . . Yes, I know high speeds can—"

Cut off again by the emphatic—some might say, bossy—older woman, Belle cupped her hand over the phone's mouthpiece and whispered, "Do we have any stuff to eat?"

"As in a meal?" Rosco whispered back.

"Or crackers and cheese? Actually, I'm famished . . ."

Unfortunately, Sara overheard the last word in this dialogue. The words that rumbled through the receiver were loud enough for Rosco to hear. "You haven't eaten, young lady! I knew it! And I assume that darling husband of yours didn't properly stock the larder in anticipation of your return. Men are perfectly hopeless when it comes to the domestic arts. My late husband couldn't have told you the difference between a *pâte brisée* and a *pâté de foie gras* . . . Unless he'd tasted both, of course—"

"We don't have a larder, Sara," Belle finally interjected.

"You'll come over at once, my dear! Emma has concocted the most delightful tomato aspic—"

"But I just walked in the door." Belle looked up in appeal to Rosco, who merely shook his head in bemused resignation.

"You two lovebirds can relinquish each other's company for an hour, I'm sure." The grand old lady's voice continued to crackle through the phone. "Anyway, Rosco's working on that despicable case, with those despicable people, and I'm sure he can't be lollygagging around, making google eyes at you—"

"But—"

"I won't hear a word of objection, my dear child. I'm going to feed you, and that's the end of the discussion. You may bring that man of yours along if you wish. If I know him at all—and I'm proud to say that I do—I assume he's also in need of a decent repast . . ."

Rosco mimed a laughing *I've got work to do* while Belle continued to cradle the phone. Her father was dead; her mother was dead; and Sara, generous and nurturing to a fault, suddenly presented a picture of the most ideal combination of parent/mentor/friend that anyone might wish.

"I'll be there in half an hour," was Belle's quiet response. "But I won't bring Rosco. And Sara . . . thanks."

CHAPTER

10

A lone in the house, Rosco decided to postpone returning to his office long enough to carry the boxes shipped from Florida upstairs to the spare bedroom. If left to her own devices, his wife would probably begin sorting through the cartons' contents in the front hall; and the house's design scheme—such as it was—would suffer. Belle didn't believe in expending energy on mundane things like tidiness and order. Clutter to her was freedom. The haphazard piles of books, the pillows tossed off the chair, were art.

Kit decided to make herself useful, as well, although the puppy's idea of work was to scurry after a squeaking ball that repeatedly leaped or rolled away. She gave herself wholly to the effort, anticipating hours spent at the chase; Rosco allotted twenty minutes to his activity before resuming the Leeland-Marine case. These differing canine and human viewpoints were bound to collide.

Which they did when Rosco lifted his foot from the

second-to-last riser in preparation for carting the fourth
cardboard box down the upstairs hall. Kit's neon red ball
was where the wooden landing should have been; and
Rosco, lacking her nimble paws, was poorly equipped to balance atop it. He fell forward; the box slipped back, caroming
down the steps with a number of mighty thuds while Kit,
entranced with the new game, raced after the now-splitting
carton, barking and trying to catch fragments of bank statements, tax returns, and other financial detritus in her mouth.

"Kit!" Rosco ordered. "Kit! No! *Baaaad* girl."

As Kit well knew, this admonition was absurd. Fun wasn't
fun without a little noise and discussion. And because she
didn't possess a tail, she wagged her entire body in glee while
Rosco descended the stairs gathering spilled paperwork. For
good measure, the puppy began to munch a particularly
chewy morsel lined with green and white and dotted with a
good deal of ink. She added a teasing growl to her act.

"Come on, Kit. I've got to get back to the office . . . Come
on, girl . . . Drop it . . ." Rosco sighed, bent down, and
coaxed the damp paper from the dog's mouth. Then he stared
at the still-legible lettering. His first instinct was to phone
Belle immediately. His second thought was, *No, let her enjoy
her lunch in peace.*

Belle spooned up another piece of tomato aspic. Sara had
been correct. It was delicious—and what's more, it
seemed the supreme "comfort food." Tomato aspic was a dish
served solely in grandmotherly houses.

"Thank you, Emma," Belle said as the woman Sara referred
to as her "upstairs maid—and full-time keeper of the castle"

poured another glass of iced tea from a silver pitcher bespeck-
led with droplets of frost.

The year, Belle decided, could have been any one prior to
World War II. Not that she'd been around to witness such
luxuries as formal luncheons served in stately, family dining
rooms, but Sara had; and her sense of what was proper and fit-
ting had obviously been learned at an early age. Tomato aspic
served on a chilled glass plate, luncheon-sized linen napkins
as opposed to the towel-sized damask ones reserved for dinner. An "upstairs maid" when, in truth, Sara's ancestral home,
White Caps, had only a single housekeeper. Belle briefly wondered how Emma put up with her mistress's old-fashioned
foibles, but then she realized how close the two women were
in age. Each held the long-dead past in loving esteem.

"Miss Belle." A round porcelain serving dish specially constructed to hold deviled eggs was proffered.

Belle beamed at Emma.

"Go ahead, my dear," said Sara. "Take as many as you wish.
Take two . . . I jest, of course. Those were the words my
paternal grandmother used to say when she passed around a
box of bonbons . . . 'Take as many as you wish, Sara, child.
Take two.'" Sara's intensely blue eyes grew misty with nostal-
gia. "Why do you suppose a lady old enough to be a great-
grandmother would miss her own grandmother? It makes no
sense. If she were still among the living, the woman would be
at least one hundred forty . . ." A sound like a tiny sigh
escaped Sara's stalwart frame. "At any rate, Belle, eat your fill.
Emma will be deeply discouraged if you pass up her concoc-
tion. It was she who suggested we serve your favorite
comestible. Wasn't it, Emma?"

"Yes, madam."

Good will, like an electrical current, flowed between White Caps' two elderly denizens.

Belle helped herself to not two or three or even four, but five deviled eggs, then proceeded to nibble her way through each delicious one.

"Now, tell me again, dear, about your father's boat, and Mr. Horace Llewellen."

But before Belle could commence, Sara, in typical fashion, reverted to her earlier topic. "My grandmother also used to admonish me with the adage that the greatest personal attribute was courage. Because if one did not possess courage, one could not cleave to any other emotion . . ." Again, she shifted tack with a wistful: "I'd like to meet this Woody character. He sounds quite intriguing."

"From the hasty retreat he beat when he learned of my father's death, I don't imagine that's in the cards."

"Ah, for the vagabond life! Before my brother, Hal, ran for the Senate, he 'flirted' with the notion of such a romantic existence. Allegedly, he was a member of the diplomatic corps at the time. That's what he told everyone, at any rate. However, it was perfectly obvious that he had connections to the Central Intelligence Agency, or the OSS, as it was called back when . . . I used to jest that the number of Russian accents floating about this house might equip several productions of *Uncle Vanya*. Hal, of course, didn't enjoy the riposte. He's always been a stickler for exactitude. Despite his alleged desire for the dramatic, he had no sense of fun whatsoever— even as a toddler . . . That's why he didn't make it as a *spook*."

Belle smiled.

"You look amused, young lady. You don't imagine an old woman like me knows words like *spook*."

"I'm smiling at your description of the senator, Sara. You sounded as if you're still an eight-year-old in high dudgeon."

"Age doesn't alter one's outlook on the world, Belle. The essential person is always there. Sometimes, I'm perfectly horrified to look at myself in the mirror and see an ancient *crone* staring back. I feel no different than I did at forty or even sixty; why shouldn't my face and body match my spirit?" Then Sara again changed focus. "I'm sorry about this Deborah person, Belle dear. However, you can't be certain they were romantically involved . . . Perhaps, what you sensed from the woman was a pure case of hero worship."

When Belle didn't reply, Sara herself grew silent, and the room's stillness was only occasionally disturbed by the distant ministerings of Emma in her kitchen kingdom.

Finally, Sara spoke again. "Men can do foolish things when they're lonely . . ."

Belle shrugged her shoulders, but her friend was too perceptive to be put off by such an ineffectual dismissal.

"It didn't mean your father loved you any less."

"Oh, I wouldn't have minded knowing about Debbie—"

Sara's patrician eyebrows arched in disbelief, but her guest pushed past the unspoken critique. "I wouldn't have minded if Father had told me . . . if I'd *known.* What troubles me is the secrecy of it all—"

"The older we grow, Belle dear, the more shadowy certain portions of our lives become. I'm sure it would surprise you to discover I'd been quite a coquette in my day. A *hoyden,* in the words of my grandmama. All you know of me is the octogenarian residing over a rather antiquated domain called White Caps . . . Don't laugh, dear . . . I'm proud to say that I have my secrets, too."

* * *

It was the sound of his wife's footsteps downstairs on the front porch that made Rosco finally lift his eyes from his steady perusal of Theodore Graham's financial records. He glanced at his watch, noting with astonishment that he'd been at work for nearly two hours. He rubbed at his eye sockets, then slowly walked down the stairs. He wasn't certain how Belle would receive his news.

"Rosco!" Her pleased tone was mingled with more than a dose of confusion. "I saw your Jeep outside . . . I thought you were going to the office to wrestle with the Leland-Marine mess . . ." She gave him a long kiss. "This is nice . . . a nice surprise." She pulled back and gazed at him. "Does this mean we have the afternoon to play?"

Rosco smiled; it wasn't one of his best.

"Uh-oh, that's not the famous Polycrates 'let's play' smile; that's more like the famous Polycrates 'I'm thinking' smile."

"I tripped over Kit on the steps."

"Are you all right?"

"I was carrying your dad's stuff upstairs. One of the cartons broke."

"But you're okay?"

"Oh, yeah, I'm fine . . . but I decided to begin organizing his paperwork . . . Rather than just stuff it all back in the box."

"Darn," Belle said, giving him another kiss, "it's the 'I'm thinking' smile."

Rosco held up the piece of paper that Kit had so helpfully gnawed. "Want to take a guess at what this is?"

CHAPTER

11

Rosco waved the limp slip of paper between them as if trying to air-dry it. "This is what's left of a receipt—albeit slightly chewed and drooled on."

"So?" Belle responded. She was still unwilling to switch over to Rosco's serious tone.

"I found it in your father's papers . . . Or I should say Kit found it . . . Did you know that your father went to Belize?"

"Hmmm? Really . . . ? Well, I guess it had something to do with his research on the Olmec people. I assumed the culture was centered in what is now Mexico, but perhaps he found traces of the civilization elsewhere."

"Belle, *Belize* isn't the point. The point is: How do you think I discovered he went there?"

"I don't know, Rosco. Is that a hotel bill?"

"No, but that's an interesting thought . . . Because now that you mention it, I actually *didn't* find any hotel bills, or dinner receipts, for that matter. And his records are immaculate—"

"Did you doubt they would be?" Belle's tone was teasing. "I told you that, in my case, the apple fell *very* far from the parental tree . . ."

But Rosco had already moved forward with his train of thought. "Perhaps your father stayed with an academic institution down there . . . or maybe he had friends?"

"It's possible . . . Although, I don't have a clue who those friends might have been."

Rosco studied her. He didn't speak for a moment. "The reason I know about the trip, is because of this." Again, he lifted the paper Kit had so diligently chewed. "It's a plane ticket stub, Belle. The name 'Graham' is on it. Your dad flew there . . . on an airplane."

Belle looked dumbfounded. She shook her head while an expression of utter disbelief swept across her face. "Are you sure?" She pulled the receipt from Rosco's hand. "Theodore Graham . . ." she read aloud. "But my father was terrified of planes. He wouldn't fly if his life depended on it."

"Well, he did fly, Belle. He went to Belize. Not once, but three times."

"By plane? Each time?"

"Yep."

"Where are the other tickets?"

"Upstairs. With the rest of his stuff."

"I can't believe this."

"Well, believe it . . . Granted, it's the only way—or I should say *simplest* way to get from Florida to Belize. I can't imagine there are many regular shipping runs. And here's the other thing—each time he left from the Tampa Airport, but the receipts are dated well before he moved to Florida's west coast. If he was living in Marathon at the time, why didn't he leave from the Miami Airport?"

"But he never traveled *anywhere* by plane, only by rail or automobile . . . Thus his train trip up here to visit us . . . as well as his aborted journey to join our wedding."

"He never went to Europe?" Rosco found it difficult to believe that a worldly type like Theodore A. Graham had never crossed the *Pond*.

"By ship . . . sure. That was long before I was born. Once the transatlantic runs dried up, I don't think my parents even considered going back."

"Well . . ." Rosco took a deep breath and tried to feign an aura of indifference. "Like I said, if he needed to get to Belize, flying might have been his only option . . . You know, gulp down a few Valium and grin and bear it, right?"

Belle remained silent, so Rosco took her hand and gave it a light squeeze. "Okay . . . So, here we are . . . What would you like to do with this information?"

"What do you mean: *do?*"

"I think you have to make a decision, Belle. We can close up this Pandora's Box we've opened, and move your dad's belongings to the attic. Or we can look for an explanation for this uncharacteristic behavior. It's not a decision I can make, though; it has to come from you. And to be honest, I think digging into the past is liable to cause you pain. A lot of pain."

Bell squeezed his hand in return. "Thanks."

"My suggestion is to tape up the box, and tackle it in six months or so—after you've put some distance between yourself and the entire matter."

Belle was quiet for a long minute. "Is there more? More 'uncharacteristic behavior,' I mean?"

"There are other oddities, yes. However, your dad's gone . . . I suggest you let sleeping dogs lie."

Belle's pensive face broke into a rueful smile. "Have you ever known me to let sleeping dogs lie, Rosco? Have you? Kit notwithstanding . . ."

Rosco smiled back at her, his expression filled with concern and love. After a moment, he continued. "Okay. Here's what we have . . ." He stressed the word *we*, which Belle acknowledged with a grateful nod. "*We* have three trips to Belize via Tampa. Now, the only people who might have an explanation are this Woody guy, or Deborah Hurley . . . You've already attempted to track down Woody—to no avail . . . So, do you want to call Debbie yourself, or should I—acting in an official capacity?"

Belle thought for a second. "I'll phone her. We have a relationship . . . sort of. I've got her number in my office."

As they walked to the rear of the house, and an excessively crossword-puzzle-themed room that served as Belle's home office, Rosco placed his arm over her shoulder. "I love you, Belle. Anytime you want to call it quits on this . . . investigation, just let me know."

"I will."

She crossed to a filing cabinet, removed a manila folder, placed it on her desk, then picked up her phone and tapped in Debbie's number. It was answered on the second ring by a male voice.

"Hurley residence."

"Yes. Is this Mr. Hurley, by any chance?"

"Yes, ma'am."

"Mr. Hurley, this is Belle Graham calling . . . Ted Graham's daughter—"

"Oh, yes . . . Deb mentioned she'd seen you when you were down visiting." The voice was surprisingly free of tension or animosity, and Belle began wondering just what Debbie had *mentioned*. "I'm sorry about your dad, Mrs. Graham. It came as a shock to all of us down here. He was a great guy. Everyone was real fond of him."

"Thank you, Mr. Hurley—"

"Mike. Call me Mike. Please."

"Thank you . . ." Belle took a breath for courage. "Mike, I was wondering if I could speak with Debbie for a second?"

"She just stepped out, but I expect her back in about twenty minutes. She went to rent a movie. Would you like her to call you when she gets in?"

"Thanks. Yes. She's got my number."

"Is this about the sale of your dad's apartment?"

Belle frowned, uncomfortable once again with how interwoven these strangers' lives were with her father's. "No. I haven't heard anything from the broker." She hesitated. "Have you?"

"Not unless Deb knows something I don't." Another brief pause ensued. "Look, Mrs. Graham, please let us know if we can do anything for you . . . It's not easy handling these situations long distance, and we're here to help if we can. What I mean to say is: the offer still stands even if Deb is no longer in your family's employ."

Belle found herself smiling at the polite formality of Mike Hurley's words as well as his obviously genuine suggestion of help. "Thank you, Mike . . . And call me Belle, okay?"

"Will do."

Belle placed the receiver back in its cradle and slumped into her chair. "Well, he seems like a nice enough guy. Too bad he got hooked up with Debbie . . . Although maybe he'll never learn what her true feelings for my father were."

"You don't know for certain she wasn't simply what she appeared, Belle: the starstruck young assistant. I need to see more proof before jumping to far-out conclusions."

She didn't answer immediately. "That's what Sara said, too . . . But I was there, Rosco. And intuition tells me there was another relationship at work."

Rosco thought. "What does Mike do?"

"Deborah said he was down there T-A-D." Belle grinned for the first time in many, many minutes, although as an expression of mirth, it was unconvincing. "I bet you don't know what that means."

Rosco returned his own slow smile. "Temporary Assigned Duty . . . So, he's in the military."

Again, Belle tried for a light approach. "Yes, Mr. Know-it-all."

Rosco rubbed his chin. He was clearly pondering this new piece of information. "And since there aren't any large military installations in the immediate vicinity, I would guess he's with the Coast Guard. How long did Deborah say they'd been down in Florida?"

"She didn't. Why?"

"Just curious. If Mike is T-A-D, they've probably been in Florida less than a year—"

The telephone rang out at that moment. Startled, Belle jumped while Rosco regarded her, noting how tense and anxious she was beneath her habitual I-can-handle-it exterior. "Belle Graham speaking."

"This is Deborah Hurley." Unlike her husband's, the tone was frosty.

"Debbie. Good . . . Thank you for calling me back so promptly."

A long pause greeted Belle's effort at politeness. Then Debbie spoke again. "Mike said you needed to talk to me."

This time it was Belle who hesitated. Part of her wanted to solve the problem of her father's mysterious journeys; another part now sincerely wanted to avoid all future contact with Deborah Hurley. Mike's kind—and trusting—voice seemed to clamor in her ears. "Yes, I did, Debbie . . ." she finally said. "I've been sorting some of my father's paperwork and I came across a receipt for a round-trip Cen-Am plane ticket from Tampa to Belize."

The response to this statement was stony silence.

Belle shut her eyes, then forced them open. "It's dated seven months ago. Last February. I know my father hated to fly, so I was a little surprised—to say the least. Can you shed some light on this?"

Debbie didn't answer for a moment. When she did, her words were stiff, as though the speech had been practiced. "Look, I don't know what you're thinking my relationship with your father was, Belle . . . if I took trips with him, or things like that . . . What he hired me to do was research— and some secretarial work. That's all. And I've got to tell you that your . . . your suspicions are making me feel real uncomfortable . . . They'd make Mike feel uncomfortable, too, if he knew. I mean, my husband's a great guy, and I don't like you—"

"Debbie . . . Deborah, I'm not asking you to explain your relationship with my father, and I'm certainly not about to interfere in your marriage. Or to infer *any* kind of innuendo with your husband . . . I'm only asking if you have any idea why my father flew to Belize?"

"No."

"And you don't recall him leaving the country for seven days last February?"

"I wasn't working for Ted back then . . . Besides, February was a tough time for me. Mike and I had to go back up to New Jersey to deal with my kid sister . . . She died on Valentine's Day . . . We were expecting it . . . But still . . ." Debbie Hurley's speech ceased while Belle opened her mouth to respond, then realized any words of consolation would sound forced and false.

"So . . . so, I don't have any idea what your dad did—or where he went—during that time. All I can say is that he was really kind when he interviewed me, and I told him about my sister . . . He was really, really nice. . . . like he always was . . ." Debbie's voice threatened to crack; again, she paused. When she finally resumed talking, her composure had returned. "Ted never told me—or Mike—that he didn't like to fly," she said before hanging up.

After what seemed an eon, Belle returned the silent receiver to its cradle. Her brain felt bludgeoned with contradictory information and with the many personalities that apparently had been her father. She squinted her eyes; she tried to focus her thoughts. "Deborah said . . . Deborah said . . ."

"I heard that much," Rosco answered. He was tempted to put his arms around her, but sensed she needed space. "I'm sorry to say we've got another unsolved problem," he finally added.

CHAPTER

12

Belle shook her head; her confusion was absolute. "So, what are you trying to tell me, Rosco?"

"That's just it; I don't know." He held up a document she recognized: the sales receipt for *Wooden Shoe*. "The receipt is dated four years ago . . . for ninety-seven thousand dollars . . . A lot of moolah—even by today's standards. But for the life of me, I can't figure out where all the money came from."

Belle didn't respond for a moment; her brow was knotted in concentration. "I didn't focus on the financial aspect of *Wooden Shoe*'s purchase when I was down there . . . I should have . . ." From her position at her desk, she looked up and away from Rosco, instead gazing out the windows to the small and cozy garden beyond the house. The golden afternoon light of an August in New England bathed the hydrangea bushes and pots of petunias and lobelias in a warm, inviting glow. It was a scene made for patio chairs and glasses of lemonade, for the sounds of crickets chirruping or of seagulls lofting in on the harbor's salt breeze, but Belle was immune to the picturesque appeal. "It was just that everything came as such a surprise when I was down there . . ."

Rosco gave her shoulder a comforting squeeze. "I know . . . And I'll say it again: I wish I'd been there with you."

Belle turned back to him, her gaze hurrying past the crossword motif on the curtains, the captains' chairs decked out in black and white canvas, the wooden floor painted in large, bold squares to match. "You're a good person, Rosco."

He didn't answer for a minute. "What's troubling me is that there's no entry in your father's bank records to indicate a withdrawal in the amount necessary to purchase a good-sized motorboat . . . nowhere in the last six years—as far back as he kept files. Now, he could possibly have borrowed against his investment account and raised the cash. Current value is sitting around one hundred twenty-five thousand, but there's no sign that he ever applied for, or received, such a loan . . . Or made any regular type of payments."

Belle raised her hand to her forehead, but her concerned frown didn't abate. "The yacht broker said Father and Woody paid for the boat in cash . . . but I never suspected he meant tens and twenties."

Rosco smiled softly. "I doubt that Woody and Ted were walking around carrying a sail bag stuffed with ninety-seven thousand dollars in cold cash, so it must have been a cashier's check or something—drawn on a bank account we know nothing about."

"Well, it couldn't have been an account of my father's. Remember, the first thing the Florida probate people did was run his Social Security number through the system. I guarantee you he had no accounts other than what appears in the paperwork I shipped up from Florida. Even a small thing like a safe-deposit box would have shown up."

"I know . . ." Rosco rubbed the back of his neck. "And speaking of Social Security, I started looking at the deposit columns, too. Your father had just started on direct deposit of his S-S check last year. And his investment account automatically transferred any dividend income straight into his checking account, as well . . . Ever since the boat was purchased, there have been deposits of five thousand dollars made twice a year—on the fifteenth of March and the fifteenth of September, like clockwork."

Belle sat up a little straighter in her chair. "So that would bolster any theory that my father had lent the money to Woody, and was being paid back on a regular basis."

"That's what I was thinking. Of course, there's no proof that it was Woody who made those payments, but at ten thou a year, he would've paid back forty-five grand so far. Obviously your father had placed the owner's papers in the envelope for Woody, and hidden it, so that if—and when—he died, Woody would own the boat free and clear . . . Without having to forfeit any inheritance tax to the Feds or the state of Florida."

"That makes sense." Belle said this in a not entirely convincing tone.

"But it still doesn't explain where this ninety-seven thousand came from in the first place."

"No . . ."

"Or why, when I told Woody about Father's death, he didn't ask if there'd been any documents—or even a letter—left to his attention—"

"We're back to the fact that your father didn't know he was going to die, Belle."

"Right," she agreed. "But that doesn't mean that when he

was confronted with the information, Woody wouldn't have made a query or two—"

"Which might well indicate that the material your father hid behind the photo was no longer relevant."

"I guess . . ." Belle sighed.

"Let's return to the monetary situation," Rosco finally said. "Now, I can phone the bank, talk to his financial advisor . . . I can call the yacht broker, but they're all going to give me the same reply: 'That's not the type of information we supply over the telephone.' I hate to say this, but the only way we're going to get answers is for me—or both of us—to go back down to Florida and ask questions in person . . . And find Woody. He's the key to all of this."

"And Father's supposed fear of flying . . . Maybe we—"

The simultaneous eruption of noise—the doorbell chiming, Kit barking at the intrusion, and the fax machine ringing—burst upon the conversation like the arrival of a high school marching band. Belle jumped; Rosco very nearly did as well.

"Sounds like we're under siege," he said. "I'll get the door . . . And I'm expecting that fax. It should be from American Express."

Belle walked to the fax machine while Rosco followed Kit to the front door. A minute later he returned carrying a thick manila envelope.

"It was a messenger from the *Crier*. For the illustrious crossword editor." He set the package on Belle's desk.

"Arrgh . . . More puzzles for my compendium. I really wish I hadn't taken on this project. I should have agreed to a collection of my own puzzles, and let it go at that . . . Look how thick this envelope is." Belle dropped it on her desk. "It's going to take me forever to get through all these . . ." She pushed the manila envelope aside, unopened. "What's this fax from American Express about?"

"When we canceled your father's credit cards, we were sent closing statements—but not from Am-Ex. I called them earlier today and was told it had been mailed over a week ago, so I gather it got lost in the postal system. Anyway, they're forwarding a duplicate, but offered to fax a copy in the meantime."

Rosco took the fax from Belle and glanced it over. "It's interesting that your dad paid for those plane tickets in cash, rather than using a credit card."

"Why do you think that was?"

"I . . . don't . . . know," was Rosco's distracted answer. He'd clearly moved to another line of thought as he studied the transactions on Ted's final American Express statement.

Belle noted his furrowed brow. "What's wrong? I don't like that look on your face."

"It seems your father purchased *two* train tickets when he came up here."

"Two?"

"Mmmm . . ."

"But . . . But that means someone was traveling with him . . . Who?"

"No, wait. I was mistaken . . . It was a single fare, but one ticket took him from Tampa, Florida, to Trenton, New Jersey; and the second ticket is for Trenton through to Newcastle. So he never did change trains in New York, as you thought."

"Wait . . . Dad stopped in Trenton?"

"Yep. He also picked up a Jarvis rental car at the Trenton train station."

Belle walked behind Rosco and peered over his shoulder at

the Am-Ex statement. "Princeton . . ." she murmured. "He must have driven from Trenton to Princeton for some reason. The Florida train doesn't stop in Princeton . . ." Belle paused. "But I wonder why he never told me he was going there—"

"Well, it obviously wasn't a long stay . . . twenty-four hours. Forty-seven dollars sounds like a one-day rental to me. The Jarvis charge is posted on the thirteenth, the day your father was due to arrive in Newcastle—meaning that he might have rented it on the twelfth and spent the night in Princeton. On the other hand, there are no hotel charges . . ."

"He must have been a guest at someone's house . . ." Even as she posed the theory, Belle's brain began challenging it. *Who?* she wondered. *Why can't I name even one person?*

"Okay . . . So, a hotel might not have been necessary. But I'm still confused about the whereabouts of the Jarvis agreement. Not only didn't the Boston Police find any train ticket stubs in your dad's possession; there was no sign of rental car papers, either. And obviously nothing in the luggage they returned to us."

"Would Father have thrown them out?" Before the words were out of her mouth, Belle realized it was a stupid question.

Rosco gave her an "are you nuts?" look. "His records are pristine—six years and not a thing's out of order. He kept those airplane receipts, didn't he?"

She moved back to her desk and sat. "I don't know . . . Maybe . . . Maybe Father was beginning to lose his cognitive skills . . . He did have a heart attack less than twelve hours after returning the rental car. Perhaps coronary disease can affect thought processes . . . or alter habitual modes of behavior . . ."

Rosco shook his head in thought. "Could be, I guess . . . But my suggestion is that I go down to New Jersey and look into this. It'll only take a day, and maybe I can unearth some explanations."

Belle considered the suggestion. "I'll go with you."

"You could, Belle . . . Obviously, you could . . ." He paused, searching for words. "But perhaps it's better that I nose around in more of a professional investigator mode . . . and not as your husband."

Belle stared at the floor. "And you don't believe a 'daughter looking for the truth' approach is going to work as well?"

"To be honest? No. Folks have a way of overcompensating with people they think are connected to law enforcement . . . They say more than they should—or far less than is normal . . . Either way they send up a flag. We need closure here, Belle . . . You may be right in thinking that a heart condition was governing your dad's final actions, but I'd feel a lot better knowing exactly what transpired."

She nodded her head in quiet agreement while Rosco placed his hands on her shoulders and massaged them lightly. "I need to prepare a few docs for the lawyers on the Leland-Marine thing. That's going to take me most of tomorrow, but I can drive down to Princeton the next day."

Belle remained quiet for a moment. "What about Florida?"

"Let's see what turns up in the Garden State first."

Again, she hesitated before forming a reply. "I can't help but feel I should go with you. Maybe, it's guilt talking, but it doesn't seem right for me to sit here in Newcastle while you—"

"Obviously, you're welcome to accompany me—*more* than welcome. But experience tells me the official PI mode is what we need here. Besides, remember we're in this thing together . . . Whatever I learn is information for us both to share . . . 'All for one and one for all'? Isn't that the quotation?"

Belle· smiled briefly. "Close enough . . . But there were three musketeers, not two . . ."

Kit took this as a cue to let out a bark and roll onto her back.

Across

1. Cleo's downfall
4. In the chips
7. School grp.
10. CIA predecessor
13. Blow-hard
15. Window treatments
17. Jousted
18. Some falls
19. LEGAL HALTS
20. CHOPIN'S #9, TO SOME
21. Neat as a pin
24. Summer drinks
25. Fall behind
28. LEON'S ISRAEL, E.G.
30. Post LBJ
31. Okay
32. What pa does with his riata?
34. Diggin' it
35. DOCTOR'S INPUT
38. Jai__
40. Reason for alimony?
43. 61-Across's prize
44. Dr. of rap
45. "FALSTAFF," TO VERDI
46. __Plaines
47. Rip
48. Town on the Meurthe
49. Darlings
50. "The Greatest"
51. "La Traviata" tenor
54. Skirt pocket
58. BAD NEWS AT A BEER BUST?
59. Eat
60. UFO passengers
61. Grads to be
62. Gel
63. Q-U link

Down

1. Stomach muscles, abbr.
2. Drain
3. Links grp.
4. INITIAL CHOICE
5. Simians
6. Spread hay
7. Bad hair day for Leo?
8. BOTTLE CAP INSTRUCTIONS
9. Black__
10. "__Life to Live"
11. Cpl's boss
12. Drafting grp.
14. TILLS
16. Parisian pronoun
20. Club soda and tonic
21. __'dino, Russia
22. Pitcher's stat.
23. Errors
25. Glove oil
26. Picnic pest
27. Washington or Hamilton; abbr.
29. Fair grade
31. CANON PRODUCTS
33. CONCORD PILOTS
36. Long or Block, abbr.
37. Leaning
38. Total
39. Fib
41. Chem-__
42. Query enc.
44. "__than a doornail"
47. 61-Across, usually
49. Start to amble?
50. Lotion ingredient
51. Pub pint
52. Building site
53. CAMERA SETTINGS

SIGNS OF THE TIMES

54. Some computers
55. Sumerian world of the dead
56. Some hosp. workers
57. Asian holiday

CHAPTER

13

"*S*igns of the Times," Belle mused aloud. "Clever . . . a nice game within a game . . ." She'd gathered the latest submissions to her crossword collection, working through each one individually as she always did, then arranging the puzzles in descending order of wit and intellect. The one entitled *Signs of the Times* was the clear favorite of the group.

"19-Across: *LEGAL HALTS* . . . 20-Across: *CHOPIN'S #9, TO SOME.* . . . Good . . . good . . . 58-Across: *BAD NEWS AT A BEER BUST?*" Belle chuckled softly as she finished inking in answers with her favorite red ballpoint pen, then added a small and carefully worked diagram to complete the page. "Why didn't I ever dream up a cryptic as ingenious as this?"

She looked at the constructor's name; it was not one she recognized. She added it to the notebook listing submissions to her forthcoming puzzle extravaganza. "What do you think, Kit? This one's a definite keeper, wouldn't you say?"

The puppy, unmoving by the garden door, didn't turn her head or make a sound. She'd been in that position ever since Rosco had left for New Jersey.

"C'mon, Kitty . . . Come on, girl . . . He'll be back soon."

Kit's brown ears only flattened further on the black and white floor.

Belle rose and walked to her, bending down to stroke the soft fur. "It's okay, Kit. Really . . ." Belle sighed; her fingers reflexively continued to pat the dog's back, but her thoughts argued a quick *No, it's not okay!*—then raced ahead to wonder for the one-hundredth time since Rosco had left how a person as seemingly ordinary and unenigmatic as her father could leave behind such a welter of problematic questions.

"I'll tell you what, Kitty. How about we go for a good, long walk?"

Rosco had calculated the drive from Newcastle to Trenton to take somewhere in the neighborhood of six hours; down and back—twelve. A lot of driving for one day, but he was unwilling to give up his "newlywed" status—i.e. spend the night alone in some cheesy motel along the New Jersey Turnpike— so he'd set the alarm for 5 A.M.

Belle had, of course, awakened as well, and feigned mock surprise at the fact that he'd opted to look at a map before jumping into his Jeep and darting onto the southbound ramp of Interstate 95. She had also been quite impressed that he'd decided to actually take the map of New Jersey with him; and Rosco now found himself smiling as he cruised down the Jersey Turnpike, recalling her parting shot: "You're taking a *map*! Whatever *for*? Oh, that's right . . . no air-conditioning in your car; I guess you'll need to fan yourself with something."

He'd said, "Ho, ho, ho," kissed her deeply, and followed it with, "I love you. See you tonight. Late."

Now, five hours into his drive south, he'd had plenty of time to consider all the worms that had crawled out of the woodwork since Belle's father had died. And the longer he drove, the more he deliberated, and the more suspicious these events seemed. There had been the flights to Belize, the missing train tickets, a missing rental car agreement, and no sign of a hotel receipt for that man's last night on earth—presumably, somewhere in New Jersey. All these lost items could have had a simple explanation—*if* Theodore Graham had been a haphazard individual. Having never met him, that had been Rosco's initial assessment: another scatterbrained professorial type, unconcerned with trivial matters such as receipts and stubs. But after dissecting Ted's financial records, Rosco had realized that nothing could have been farther from the truth. This was a person who was organized to the nth degree.

And then there was the lingering question of where the ninety-seven thousand dollars for Woody's Hatteras had come from. A problem that could be answered only by Woody himself—but one that also could have a logical explanation.

Rosco had refrained from transmitting his more serious concerns to Belle partly because he didn't want to worry her, but also because all he possessed was a handful of queries. As there seemed to be no evidence of foul play, why burden her?

But the many pieces of that deliberation had occurred back in Newcastle. Now that he'd had the long solo drive to analyze the situation, he'd convinced himself that something was most definitely wrong. Someone had taken Theodore Graham's train ticket and rental car agreement—which would indicate that someone was trying to conceal the fact that Ted had visited Princeton.

Then a far more grievous idea began nagging at Rosco: That same person might have gone so far as to have killed Belle's father.

These deductions left Rosco trembling slightly as he eased his Jeep into a parking space on Clinton Avenue, directly in front of the Trenton train station. The notion that his wife's father might have been murdered had turned his stomach into knots.

From habit, he reached up and flipped down the Jeep's sunvisor, displaying a Newcastle Police Department OFFICIAL BUSINESS placard, but then returned it to its original position, realizing it would carry little weight with the Trenton parking authorities. He stepped from the car, dropped two quarters into the meter, and surveyed the area. The station was low and modern in a 1970s sort of way—*Not a great era for architecture,* Rosco thought as he noted four taxis queued up in front of the station, the drivers standing in a bunch alongside the first cab telling jokes and smoking cigarettes. They looked as if they hadn't had a fare in hours and didn't much care; they seemed happy to enjoy the August sunshine. Rosco crossed behind them and entered the station.

Unlike many of the large older stations on Amtrak's East Coast line, the facility in Trenton had low, depressing ceilings. It appeared little more than a long corridor stretching over the tracks below. Services appeared to be minimal: four ticket windows, only one of which was open, a newsstand, a shoeshine area that looked permanently closed, a coffee vendor working out of a pushcart, which also offered smashed doughnuts sealed in cellophane, and a bank of self-service ticket machines. At the far end of the corridor Rosco spotted a sign reading RENTAL CARS.

He ambled toward the sign. When he reached the halfway point, he stopped and peered out of the large window at the tracks below. A train was just arriving from Philadelphia. Two passengers exited, and the train pushed on toward New York and Boston. Rosco continued down the corridor, through the glass door, and approached the Jarvis Rental Car counter. It was manned by a young black man who looked to be all of sixteen, although Rosco assumed there was an age requirement to get this managerial post. The man wore an orange Jarvis jumpsuit, with his name, SHAWN, embroidered on the left-hand pocket. He looked up from a copy of the *Sports Illustrated* swimsuit edition as Rosco neared.

"Good morning," he said, closing the magazine. "Can I help you?"

"Well, I hope so." Rosco pulled the American Express fax from his leather case. "I'm having a bit of a discrepancy with Am-Ex over a charge, and I was wondering if you could help me out."

"I will if I can. What's the problem?"

Rosco turned the fax around so that Shawn could read it and pointed to the Jarvis charge. "You see this charge for forty-seven dollars?"

"Yes, sir."

"Well, this is my father-in-law's statement, and I'm trying to verify all of these charges. The problem is, I can't find his copy of the rental agreement anywhere, so I thought I'd stop in and see if you might be able to print up another for me."

Shawn picked the fax up and looked it over. "Mr. Graham, huh?"

"Right."

"Why doesn't he stop by for it himself?"

Rosco debated which approach would work best with Shawn, and opted for something close to the truth. "Well, Mr. Graham is, I should say was, my father-in-law. He passed away. I'm running down these charges to clear up his estate, and this is the only one I don't have a receipt for."

"Jeez, sorry to hear about that." Shawn seemed sincerely upset at the news. "Wow . . . Yeah, sure, uh . . . That's no problem, mister, but I can tell you this charge is correct. Forty-seven dollars and fifty-two cents. That's the one-day charge for a midsized with the Triple-A discount and unlimited mileage. Comes out the same every time, as long as they don't take the extra insurance and return the car with a full tank."

"It sounded right, but I should take the printout just so everything's in order."

"No problem. Let me punch this code number into the computer. It's odd, though. He seemed to be a stickler for details. I'm surprised he lost the original."

"You remember him?" Rosco said, making no attempt to hide his surprise.

"Yeah," Shawn said, glancing at the fax again. "Mr. Graham, right? Like the crackers? You know, I thought he was gonna be a problem . . . on accounta' my being black . . . He had that look . . . I can usually spot the type. But he was a good guy. Bought me a Krimpet."

"A what?"

"I remember because he rented the car on the twelfth. And I was moanin' and groanin' because I had to work the next day, the thirteenth—which happens to be my birthday. Anyway, your father-in-law was real sympathetic about it; you know, really friendly. Especially considering the fact that his train was an hour late . . . And then, when he comes back with the car, on the thirteenth, he gives me a TastyKake Krimpet and says, 'Happy Birthday.' Yeah, a good guy."

"A Krimpet?"

"It's a butterscotch cake. Small, like a Drake's Cake? You're not from around here, are you?"

"No, I'm from the Boston area," Rosco said as he watched Shawn tear Ted's rental agreement from the computer's printer.

"Right, that's where Mr. Graham said he was heading. Massachusetts. Jeez, I'm real sorry to hear about this." He handed Rosco the printout, and Rosco scanned it quickly.

"Whoa," he said as he noticed the mileage, "there were a hundred and twelve miles posted on here. I'd assumed my father-in-law only went over to Princeton and back."

Shawn shrugged. "Who knows? Princeton's like ten or fifteen miles, tops. Guess he went somewhere else. Maybe the other guy knows where he went?"

"The other guy?"

"He had another guy with him when he returned the car. Didn't do any talking, the guy didn't . . . Seemed kinda steamed up about something."

"What did this other man look like?"

"I don't know . . . Regular. Just a regular white guy."

"How old was he?"

"Kinda old, you know, maybe your age. He had a Yankees hat on, so it was hard to tell."

"I'm thirty-eight. Is that old?"

"Wow, yeah, maybe he was younger. I don't know. But hey, he coulda been bald under that hat, for all I know. Then he would have been real old, right?" Shawn chuckled.

Rosco didn't respond to the jest. Instead he posed another

question, "Anything else you remember about this 'white guy'?"

Shawn shook his head. "Not really. He was the khakis-and-polo-shirt type . . . You know, the type of white guy that lives around Princeton. Probably works in New York or something . . . He didn't give me the time of day. Wasn't exactly nasty, but . . . Hey, you know the type."

"Anything else you can tell me? His height? Or weight?"

"He was just a regular guy . . . maybe a little taller than you . . . but I don't know . . . To tell you the truth, mister, I don't pay much attention unless people are real nice—or real obnoxious. Mr. Graham was the real nice type."

"And this man wasn't with my father-in-law when he picked the car up on the twelfth?"

"Nope. Mr. Graham drove off by himself."

"Did the two men board the train together?"

"Who knows? Once they walk through that glass door, they're outta my life." Shawn handed the fax back to Rosco. "Say, how did Mr. Graham die? If you don't mind me asking?"

Rosco saw no harm in telling Shawn the truth. "He had a heart attack on the train."

"Huh. And he didn't have our rental agreement on him? Sounds kinda fishy, if you ask me."

CHAPTER

14

Sliding behind the wheel of his Jeep, Rosco reset the trip gauge to zero. Although Shawn had insisted Princeton was less than fifteen miles from the Trenton train station, Rosco wanted the exact mileage, and a good idea of how long the drive could take.

"Just catch Route 1 North," Shawn had told him, "then grab the 202 exit, go through Lawrenceville, and Tiger-Town's five more miles, max."

Twenty-five minutes, and fourteen miles later, Rosco found himself pulling into a shaded parking place in front of an upscale dress shop in the center of the college town. The window display consisted of three tailored women's navy blue suits, a number of silk scarves, and a collection of leather handbags. Nothing was flashy; nothing was bold or remotely high-fashion. Self-consciously, Rosco considered his own attire. His fondness for not wearing socks would do fine in this classic Ivy League burg, but he suspected he just might be the only person shod in black shoes this side of New York City.

He glanced at the trip gauge a second time. Fourteen miles to Princeton, and fourteen miles back: twenty-eight miles total. Belle's father had driven a hundred and twelve miles. How, and when, had he added an additional eighty-four miles? According to the rental agreement, he'd picked up the car at 10:02 A.M. on the twelfth, and returned it on the thirteenth in time to catch the 9:27 A.M. train to Newcastle. Rosco opened the map of New Jersey. Calculating an eighty-mile round trip, he drew a circle that incorporated every area within forty miles of Princeton.

"He could've gone anywhere—even Pennsylvania," Rosco mumbled while sliding the map back into the glove compartment. "Well, let's see what Tiger-Town can tell me."

Princeton had a reputation for being picture-perfect, and Rosco could find nothing to contradict the assessment. The main drag, Nassau Street, separated the village from the university; as the school had grown to the south, the town had expanded northward. The process had begun during the eighteenth century, making the town and college quintessentially Old School.

Shop signs were carved from wood and painted in subdued shades of green, brown, blue, and red, with attractive gold-leaf lettering. A bookstore appeared to offer only an assortment of orange-spined *Penguin Classics,* while the music seller exhibited an ancient Victrola, with an antique RCA dog perched alongside—thereby almost camouflaging the racks and racks of CDs lining its interior walls. The men's clothing shops offered variations of herringbone, houndstooth, tweed, khaki—and the requisite Ivy League blue blazers. However, each display had the addition of at least one orange-and-black

Princeton University trinket—coffee mug, pennant, toy stuffed tiger, etc.

The heat of the August afternoon made the fall garments seem out of place, but Rosco realized that the average male student probably arrived with a collection of shorts and T-shirts. By October those same students would be freezing—leaving little option but to scoot across Nassau Street with Dad's credit card and get with the program. He figured the girls would be better prepared; girls usually were.

He dropped a handful of quarters into the parking meter and turned his attention to the university. The buildings were primarily brick and graystone, the architecture neo-Gothic, Tudor, or Georgian; and each edifice was covered with the requisite splotches of thick and glossy ivy. The scene was almost too idyllic.

Crosswalks painted in white and yellow led the way into the campus; as Rosco entered one, all traffic came to an abrupt halt. He strolled across Nassau, and passed through an archway that seemed to be the only vehicular entrance to the university. A uniformed campus policeman sat in a guard booth poring over a newspaper. As the majority of the student body wouldn't be returning until later in the month, the school grounds were noticeably deserted, and the guard decidedly unconcerned.

Rosco approached the booth and rapped on the window. "I parked on the street . . . But should I have driven onto the campus itself?"

The guard regarded him thoughtfully. "Wilson School?"

"Pardon me?"

"Are you looking for the Wilson School?"

"Ah, no . . . No, I have an appointment at the Anthropology Department."

The guard nodded slowly. "Anthropology, huh? . . . I would have picked you for Diplomacy. They're the only ones who wear black shoes around here. Anyway, if you're checking into a dorm, you can drive onto the campus. But only to unload, because there's no unattended parking. We tow . . . You registering?"

Rosco chuckled. "I'm a little old for college, don't you think?"

"You wouldn't think like that if you'd been here as long as I have. Hey, we've got geezers who've been studying for forty years. After a while, you can't tell them from the professors."

"Right. Anyway, I'm not planning to study at Princeton, I have an interview with Professor Araignée—"

"Don't know him."

"According to the secretary, it's a her, not a him."

"Ahhh."

There was a long silence while the guard returned to his paper and Rosco gazed at the expansive campus. "You don't happen to know which building the Anthropology Department is in, do you?"

"Aaron Burr Hall."

After another pause, Rosco cleared his throat. "Actually, I'm a visitor here. Could you point me in the right direction?"

"It's easier to go back out to Nassau." An abbreviated gesture accompanied the words. "You make a right there . . . After about three hundred yards, you come to an intersection. It's on the corner. Can't miss it."

"Thanks."

"The building's got ivy growing on it."

Rosco raised an eyebrow. "Thanks for the tip."

CHAPTER

15

The first thing Rosco had noticed was the skull. No, that was the second. The first had been Marie-Claude Araignée's husky French accent—followed by Marie-Claude herself: a woman almost vibrating with sensuality, a woman who'd been around the block more than a few times and who knew what she wanted and how to get it.

"Teddy?" she repeated in a guttural drawl. "Of course, I knew Teddy. And to think he can be dead . . . *C'est impossible . . . Impossible!* . . . Of course, I read the—how you say it?—obituary in the local newspaper . . ." She sighed. *"C'est terrible . . .* Teddy . . ." The way she spoke the name made Rosco think of a soft and much-loved stuffed bear. Marie-Claude sighed again, lit a cigarette, glanced at Rosco as if insisting that only the most boorish of males would deny her permission to smoke, then added a coquettish, "You Americans are so silly about this tobacco. *La vie est . . . Pardon . . .*

Life is too brief to worry about the small things. Obviously, far too brief. Look at Teddy . . ."

Rosco didn't answer, but his eyes inadvertently strayed to the skull atop Marie-Claude's desk.

"An interesting example that, *oui?*" She held the cigarette in her lips and lifted the skull, rolling it admiringly in her hands. "It is one of the prizes of the *collection* . . ." Another slow drag on her cigarette while the "prize" was gently returned to the desk. Marie-Claude gazed provocatively at Rosco. "The infamous nineteenth-century murderer and cut-throat, Bobby Sutcliffe . . . He makes interesting company, *non?* Of course, Bobby belongs in the case with the others. But what can I say? One of the privileges of power . . . I have *Monsieur* Sutcliffe with me all the day long . . ."

Rosco was about to return to his previous question about Belle's father and his most recent connection to Princeton's Anthropology Department, but Marie-Claude cut him off. "You must see many *corps* . . . corpses in your line of work, Mr. Polycrates."

"Fortunately, no." Rosco tried to smile.

"*Tant pis* . . . too bad . . . They make such fascinating subjects . . . But, of course, you must desire to see the *fameuse* Bartell Collection." Marie-Claude stood abruptly, her very unprofessorial high sling-back heels and clingy silk dress making her look as if she were ready for an evening *soirée*. "Everyone wants to view the Bartell heads . . . Teddy, of course, adored them. Real bone, you know, instead of the stone statues he was intent on writing about. Real people who were once truly breathing . . ." She sighed for a third time.

"So, you knew about Professor Graham's most recent work?"

"But, of course! . . . And how typical of Teddy to adopt a

subject that was so—how you say?—physically challenging . . . It is not easy to journey into Central and South America if one refuses to board an *aeroplane*."

"But he—" Rosco began.

But Marie-Claude had already left the room, beckoning to Rosco as she stood within the doorway. "We have specimens dating from as early as the seventeenth century . . . Bartell was a most unusual benefactor; a *Renaissance* man dwelling in America in the mid-1800s. He collected the various crania we now have on view, bribed ship captains to smuggle them into the country . . . bribed executioners, *aussi,* I am thinking . . . Then he measured each one, filled the brain cavities with sand in order to weigh them and determine volume. He hoped to understand the individual's capacity for intelligence . . . But you must know this *information*—?"

Rosco, following behind, merely answered, "If Professor Graham refused to fly, how did he accomplish his fieldwork?"

"*Je ne sais pas* . . . I don't know and he never offered to tell me. Ahh, I have no answer." She led the way through a dimly lit and poorly air-conditioned interior exhibition hall. "I was comfortable knowing he had . . . places in his life in which I had no part."

"Did he ever mention a man named Horace Llewellen?"

"He might have . . . but I don't remember . . . Teddy and I talked of many things when he visited. . . . including the skulls . . . many times the skulls."

"Were they part of Professor Graham's studies?"

Marie-Claude laughed slightly. "Well, not precisely . . . This latest craze of his was more archeological than anthropological, you know . . . When one is not bound by an institution such as this, one can indulge in a side trip every now and then." She snapped on a light switch, and a vast relic of a mahogany display case began to hum with a bluish neon glow. "Voilà . . . We also inherited the specially constructed *étagères* our benefactor designed for his display . . ."

Rosco avoided looking into the row upon row of gaping eyesockets, the jawbones from which protruded brown and broken teeth. "I'm not sure I understand, Professor Araignée . . . Why do you mean Theodore Graham wasn't 'precisely' studying the Bartell collection?"

In response, Marie-Claude turned a high-voltage smile upon him. "Do you know what the word *araignée* means in French, Mr. Polycrates? Spider . . . Black widow was what some vicious people said behind my back when my poor husband disappeared . . . So mean, you Americans can be some-times . . . Teddy was such a *confort* in those days . . . a comfort—"

Rosco felt as if he were spinning in circles. He pulled out his notebook in hopes that the lined paper could bring order to this peculiar conversation. "And when was that?"

"When darling François disappeared? . . . *Pardon,* Franklin . . . although I always called him François. Frank is such a Teu-tonic name . . . so nasal—"

"I was referring to the days when 'Teddy' proved such a 'comfort.' "

"Well, clearly that was when I found François gone." She spun back to the display case. "Look, here we have the head of a male . . . a German giant from the late seventeenth cen-tury—so the *information* tells us. Beside him is the cranium of a girl from the same region, most probably in her late teens . . . very *petite,* she was purported to be when living . . . although, as you will note, not in the least malformed—"

"And your husband—excuse my bluntness—your husband deserted you, Professor Araignée?"

"Deserted . . . ? Ah, *non* . . . François simply vanished."

Rosco frowned and wrote her words in his notebook.

"We were in Guatemala, *Monsieur* Polycrates. Four years ago, last winter. The police there sent out his photograph, contacted airports, and so forth. He'd been piloting his own plane, you know . . . Being Latin men, the local *gendarmes* reasoned that it is not uncommon for a man to forsake his wife for a younger female . . . They also spent time theorizing that he might have been murdered, and the *corps,* well . . . you are a detective. You may supply the words." Her words crackled with anger, then the rage subsided, leaving her tone pensive and subdued. "François's body was never found. Nor was his *aeroplane* . . . So quick, he was gone . . . Nothing like his darling last name . . . Mossback . . . a dear slowpoke of a turtle . . . Slowpoke, Yes? That is the correct expression?"

A dozen questions sprang into Rosco's brain, but he warned himself to stay on track. It was Theodore Graham's final days he was investigating, not Franklin Mossback's.

"And that's when you met Professor Graham? When he became such a *comfort*?"

"Oh, no. I'd met him before. François and I both knew Teddy."

"You knew him when he was teaching here?"

"*Non* . . . *non* . . . Teddy had already retired from academia when we three were introduced. He'd become a wanderer . . . an intellectual *vagabond* . . . free of the tiresome constraints of faculty life. You must understand, though, François was very keen on Teddy . . . It was not until . . . well, later that—"

"I understand . . . It's Professor Graham's most recent history I'm interested in. Specifically, what he did during the day and evening of August twelfth—"

"Oh, but the latter part of your question is so simple! He

stayed the night with me! I took him to hear a lecture given by this president of—how you say?—the Savante Company. No, no . . . Savante *Group* . . . It was a subject far from Teddy's sphere: energy production, fossil fuels, and so forth, but he was extremely anxious about drilling practices in Veracruz, in Mexico. That was the *habitat* of the Olmec peoples. I'm afraid he became rather aggressive in his questions after the talk, and there was a bit of a dust-up. That is an expression, no?"

Rosco considered her remarks. A public argument seemed out of character for someone as outwardly restrained as Ted Graham. And Belle had often mentioned that he'd never raised his voice. "What sort of 'dust-up,' Professor Araingée?"

"Oh, Teddy was concerned with potential damage to Olmec sites . . . that sort of thing—pollution of the land and seas. He finally stated that oil producers 'manifested barbarous insensitivity.'"

Rosco raised his eyebrows. "That must not have sat well with the president of Savante."

"It didn't." Marie-Claude laughed. "But Teddy could be so wonderfully . . . *viril* when he chose to be. 'Damn the polluters!' . . . That sort of rousing speech . . . His argument with Savante certainly proved an *inspiration*."

Rosco remained quiet a moment. "So . . . returning to Professor Graham's arrival on the day of the twelfth. What time was that?"

Marie-Claude chuckled again. "You Americans! So precise about the hours! He arrived when he always arrived . . . at six or seven in the evening . . . something like that—"

"And he left you at what time?"

"*Monsieur* Polycrates! You realize that I am an adult . . . Consenting adults, I believe your expression is? Teddy left me in the morning. The sun was up. You may supply the rest."

"And you don't know what he did before appearing on your doorstep? He apparently took an eighty-mile drive. You don't know where he might have gone, do you?"

"Teddy was also an adult, *monsieur*."

Rosco stifled a frustrated sigh. International diplomacy wasn't proving to be his strong suit—black shoes or not. "Is there someone else in Princeton who might be able to supply additional information?"

Marie-Claude squinted her eyes. For the first time, Rosco noticed they were very green. Like emeralds glowing with an interior light. "As I said, Teddy was retired when we met. He was no longer part of the *université,* and his sojourns here after François was gone, well, I will be discreet . . . They were not times of man-to-man chitchat. He did, however, still possess one *comrade* from the old days . . . one friend with whom he talked on occasion."

"Professor Graham drove someone—a man—to the Trenton train station with him. Was that the same friend?"

Marie-Claude Araignée shook her head. "*Ah, non, c'est impossible* . . . Roger is away on sabbatical . . . *en Chine,* I believe . . . doing research on the lost cities of the Gobi Desert. Roger Page is his *nom* . . . Also a member of the *université* faculty. He would know if Teddy had other male acquaintances with whom he spoke . . . Although, as I mentioned, he will be out of the country for several more months."

Rosco jotted down the name. "Would Deborah Hurley have contact information on Roger Page?"

The green eyes flashed. "I know of no Deborah Hurley."

"Professor Graham's research assistant . . . in Florida."

"Teddy never mentioned such a person."

So much for Marie-Claude's proud avowal of the benefits

of privacy among consenting adults. Rosco backtracked. Quickly. "So, you can't tell me who might have accompanied Professor Graham to Trenton on the morning of August thirteenth?"

"Perhaps you should pose the question to this *Mademoiselle* Hurley—"

"It's *Mrs.* Hurley."

Marie-Claude shrugged, then abruptly turned away and switched off the light filling the glass-fronted display case holding the Bartell collection. "I know nothing about this *Madame* Hurley, and I cannot tell you what Teddy did—or with whom he consorted—after he left my company." Then she looked at Rosco again, her expression now serene and inscrutable. "*C'est trés triste, n'est-ce pas?* It is very sad. The heart is a such fragile instrument. Bones are so much more durable . . ."

CHAPTER

16

Rosco grabbed his phone the moment he climbed into his Jeep, punched in New York City Information, requested a listing for the Savante Group, Incorporated, and rapidly jabbed out more numbers. After a minute, the switchboard put him through to the Office of the President and CEO where a receptionist reluctantly connected him to an assistant, who then uncategorically stated that Mr. Oclen was unavailable—even to members of the press, which was the alias Rosco had chosen.

"But this is the same Carl Oclen who spoke at Princeton University on August twelfth?" Rosco asked.

"Mr. Oclen did not address the university. He was entertained at the Harcourt Corporate Center. And you represent which newspaper, Mr.—?"

"Duncan. Tom Duncan. Of the *Evening Crier*, Newcastle, Massachusetts," was Rosco's quick lie. "I understand there was some unpleasantness during Mr. Oclen's presentation."

He added a placating "Sir . . ." then continued with a hurried, "I gather a number of people made attempts to put Mr. Oclen in the hot seat. Can you comment on that?"

"I advise you to contact our press office if you wish information, Mr. Duncan."

Sensing an imminent brush-off, Rosco barreled forward with another question. "Well, we always like to get it from the horse's mouth if we can—give folks an opportunity to tell their side of the story . . . Before we go to print. Can you tell me what Savante's position is in regards to oil production in Veracruz, Mexico?"

"That's Pemex's problem. Not ours."

"Pemex?"

The voice on the other end of the phone barked out a sharp, suspicious, "Who is this?"

"Tom Duncan, *The Evening Crier.* Actually, I'm on my way through New York City. If Mr. Oclen would like—"

"I don't know what hick newspaper editor told you to call Savante, Mr. Duncan, but I'd suggest you do your homework before bothering busy people. Pemex. Mexico's government-owned oil company. Savante does not participate, has not participated, does not foresee *any* participation in a state-owned monopoly. Good day, Mr.—"

Rosco blurted, "Well, what about the rest of Central America? Does Savante have operations there?"

"Our operations are a matter of public record, as with any publicly held corporation. There are channels for obtaining that information, but I'm afraid this is not one of them."

"Agreed," was Rosco's rapid reply. "But does the name 'Theodore Graham'—?"

"Good day, Mr. Duncan—"

"Is Mr. Oclen a Yankees fan?"

"What?"

"Is he a fan of the New York Yankees?"

"I wouldn't know." The receiver hit the cradle with such a bang it stung Rosco's ears.

As a true New Englander, he mumbled, "It was worth a try. How many Yankees fans can there be in the world?"

He redialed the central number, requested a copy of the corporation's annual report, then turned the key in the Jeep's ignition and began the long drive back to Massachusetts. He felt as if every question he'd asked had revealed only the need to ask twenty more: the proverbial snakes hiding under a rock.

After he'd driven past Manhattan and found a relatively quiet stretch of I-95 north of Stamford, Connecticut, Rosco again picked up his cell phone, this time calling Al Lever at the NPD. The gruff "Lever" that boomed out of the receiver was a sign that all was still right in the world.

"Al, I need a favor."

Lever sighed—one of the stagy, put-upon sighs that Belle referred to as "endearing." "I should say, 'Who is this?' but unfortunately, I know who it is . . . Look, Poly—crates, I already told ya, I don't know any more than you do on that Leland-Marine mess—"

"No, no, I already wrapped up Leland-Marine. Yesterday. This involves Theodore Graham."

The lack of response meant that Al was sitting straighter in his chair. "I don't like the way you're saying that Poly—crates . . . And I don't like the fact you're calling me on a cell phone, asking about your wife's father behind her back. Where is she?" Tough guy though he liked to appear, Al made no secret of the fact that he considered Annabella Graham to be the best thing that had ever happened to his former partner. "For that matter, where are you?"

"Heading north on 95 . . . Look, Al, I need to ask you to keep this conversation confidential—"

"I can handle that—for now . . . Not that you needed to ask . . . So, what gives with Pop Graham? A bunch of aliases? A slew of shady ladies on the side?"

"What makes you say that?"

"Sorry. That was a little out of line. What's up?"

"What can you find out about a disappearance of an American four and a half years ago in Guatemala?"

Lever laughed sardonically. "Not a damn thing, Poly—crates. You know that. I don't do international. And my connections with the Feds are somewhat strained at the moment."

"An American citizen, Al. Name of Franklin Mossback. Wife, Marie-Claude Araignée, professor of anthropology at Princeton University; French, obviously—"

"What's this got to do with old man Graham?"

"I can't tell you that now."

"Can't or won't?"

"Can't. I'm not sure what I'm fishing for."

Lever didn't immediately respond. When he did, his voice sounded tired. "I'm not trying to stonewall you, Poly—crates, but international data isn't our deal here. If you need info on this Frenchie and her—"

"It can be off the record, Al. Hearsay is fine. I don't need to know the source. I'm not trying to establish anything credible. I'm only trying to come up with some logical way to piece a puzzle together."

Lever sighed again. "Arrrgh . . . How do you spell this guy's name?"

"M-O-S-S-B-A-C-K, Franklin, as in Benjamin—"

"And the French babe, again?"

Rosco also supplied that information, then posed another question. "Have you ever heard of Pemex, Al?"

"Sure. Pemex. Cemex. Telmex. All the mexes. I bought stock in Telmex a while back . . . what a mistake. Took a damn bath—"

"Stock?"

"Stock. Shares. An investment. You got something wrong with your cell's reception, Poly—crates? Or don't you think cops follow the market? You don't think I'm working on retirement? Telmex. *Teléfonos de México* . . . Cemex is one of the world's biggest cement producers. Pemex is the oil king. You know, as in petroleum—?"

"How about the Savante Group?"

"Nah . . . The shares are way out of my range . . . They trade too rich for my blood. Not many solid oil stocks are penny-ante. What is this, Poly—crates? A lesson in intelligent investing?"

"Just pieces of a puzzle, Al. And right now, they don't even look like they came out of the same box."

CHAPTER

17

It was 8:45 P.M. by the time Rosco left I-95 at the Newcastle exit. Almost unconsciously, he found himself driving—not southward toward home—but north in the direction of tony Liberty Hill, and Sara Crane Briephs's grand domicile. It was late, Rosco knew, later than it should have been to pay an unexpected call on the town's dowager empress, but he reasoned that if anyone could advise him on how to handle the information he'd gleaned in Princeton, it would be Sara.

"Rosco!" White Caps' doyenne was outside "perambulating the nighttime gardens," as she referred to her evening strolls, when the Jeep pulled into the drive. In the harsh glare of the headlights, Sara's pale skin and white hair looked almost spectral, and her tall, slim body gaunt and disturbingly unhealthy. Rosco switched off his headlights. He hated to see her looking old. Looking fragile.

"Dear boy, whatever is the matter? You haven't seen a ghost, have you?"

"I'm sorry to bother you so late, Sara."

Her cane flicked dismissively across the gravel drive. "You're always welcome here, Rosco. You know that . . . I take it things did not go well down in the southlands of New Jersey."

"How did you know I was there?"

In answer, Sara hooked her hand into the crook of his arm: a lady from another era walking decorously with a male companion. "Your wife, of course. She'll be worried if you're not home soon." As she spoke, Sara steered their steps in the direction of the house. "We'll sit for a minute or two so you can tell me your troubles."

Rosco was about to reply, but Sara in her calm and understanding fashion seemed to have already intuited a good portion of his worries. "It's always difficult to discover lives that seemed so straightforward are in fact fraught with contradictions—sometimes even a nasty secret or two. I told Belle the same thing when she was fretting over the existence of this Deborah person . . . Parent or child, brother, sister: no one has the right to stand in judgment of another's motives, another's life decisions. Even husbands and wives, Rosco, and those are relationships established by mutual choice—as you well know."

The two entered the house after Rosco had batted aside the many moths that eagerly flocked around the door's exterior light. The August night was warm but pleasant; the scent of the not-too-distant ocean lingered in the air: a perfect end to a summer's day.

"Maybe it's my age, Rosco . . . maybe I'm turning batty and forgetful, but I can't help but recall my youth on evenings like this . . . No, recall is too weak a word. I can't help but be *returned* to childhood. I feel as free and full of excitement as if I were on school holiday, as if all I had to do tomorrow was play games with my friends on a hot and sandy beach." Sara briefly squeezed Rosco's arm as they proceeded into her sitting room, where she assumed her customary chair, a high-backed velvet-cushioned contraption that almost resembled a throne. "So, dear boy, what dire news have you discovered about Theodore Graham?"

Rosco told her. Sara remained silent as the story unfolded, merely nodding her head or leaning a thoughtful chin into her cupped and delicate fingers. When Rosco had finished his tale, she didn't speak for several long moments, then finally said, "I gather you're wondering how much of this to share with Belle."

Rosco nodded.

"Why is that, dear boy? Your wife is what my generation would have called a 'modern woman.' Surely, she will understand the situation with *Madame* Araignée—"

"Oh, I agree with that, Sara . . ."

"It's something else, then?"

"I'm not sure . . . The 'disappearance' of Franklin Mossback doesn't feel right . . . The whole Central America connection . . . especially in light of Belle's father's repeated flights to Belize."

"Belize *is* not Guatemala, Rosco."

He nodded. "I'm aware that I might be leaping to major erroneous conclusions . . . It may be no odder than one person vanishing in the French Alps while another has business in Rome. Still . . ."

"You realize you could be looking at pure coincidence in the case of Mossback, Rosco. Unwary tourists often find themselves in untenable positions. Especially those flying private planes in uninhabited and mountainous regions."

"I know that, Sara . . . But my gut instinct tells me there's trouble hiding here somewhere . . . This mysterious Woody character . . . all the money for the boat . . . Anyway, I phoned Al on my way back up here. I asked him to check into Mossback's status."

A smile wreathed Sara's face. "Darling Albert . . . You know how fond I am of him, Rosco . . . However, I don't believe a member of the local police force will have sufficient clout to garner pertinent information from the tight-lipped Washington powers-that-be. Albert will be told that Franklin Mossback was deemed a missing national . . . and that the case was successfully retired—"

"Al was afraid of that—"

"However, I *do* have clout. I'll simply telephone Hal's right-hand man, and ask him to contact State . . . On the q.t., of course. And don't forget that my dear brother is a Princeton man as well. He can be a fountain of information . . . although the difficulty comes in locating the valve that controls the water flow."

Rosco considered her suggestion. "I don't like to involve you, Sara . . ."

The proud face was suddenly creased with sorrow. "Rosco, my dear, what good am I if I cannot help my closest friends?"

Rosco smiled at her. "Thanks, Sara." Then again grew silent.

"You're still not confiding everything in me."

"You're right." He stood and walked over to the mantel, staring absently at the Delft clock and the vases filled with roses that flanked it. "I have a nasty hunch that Theodore Graham may have been murdered, Sara."

"And you don't know whether to share your suspicions with Belle?"

Rosco turned around and regarded his hostess. "No, I don't."

"There's only one answer to that Rosco: Yes. Of course, you must tell her."

CHAPTER

18

"Where have you been? I was starting to worry." Belle, buoyant, tripping over Kit, who was also rushing to meet her favorite human male, accidentally let the screen door bang behind Rosco's tired back. The crash echoed through the house, through the quiet of the peaceful New England street. It was a timeless sound of a summer's night; the only thing missing was a dog barking, but Kit preferred her own short yips of canine conversation.

"You look absolutely done-in . . . I wish I'd persuaded you to spend the night down in New Jersey."

Rosco sank down into a chair—one of Belle's thrift-shop finds: an upholstered number with a bold geranium print that looked as if it belonged in a 1950s resort hotel. "I stopped by Sara's on my way home."

"Sara's?" Belle's tone changed instantly. It was subdued, cautious. She sat on the arm of the chair beside him.

"Your dad never mentioned a fellow Princeton professor named Franklin Mossback, did he?"

Belle shook her head.

"Or his wife? The woman I went down to interview, it turns out."

"The spider lady?"

Rosco looked up sharply. "How did you know she was called that?"

"Her name . . . Araignée . . . I just translated . . ." Belle regarded him, her expression both wary and searching. "What happened in Princeton?"

Rosco put his arm around her waist. After a moment, he said, "Whose idea was it to have your father arrive here on August thirteenth?"

"Mine, I guess . . . I thought the height of summer would be a good time to show him around . . . The town and bay look so pretty, and there's plenty to do . . . all the cultural activities, and the touristy ones, too. Plus a relief from the Florida heat." Belle thought a moment. "Actually, I think I'm wrong about my input . . . I think the specific date was Father's idea . . . I suggested August, but he chose the thirteenth. Why do you ask?"

Rosco turned slightly toward her, raising his other arm to touch her bare and suntanned knees.

"You suspect something's wrong, don't you?"

When he didn't respond, she paused only for a fraction of a second, then hurried ahead as if her speech had been outlined long before. "You think someone killed my father, don't you? A person on the train . . . You were worried about that when you left this morning . . . You didn't tell me, but that was what you were mulling over . . . And probably yesterday, too."

"I didn't have anything to go on . . . just a gut sense that all wasn't as it appeared."

"Yes . . ." Belle admitted with some finality. "I imagine you and I came up with an identical—"

The phone rang at that moment, startling them both as the noise knifed through the stillness. "Oh, honestly!" she grumbled. "It's nearly eleven o'clock at night! I'm going to let the machine get it."

"It could be Sara."

Belle gave Rosco a look that was part puzzlement, part jealousy. "I don't know why you had to talk to Sara first. I'm not a toddler who needs to be protected."

"I realize that, Belle . . . But I didn't want you upset if my suspicions prove unfounded."

"But we've been worrying about the same thing—Not to mention, when you would finally get home—" But her words were interrupted by the voice being recorded on the answering machine. "Security . . . Sanibel . . . Theodore Graham's apartment . . . a break-in—"

Belle flew into her office and grabbed the phone. Rosco followed close behind. The many crossword puzzles she'd spread throughout the room fluttered in the disturbed air. "I see . . ." she said into the receiver. "And when did it happen?" She glanced at her watch. "But that's only twenty minutes ago . . . Oh, I understand . . . So, the night shift *discovered* the door had been forced at that time. The burglary could have occurred an hour or more before . . ."

Belle didn't speak for the next minute. She was too busy listening. Rosco watched her face for signs of what was transpiring, but she seemed as perplexed as he. He sat in a canvas captain's chair, realizing too late he'd squashed one of the puzzles she'd been assessing for her collection. "So, nothing was taken . . . ? That you could 'detect' . . . ? I don't understand. What do you mean by 'signs of a search' . . . ?" Again, Belle remained silent, at length adding, "Well, my father's personal effects are with—" Rosco raised a hand in gentle warning. She nodded her comprehension.

"His effects are in a storage facility. Only furniture and a couple of pieces of clothing remain in the apartment . . . But if nothing was left in the dresser drawers . . . ? I see . . . Okay . . . Yes, I'll contact my father's former secretary, and inform her. She no longer has keys to the apartment, but I'll ask her to get in touch with you. The locks will need to be . . . Okay . . . Yes . . . The police . . ." Belle scribbled names on a piece of scrap paper, then finally concluded the conversation with a grateful: "No, of course, it's not good news. But I appreciate your diligence . . ." Then she hung up and turned to Rosco.

"Your father's apartment's been ransacked," was all he said.

"The term Security used was 'signs of a search.'"

Rosco stood and walked to her. He held the crushed crossword in his hand. "Sorry about this—"

"Oh, who cares about the damn thing!" She grabbed it out of his hand and dropped it on the desk. "The same person submitted two at the same time . . . I'll publish the other one, the stop sign puzzle I showed you . . ." Her voice started to break, but her words kept streaming out. "Just look at the title. *It Hurts So* . . ."

Rosco took her in his arms. "This could be simply a nasty coincidence, Belle . . . Kids breaking in, hunting for cash . . . They find the place virtually empty and turn it upside down out of spite—"

"You don't believe that, Rosco."

In answer he hugged her tighter and finally said, "Do you want me to phone Deborah Hurley?"

"No, I'll do it . . ." Belle sat again, and hunted for the Hurleys' listing. Her shoulders sagged as she picked up the receiver and punched in numbers. When an answering machine picked up, her head drooped as well. "Debbie, this is Belle Graham. Sorry to phone so late, but I'm afraid I've got an emergency . . . Someone broke into my father's apartment. Would you mind doing me a favor and contacting Security? They're expecting your call." Belle left the pertinent information, then concluded with a weary: "I really appreciate your help . . . Call me back . . . I'll give you Rosco's pager number if that's an easier way for you to contact me." She supplied the information, dropped the phone back into the cradle, then immediately retrieved it, this time leaving a similar message for the realtor in charge of selling the condo.

Finally she looked at Rosco.

"I'll handle the Sanibel Police, if you'd like," he said.

"Thanks . . . but I think we should do it together." She stood, crossed over to him, and gave him a loving kiss. Then her expression turned serious again. "What I don't understand is this: If Father was killed, why wouldn't the police in Boston have been suspicious of foul play? Wouldn't there have been signs of . . . of something? A struggle . . . or something? Why didn't they even suggest an autopsy?"

"Obviously, there was no substantive evidence to make them question their initial supposition . . . And at your father's age, a heart attack seems a pretty logical bet."

Belle nodded slowly, but didn't speak.

"I'm going to suggest we do something that may seem unpleasant, Belle . . . I'm going to suggest that you and I go down to police headquarters first thing tomorrow morning, and have a chat with Carlyle at the city morgue."

"But he had nothing to do with Father's—"

"I know that. But if anyone can provide us with information on murder methods that are difficult to physically detect—or trace—it's Carlyle."

Across

1. About; abbr.
4. Diner offering
8. __Rios
12. RAF kin
14. Resound
15. "What Do You Know About Love" artist
17. Exchange premium
18. 1956 McCormack film
20. Some limerick writers
22. Sonnet's end
23. Feline utterance
24. Scottish John
25. Loot
28. 1973 Sheen film
33. "American Gothic" artist
34. Silkwood and Brockovich
35. Be beholding
36. Chemical suffix
37. Magistrates of Venice
38. Part of AT&T
39. German article
40. Swell
41. Jack's gal
42. 1994 Barrymore film
44. Teases
46. Sound of frustration
47. NYC subway line
48. Lava, e.g.
51. Pink poodles, to some
56. 1972 Bridges film
58. Always
59. Lady of song
60. Brute lead-in?
61. Seaweed product
62. Employer
63. Mar
64. Draft org.

Down

1. Hermit or king
2. Young Frankenstein's love
3. Bust
4. Sexual lead-in
5. 46-Across, in Berlin
6. "__Got You," Patsy Cline hit
7. Quoit peg
8. Trials
9. Certain small plane
10. Hot in Haarlem
11. Hosea
13. Used bread on the gravy
16. Tampa time; abbr.
19. Stage whispers
21. Yours and mine
25. Geek
26. Ancient Greek land
27. "And found ___ in wand'ring mazes," Milton
28. A.L. batting champ, '85—'88
29. Aweather, opp.
30. Out to lunch
31. Lived
32. Hawks
34. Drum solo
37. North Carolina town
40. Some large digits
41. Area west of the Dead Sea
43. Some loafers
44. Straighten
45. Industrious type
48. Compass point; abbr.
49. Ontario lake
50. Taro root
51. Maine seaport
52. One opposed
53. Part of S&L
54. Some are herbal

IT HURTS SO . . .

55. Trips up
57. Workout target

Carlyle, Newcastle's chief medical examiner, had never been one of Rosco's favorite people; and the feeling was more than mutual. When Rosco had been with the police department, his run-ins with Carlyle had often been "testy," to say the least. Rosco was the type who tended to go with his hunches while Carlyle invariably insisted on sticking to the facts, and only the facts. Their differing methodologies had produced decided dissension when Rosco's hunches panned out to be more accurate than Carlyle's facts—a situation that had occurred more than once. It was for this reason that Rosco had enlisted the assistance of his former partner to help break the ice with the ME.

"You just have to know how to handle the guy," Lever said as he, Belle, and Rosco stepped from the elevator in the basement of the Newcastle Police building. "You have to be willing to use some well-placed flattery . . ."

Belle glanced down at the gray linoleum floor tiles, and then at the institutional green walls. Fluorescent lighting illuminated the hallway, giving everything and everyone a cold and sickly look. Halfway down the hall Lever opened a heavy glass-paneled door and held it for Belle and Rosco. When they stepped into the morgue, their nostrils were attacked by a strong chemical odor, and their bodies experienced a noticeable drop in temperature, making the sunny August morning outside seem no more than a distant memory.

Carlyle was at the far end of the room standing at a stainless steel examining table. A corpse was stretched out in front of him, and his assistant, Estelle, was hanging over his shoulder like a hungry vulture. He removed some unrecognizable piece of human tissue from the corpse and handed it to Estelle.

"Let's get a weight on that before we move on." Carlyle then glanced toward the doorway and noticed his three visitors. "Is it ten o'clock already?"

"Yep," Lever said with a not-too-convincing smile. "We'll just wait over here until you're done with that . . . piece of business . . . Take your time." Despite a career that entailed frequent visits to the morgue, Lever had never become inured to its grim ambience. His stomach churned every time he stepped through the door.

Carlyle stripped off his latex gloves and deposited them into a receptacle marked BIO-WASTE. "Estelle can finish that one up," he said as he approached. "Cut-and-dried. It'll be the last time that schnook ever fools around with a married woman . . . Lead poisoning—in the form of a .38-caliber slug to the heart." He directed the entire conversation toward Lever, as if Belle and Rosco weren't in the room. "I understand Polycrates is now questioning the judgment of the

Boston Police Department. How's it go? The more things change, the more they stay the same? Well, better them than me. What's all this about?"

Lever looked at Rosco and gave him a shrug that said: *The floor is all yours.*

Rosco cleared his throat slightly. "I don't know if you heard, but Belle's father passed away on an Amtrak train back on the thirteenth. The Boston ME found nothing suspicious and deemed it a heart attack. The body was returned to a Newcastle mortuary and buried three days later."

During Rosco's brief speech, Carlyle's face changed from a stone-cold, all-business expression to a look that resembled compassion—an emotion Rosco had never seen the ME register before.

"I'm sorry," Carlyle mumbled as he brought his eyes to meet Belle's. "Someone gave me a bunch of wrong information. I had no idea it was your *father* on the train. In this business everyone tends to be referred to as a *John Doe*. And of course, there's a kind of ME's gossip network in New England—everyone talks about everyone else's business. Anything interesting, death-wise, gets thrown over the transom—so to speak . . . I'm sorry . . . I wouldn't have been so . . . well . . ."

Rosco and Lever were left speechless by the ME's admission—to say nothing of his gallant manner. Belle extended her hand. "It's nice to finally meet you . . . I've heard a lot about you."

Carlyle nodded in Rosco's direction. "Well, if you've been listening to him, you've most likely been given some misinformation as well."

Belle smiled. "I know; he can be a little hardheaded sometimes. But I'm working on that."

"I apologize for my lack of tact—"

"It's okay. Really . . ."

Lever scowled. For a moment he wondered whether the morgue chemicals had begun to affect Carlyle's brain. The man hadn't displayed an ounce of human kindness in his life. "What Belle and Rosco were wondering," he interjected, "is this: Is it possible that Theodore Graham could have died under circumstances that might have been less than *natural*? And could that cause of death have eluded the medical examiner in Boston?"

"I.e.," Carlyle said, still looking at Belle, "you have reason to believe we're looking at a homicide?"

She took in a deep breath. "There's nothing substantiative to prove that. It's just . . . well . . . There have been a lot of strange questions popping up."

Carlyle pointed to a round table with six folding chairs scattered around it. "Why don't we sit."

Lever picked up the petrie dish that had been designated "morgue ashtray," and lit a cigarette. He dropped the match in the dish. As an afterthought he said, "This doesn't bother anyone, does it?" No one troubled to answer.

"I know this is a sensitive topic," Carlyle said after everyone was settled, "so, Belle, please let me know if I'm being too blunt. It can be my nature at times . . . Okay, back to the gossip drifting over the proverbial transom . . . A body turns up on a train . . . ? People in my field begin to talk . . . Now, I'm not saying the man in Boston did anything wrong or made any errors in judgment, because I might well have made the same analysis if I'd been the first one to examine your father—"

"But it's possible Boston could have missed important evidence," Rosco said, interrupting.

Carlyle ignored him and continued to focus on Belle. "It's virtually impossible that the ME in Boston would have missed anything physical: torn or rumbled clothing, bruises, contusions, et cetera. He would have also noticed any nose or ear bleeding or swelling, fluid discharge, dilation of the eyes, or skin discoloration. All of these things would have indicated that things were not right, not 'natural' as Al says . . . and he would have pushed for an autopsy."

"But he didn't," Lever said as smoke drifted from his nostrils.

"Obviously he saw nothing out of place. But then again, he had no real reason to suspect anything was wrong. From what I understand, your father's body had been removed from the train before the ME arrived on the scene—allowing Amtrak to return the train to service. That's a frustrating situation for any ME. We're better judges, when it comes to analyzing a suspicious situation, than your average beat cop—or train conductor. For instance, the position of the body at time of death can tell us a lot. The man in Boston didn't have an opportunity to make that type of assessment. Another factor to consider is that your father wasn't a local Bostonian."

"What does that have to do with it?" Belle asked.

"Well, the police would have had an immediate history. They would have been able to discover if the *John Doe* had a nefarious past, if he owed large sums of money, if he had an unhappy family life, had recently quarreled with someone, etc. The department would have been keyed into that background information, and would have studied the situation from a local angle; ergo, a lot closer."

"He's right," Lever added. "The first order of business is to contact next of kin . . . If they don't raise any questions, and if the death appears to be natural, most municipalities are very happy to let the entire business drift away."

"So you're saying there's no possible way my father could have been murdered?"

"No. No. Not at all. But the only manner in which your father could have been killed—without the Boston ME becoming suspicious—would be if he'd ingested some type of specialized poison . . . At this point, the only way to confirm the presence of such a chemical would be to exhume your father's body and perform an autopsy . . . And to be perfectly honest, Belle, after an undertaker has treated a corpse with embalming fluid, it can be difficult to get completely accurate results. We can be fairly positive, but nothing's one hundred percent."

At that moment Rosco's beeper sounded. He glanced down, tapped a button, and silently read off the number. He then pulled the beeper from his belt and handed it to Belle. "Florida. I think that's Deborah's number. Do you want me to call her back?"

"No, I'll do it."

Carlyle said, "Use the phone in my office," then stood, crossed the room, and formally opened another glass door for Belle. He returned to the table, and the three men watched her sit behind Carlyle's desk and dial the phone.

Rosco was the first to break the silence. "I was under the impression that if someone had been poisoned, it would be fairly obvious to a medical examiner."

With Belle gone, Carlyle's stony expression returned. "I guess you've been under the wrong impression, Polycrates. Why doesn't that surprise me?"

Lever rolled his eyes as the ME continued. "There are substances that can be placed in an individual's coffee, water, fruit juice, whatever, that will bring on symptoms resembling a coronary—and that can fool the casual observer.

Anectine—succinylcholine—is one of these; it's odorless and highly soluble in water . . . Of course the chemical will show up in the drinking vessel when tested, and a thorough autopsy will also reveal its presence. Then there are substances that have to be injected. Tubarine—tubocurarine chloride—has been employed in criminal cases. Symptoms resemble those of heart attack victims . . . Likewise Pavulon—pancuronium—which also presents as a probable heart attack . . . All three substances are neuromuscular blocking agents. Reaction time for each is immediate." Carlyle thought for a moment. "Pavulon's difficult to detect if an autopsy isn't performed quickly."

Lever stubbed out his cigarette in the petrie dish. "Correct me if I'm wrong, Rosco, but I'm guessing Belle isn't going to warm up to the idea of exhuming her father's remains."

"I wouldn't think so, Al . . . But who knows; she can surprise you."

"And the odds of finding a two-week-old coffee cup in Amtrak's trash are next to nil," Lever observed quietly. No one laughed.

Carlyle glanced through the glass at Belle. "Well, those are your only options, gents—if you want conclusive proof."

Unable to hear the conversation, Belle stared worriedly at the three male figures as she tapped her fingers on the desk top and waited for Deborah Hurley to answer the phone.

After the third ring she heard a male voice sing out, "Hurley residence," from the other end of the line.

"Oh, hi, Mike . . . it's Belle Graham. I'm returning Debbie's call . . . or rather, she was returning my call . . . anyway . . . I got her page. Is she there?"

"No. Sorry, Belle. It was me who paged you. I apologize for

not reaching you sooner. I got your message about the break-
in. That really stinks. Things like that don't usually go on
down here. But you know. Summer. Kids with too much time
on their hands—"

"I'm sorry to bother you with this, Mike."

"It's no bother . . . It's just that I've pulled extra duty, and
Deb left for Kings Creek yesterday to visit her aunt."

"Oh . . ."

"But I can go over to the condo and check things out if
you'd like. I already put in a call to the real estate agent. She
said you'd also left her a message."

"Yes, I did." Belle made eye contact with Rosco through
the window and gave him a small wave indicating everything
was being taken care of—at least in Florida. "Since I have you
on the phone, Mike, I wonder if you could do me another
favor?"

"If I can."

"Do you know where the Anchorage Marina is?"

"Sure. What's up?"

"If this is too much trouble, please let me know, but my
father had some sort of relationship with a man named
Horace Llewellen. He goes by the nickname of Woody.
Apparently, Woody and my father copurchased a boat called
Wooden Shoe. It's a Hatteras 42. The owner's papers were
among my father's effects, and I wanted to make sure he got
them . . . The boat is usually berthed at the Anchorage.
When I went there, however, *Wooden Shoe* was gone, and I was
told that Woody's schedule can be erratic. Would you mind
terribly stopping by the marina and seeing if he's returned?
And tell him that I'd really like to talk to him."

"Will do. No problem . . . And don't worry about your

dad's condo, Belle . . . It's too bad, but these things can happen when a property is vacant . . . I'm sure management will beef up security. Although if it was just kids hunting for the liquor cabinet and a few extra bucks, they won't be back anytime soon."

"Thanks, Mike. I really appreciate your support." Then, as an afterthought, she added a quick: "Give my best to Debbie when you talk to her."

"Will do."

As Belle stepped out of Carlyle's office, the conversation at the table ceased. Rosco turned to her; his expression was troubled.

"What did I miss?" she asked.

"Is Deborah going over to your dad's condo?" was his evasive reply.

"She's not there, but Mike is. That was him on the phone . . . What did I miss?"

Carlyle cleared his throat. He avoided looking at Belle. "I was just outlining some possible . . . well, scenarios . . . Unfortunately the only way to confirm any of them would be to perform an autopsy, which obviously means exhuming your father's remains."

Belle returned to the table but didn't sit. Rosco took her hand. "I don't know," she said softly. "There's something . . . There's something so repellent about that. It would mean treating him like . . ." She shivered briefly before nodding toward the cadaver Estelle had been dissecting. "Like . . . Like that person."

Carlyle said, "Yes, I'm afraid so," without glancing in Estelle's direction. "But it's the only way to get a definitive answer to your questions, Belle."

She shook her head and hunched her shoulders. Rosco held her hand tighter. After a moment she turned toward Carlyle. "I appreciate your honesty. I appreciate your taking time to explain . . . all of this . . . But I'd like to give your suggestion some thought—reflection, I guess. If I take a day or two, will it make your work more difficult? Do we need to do this immediately?"

"Well," Carlyle said, "if we're going to exhume the body, I wouldn't want to wait six months, but at this point a matter of a couple of days—even a week—won't change any test results."

"I just hate to see my father cut up like that . . ."

Carlyle shrugged while his mouth narrowed into a resolute line. "And I hate to see people get away with murder."

CHAPTER

20

When the phone rang at nine-twelve that night, Belle gave it an apprehensive stare. Rosco and the puppy were off on their nightly walk, and their absence made her pause before picking up the receiver. Ten hours of pondering the myriad questions surrounding her father's death hadn't brought her any closer to a decision as to whether to exhume his body; instead, it had only served to further unnerve her. Now, an unhappy hunch made her suspect that this phone call would produce additional distressing news; and she didn't want to tackle it alone. For a moment, she considered letting the machine pick up and eavesdropping on the message before deciding whether to respond in person or not. But she reasoned that was the coward's approach. *Trouble doesn't go away simply because you ignore it.*

She grabbed the receiver. "Belle Graham speaking."

The voice that greeted her was controlled—but barely. "This is Mike Hurley."

She registered his obviously troubled emotional state, but couldn't connect it to the break-in at her father's condo. Her eyes narrowed in confusion, then she proceeded as if the call and tone of voice were not only normal but expected. This entire thought process took less than a second. "Mike! Thanks so much for helping—"

"That's just it . . . I didn't . . ." He stifled what sounded like a sob, then drew a long, uneven breath.

Belle also took a breath. Whatever information Mike had to impart wasn't going to be pleasant. "You sound upset—"

"Debbie's dead." The words crashed through the line. "Her aunt . . . The police called her aunt . . ."

"Oh, my God," Belle murmured.

"They told her it was a hit-and-run . . . The guy just sped away . . ." This time Mike cried full out. Belle, at her end of the phone, was too stunned for further speech. "He just . . . just . . . Witnesses got a model type, but that's it . . ." Again, sorrow overwhelmed him. When Mike spoke again, his tone was exhausted. "I didn't get a chance to go looking for that Woody character . . . but your dad's condo's okay—"

"Never mind about Woody, Mike . . ." This time it was Belle who was momentarily speechless. *How is it possible to face the sudden death of a spouse? How is Mike going to continue to function? Make the necessary arrangements, call family and friends? How do surviving mates cope when misery rips them apart?* "I'm so sorry, Mike . . . I'm so sorry to hear this terrible news. *Your* terrible news."

"She'd just left the local library," he answered, as if his wife's connection to such a solid and nurturing institution should have protected her. "You know how much she loved poring over books—" Mike broke down again, then finally resumed his speech. "I'm going up there now. Flying up. To Deb's aunt's. I'm at the airport. I'm waiting for my flight . . . My CO gave me emergency leave."

Belle let him finish, then interjected a gentle, "Is there anything I can do to help you?"

"Oh no, I'll be okay. It's just going to take . . . It's going to take . . ." He gulped back tears. "Sorry about not finding Woody."

"That's completely unimportant, Mike—"

"She was all alone! I mean, her aunt wasn't even with her. No one was with her!"

Belle could think of no response to those words that would bring even a measure of solace. Instead she continued with her offer of help. "Mike, you know where to reach me. If there's anything I can do . . . My father would have wanted—"

Mike cut her off. "They're calling my flight. I have to go."

The line went dead.

Belle replaced the receiver with deliberate care. She shook her head; her heart felt numb with sorrow—as well as a good measure of guilt. Deborah Hurley, the young woman she'd so mistrusted. Belle could recall almost every word of their final conversation. She knew she'd been neither charitable nor kind.

Then a frown began to crease her brow. The frown grew. *Father's bird-watching notebook—the one Debbie insisted he "always" kept near him. The one that didn't appear in the effects returned by the Boston Police.* In her hurt—and jealousy—Belle realized she might have overlooked an important clue. *What if the pages contained more than simple facts about birds? What if her father had discovered something so dangerous, he was killed for his knowledge? What if Debbie Hurley, a woman so familiar with Theodore Graham's life—?*

Rosco walked into the kitchen at this moment in Belle's deliberations. He was followed noisily by Kit, who felt she deserved a treat after each walk. After all, how many other animals were forced to leave their homes in order to parade the dark streets with their human companions, marching outside when it was raining, when winter snow and sleet made the pavement slick enough to slip? Such diligence should be rewarded. Kit danced around Rosco's feet in an effort to get him to move faster.

"Okay, Kitster—" Rosco stopped in his tracks as he registered Belle's troubled expression. "What happened?"

"Debbie Hurley's dead. A hit-and-run. In Kings Creek . . . She was visiting her aunt."

Rosco stared. "Kings Creek?" he finally said, "As in Kings Creek, New Jersey?"

CHAPTER

21

The air conditioner gurgled, wheezed, then spewed a burst of semicool air into the room before again retreating to hiccoughing inertia. The man seated at the table looked up at the ancient machine, stood, walked to the window, banged on the unit once—producing another blast of unchilled and rank-smelling air—then returned to the papers spread across the table's chipped Formica surface. The design was intended to resemble walnut—a wood supremely out of place in this humid, tropical port town.

From beneath the man's sealed window, the desultory sounds of a waterfront trapped in the August heat of a southern latitude rose and fell. The noise was sluggish, enervated; even the boat engines seemed exhausted as they sputtered within waves made greasy and brown by diesel fuel. A voice called something in Spanish; an albatross or another type of sea bird squawked in alarm, then all was silent. The man at the table watched as a dark and prehistoric shape of a pelican floated by, its body momentarily shadowing his view of the blue and glaring sky. Then the pelican was gone, while the sun, despite the bird's absence, grew suddenly dimmer as clouds as opaque as paint swelled around and over it.

All at once, rain lashed at the window, at the languishing air conditioner, at the spindly palm trees dotting the quay side. The man glanced at his watch as if monitoring the precise hour and minute of the torrent's arrival, then returned to his work. In the hot room, his naked back glistened with sweat.

He pulled a dingy towel off a nearby chair, wiped his face and hands, then took up a newly sharpened pencil and carefully shaded four squares on the sheet of graph paper he had before him. He didn't utter a word, but his eyes shone with as much energy and interest as if he were deep in animated conversation.

He shaded more squares, copied letters and numbers in a precise, mechanical hand, then realized that the brief rain squall had passed and the day grown even more unbearably warm.

Another boat putt-putted by below his window—a local fishing vessel by the smell of it. A cadre of gulls screamed and whirled in its wake, and for a moment the small room was full of their greedy calls—as well as the cloying scent of rotting fish guts and blood.

The man again consulted his watch, then returned to his efforts, at length nodding approval as he outlined and shaded the crossword puzzle's final squares. Completed, the handdrawn cryptic looked as meticulously delineated as one printed in ink on crisp paper.

He stood, pulled an aged T-shirt over his faded shorts, then slid his feet into rubber sandals. Dressed for the street, he retrieved a Global Delivery envelope from the rumpled bed. The recipient and her address were already written in bold, block letters.

He slid his handiwork into the envelope, opened the door to his room, and locked it carefully behind him. The exterior passageway that ran the length of the building was still awash in rainwater and the numerous puddles that had collected on the concrete floor. A malodorous steam had begun to arise. The man coughed as the sticky air entered his lungs. For a moment he clutched the stair rail leading down to the street. He wasn't as young as he had been.

When he reached the pavement, he turned to the right. *"¿Professor, cómo está?"* he heard someone call in greeting. He raised his hand in silent reply, but kept walking; all the while thinking, *Is every elderly American a professor to these people?*

CHAPTER

22

"**B**ut what do you mean by insisting that Theodore Graham is still alive?" Sara stared at her brother as he calmly sipped his iced tea, then swirled a long silver spoon through the minty liquid. The *plink* of silver on crystal was the only sound in White Caps' drawing room, and it seemed noisier because of the closed foyer door, the windows that had been pulled fast, the weight of privacy that Hal had stipulated for their "off-the-record" conversation. "I'll supply what information I can, Sara," he'd told her when previously agreeing to this discussion. "But strictly in confidence. I further suggest that we meet in midmorning. That way we won't need Emma in constant attendance."

"The word 'insist' is yours, Sara," the senator now said. "Likewise, the assumption that Graham isn't dead. Now, what my actual words were—"

She waved an older sister's dismissive, impatient hand. "You needn't be so circumscribed with me, Hal. Nor so damnably diplomatic. We're not in the marbled halls of Washington, you know, and my home is certainly not littered with listening devices."

But more than seven decades of sibling quibbling made the senator equally quick to interrupt his sister. "What I said, Sara, was that 'movement by a man of that name was monitored two days ago—'"

"Meaning that your source at the State Department—or whomever you're speaking with—believes that Belle's father is—"

"No, Sara . . . My meaning is no more than the words indicate . . . 'Movement was monitored—'"

"Oh, honestly, Hal! How you people in government like to complicate issues! Why can't you learn to speak and act like ordinary people?"

Her brother didn't rise to the attack. Instead he smiled amiably. It was a patrician expression of contentment and serenity. For a moment, he and his sister—disagreeing as they habitually did—looked like identical twins: two white-haired and lordly heads, two pairs of shoulders set on ramrod-straight spines, brows that conveyed keen intellects—as well as a good dose of stubbornness. "Who is to say what is ordinary, Sara? Perhaps, mine is the more typical life while you, existing in the secluded environs of Newcastle—"

"I do not live in seclusion, Hal, and you know it!"

Her brother merely raised an eyebrow. His grin broadened. "A hot temper . . . quick to take offense. You'd make a poor politician."

"For which I am eternally, I repeat *eternally,* grateful . . . Especially knowing the unsavory company you often keep!"

He laughed, and took another slow sip from his glass. "I've always liked the way Emma makes this mint-flavored iced tea. It's so invigorating."

Sara glowered. "Don't you play fast and loose with me, Hal Crane. This isn't a press conference, and I'm not going to be put off by verbal sleights of hand. Is Theodore Graham dead or not? A simple yes or no will do."

"Did his daughter identify the body?"

Sara was about to protest anew, but her brother continued to regard her probingly. Finally, Sara nodded her assent. "Then who—?"

"Is the person my source 'monitored' two days ago?"

She nodded again.

"Obviously, someone who has assumed the name of the departed professor."

Sara thought for a minute or two. "Are you insinuating that this person stole Belle's father's identity?"

"I'm not *insinuating* anything, Sara—"

"Because, if that's the case, then this unknown man . . . wherever he is . . . being 'monitored' on whatever clandestine screen . . . then this unknown person doesn't know that the real Theodore A. Graham is dead—"

"I can't speak to that situation—"

"Which puts your mystery man into a murky position—"

"All conjecture, Sara, my dear. And all beyond my scope, I'm afraid."

Sara's eyes narrowed. "Horse feathers, Hal! You know far more than you're letting on."

The senator didn't respond immediately. "You requested information on another subject, Sara. Someone who apparently died in Guatemala."

"Franklin Mossback, yes. Also a professor. Also from Princeton—"

Hal put up a hand requesting her to hear him out. "I'm very fond of you, Sara. As you well know. And I deeply respect your intelligence and your steadfast loyalty to your friends. And I realize that, despite the differences in our political leanings, you also respect and love me . . . Now, I don't want to appear to be talking down to you, or skirting issues, but I cannot stress strongly enough the inherent risk in asking too many questions. Especially questions that—"

"Risk? To whom?"

"I'm not at liberty to say, Sara."

But his sister was not to be put off by this bland response. "You don't mean risk to Belle?"

"Sara. I cannot reveal more than I have already."

Her slender and expensively shod feet pounded the floor. "There you are again! With all this hush-hush spy palaver! I honestly think you do believe this house is bugged the way you go on!"

"Sara, I want you to recall that my position . . . the position I've been honored to hold for many years requires tact and diplomacy. It also entails a goodly amount of restraint . . . Keeping 'one's thoughts close to the vest,' as Pater liked to say." Hal paused. When he resumed his speech, he was every bit the elder statesman his colleagues on "The Hill" had grown to trust and admire. "One week ago, a Belizean fishing trawler carrying nine tons of cocaine was intercepted by the Coast Guard near Panama City, Florida . . . The estimated value of the shipment was nearly five hundred million dollars. Obviously, the men and/or women involved in such trafficking have a strong motivation for assuring that their goods are delivered into the right hands. Rather than those of the United States government."

"Belize—" Sara murmured, but Hal repeated his gesture requesting her silence.

"Please, Sara. Allow me to finish . . . To return to the question of Franklin Mossback: We're both aware that tourists often venture into terrain that's unfamiliar, even dangerous. Some travelers are infected with rare diseases; some sustain automobile or boating accidents—or journey in private planes that are ill equipped. And some of these people sadly die. But tragedies can happen anywhere—"

Again, Sara began to interrupt. Again, Hal pressed forward. "Bear with me, Sara. I realize you feel frustrated at what you refer to as my 'obfuscation.' And that your very kind heart wants to help your young friends put their minds at rest in regards to this obviously perplexing situation involving Dr. Graham . . . And I concur—from what information you've shared with me—that the unfolding story of his life is complicated indeed . . . However, I don't believe you fully comprehend the harm that might befall Belle and Rosco— and you—for learning more than is necessary—"

However, Sara could no longer keep silent. "Belize and Guatemala share a border . . ." She paused while her mind flew to all the facts she'd garnered, and her bright eyes grew wide and frightened. "Are you suggesting that Mossback and Graham were . . ."

Hal pressed his hands together and studied his sister. "I'm merely suggesting that this situation is far more perilous than you know."

"No, Belle, that's the extent of what Hal told me . . ." Sara sighed as she spoke. The weight of her conversation with her brother hung heavily on her heart. So heavily that the moment he'd left, she'd wheeled out her pristine 1956 Cadillac and driven to Belle's house rather than requesting the younger woman visit White Caps. Now she sat in Belle's home office wearing a pastel straw hat she used for summer "outings," and the formal white cotton gloves that served as mementos of a more graceful era. "Naturally, I badgered him for more information . . . but he wouldn't budge. Not even for you. He just kept reiterating the need for circumspection—"

"And caution," Belle interjected.

"Yes," Sara replied. "And caution. Above all. I do believe politicians must have CAUTION tattooed on their arms where normal men place BORN TO RAISE HELL." Then she sighed again. Mightily. "How's Rosco bearing up?" she asked.

"Fine," was Belle's automatic reply. "Well, no . . . That's

not true . . . He's not fine . . . Not after our conversation with Carlyle yesterday. To say nothing of that terrible phone call from Mike Hurley . . ." Belle's shoulders hunched with fatigue. "Rosco will be sorry to have missed your visit, Sara . . . but he thought it was a good time to clean up paperwork at his office . . . He insists it frees up his mind . . ." She didn't continue. Like Sara, Belle also sighed.

"He'll be sorrier when he hears the information Hal shared with me," was Sara's disconsolate reply, then she added a forceful, "I simply can't imagine how your father could have been mixed up with drug dealers."

Belle shook her head. "My only conclusion is that Father's research must have unintentionally put him in contact with . . . well, I don't know who—or what—but with someone or something that compromised his safety . . . Debbie told me he'd entitled his birding notebook 'A Murder of Crows' . . . At the time I didn't imagine it . . . No, that's wrong . . . What I felt was envy. Envy that another person could be close to a man I'd never really known . . ." She closed her eyes, and then did something wholly unexpected. She began to weep.

Sara was beside her in a flash. "There . . . there . . ." A lace-edged handkerchief was produced from an antiquated patent leather handbag. The linen smelled of cedar blocks and violet *eau de cologne.* "It's all right, dear one. A good cry will do you a world of good."

Belle sniffled unabashedly into the handkerchief. "It's just not knowing, Sara . . . And all that discussion with Al and Carlyle . . . autopsies and exhuming Father's body . . . and Debbie Hurley's death . . . It all seems so strange . . . so sudden and so strange . . . and so *awful* . . ."

Sara nodded, but didn't respond. Instead, she put her hands on the younger woman's shoulders.

"I just wish . . ." Belle began. "I just wish I'd . . . that Father and I had . . . I mean, all those wasted . . . those wasted . . ." But those thoughts were left unfinished as she began crying afresh. After several more sorrowful minutes, she began to mop up her tears and try to pull herself together. "If I knew for certain that Father had been killed . . . What I mean is, at least I could get angry."

Sara patted Belle's back; her still-gloved fingers lingered in a gesture of loving comfort. "And make every attempt to find the criminal," she announced while her mouth grew pinched and grim. "I regret that Hal wasn't more forthcoming."

Belle thought. "In light of Carlyle's suggestion, do you think you could ask the senator to continue his investigation?"

Sara shook her head. "Hal told me he 'couldn't go back to the well'—his words. He also intimated that he wasn't privy to everything that transpires in 'certain government agencies'—at the same time as he reiterated the critical need for discretion. Hal as much as stated that you could become a target, too." Sara purposely neglected to share her brother's concern that she herself might now be in jeopardy.

Belle remained silent for a long time. "I'm sorry I behaved so horribly with Debbie," she said at last. "Mike has been so helpful, and I . . . well, I had no cause to treat her as I did . . . I had no cause not to believe her—"

The doorbell clanged loudly, cutting off further speech.

"Oh, what now?" Belle fairly yelped. She flung herself out of the chair and marched through the living room. Sara, concerned, followed while Kit, keenly attuned to human emotion, decided to retreat to the stair landing. Something was amiss with this blond-haired lady who shared the puppy's home—best to avoid getting underfoot.

That same blond-haired woman grabbed the front door and yanked it open. "Yes?"

A Global Delivery truck sat on the curb; its driver stood on Belle's porch. "Annabella Graham?"

"Yes."

"Sign here."

Belle almost growled as she did so. When the transaction was completed, she was handed an envelope containing an overnight letter.

She took it, forced a tight "Thanks," then shut the door and turned the cardboard packaging to read the return address. A sudden gasp escaped her; Belle ripped open the envelope. Inside was a hand-drawn crossword puzzle. "It's from Belize," was all she could manage to say.

Across

1. Spills the beans
5. "It" game
8. The Mustangs
11. Lincoln & Johnson; e.g.
13. Dash
14. "Oh, me, oh, my"
15. Where do I do?
16. Suit to ___
17. Yew
18. Wise man's tip, part 1
21. Splitter
22. Some Londoners
24. Aztec or Incan; abbr.
25. Sawbuck
26. ___kwon do
28. New, prefix
29. Tetra type
31. Strangled
33. Wise man's tip, part 2
37. Lackluster
39. Bolts
42. Trip type
43. Lyric poem
44. Baseball stat
47. Reformer Nellie
48. 4-F
50. See 21-Down
52. Wise man's tip, part 3
55. Name meaning ruler
56. Certain shark
57. Leveled
59. Hi-___
60. Hit man?
61. January, south of the border
62. Summer drink
63. Dr. Graham
64. Gaelic

Down

1. Scouting grp.
2. Nonsurpassed
3. 04530 drop-off
4. Gaze intently
5. Certain Turk
6. ___-deucy
7. Dweeb
8. Try out a jacket or Chevy
9. Gulf Coast mammal
10. Employ
12. Build
13. Actor Novarro
14. Mime
19. Summer for 46-Down
20. Jolly Roger?
21. With 50-Across, originator of tip
23. Turf
26. ___chi ch'uan
27. Pound sound
30. Gov. arts org.
31. Some Ferraris
32. Wise one
34. Canvas
35. '50s & '60s scare
36. Heading from Brownsville to Havana
37. A little bit of French?
38. Overlooked the clue
40. Hawks and eagles
41. Dict. abbr.
44. Mistake
45. Explorer of the Northwest Territories
46. Monsieur Gide
49. Yen
50. Assumed an identity
51. Ockelman-Lake link

WORDS TO THE WISE

53. Give out
54. Weapon of the Middle Ages
55. JFK stat
58. Female rabbit

Hunched over the desk, Belle and Sara began to work the crossword's clues. "13-Down . . . The answer is RAMON as in RAMON *Novarro* . . . the star of that marvelous film epic *Ben-Hur* . . . well before your time, my dear—almost before mine, if you can imagine such a notion . . . Oh, and 15-Across: *Where do I do?* You should know the answer to that!"

Silently, Belle wrote in the letters ALTAR. She wasn't feeling even a fraction of the perkiness her puzzle partner was evincing, although in truth, Sara's determined chattiness masked her own deep-seated unease.

"And Belle, dear, this one I know without even needing to dredge up the past. *Ockelman-Lake link.* That would be KEANE, the name by which Veronica Lake was known for a brief time. You wouldn't imagine it, Belle, but I was once told I resembled that lovely blond actress . . . So tragic, the way her life ended . . ."

Belle let the old lady indulge in a rueful sigh, then interjected a tense: "But who could have—?"

"Let's ink in all the answers before we begin making conjectures, my dear. There must be a hidden message, or else why would the constructor—?"

"Exactly," Belle agreed, but her tone was abrupt and wary. "And why would he—or she—have written *Dr. Graham* as the clue to 63-Across?"

"Or made *Spills the beans* the first Across clue . . . ?" Sara took Belle's red pen from her hand, and began to write while the younger woman read aloud:

"20-Down: *Jolly Roger?* . . . 24-Across: *Aztec or Incan; abbr.* . . . *Overlooked the Clue* at 38-Down . . . 50-Down: *Assumed an identity* . . . *Hit man?* is at 60-Across . . . I don't have a good feeling about what this mystery person is trying to convey, Sara. I don't have a good feeling at all."

"Nor do I," was Sara's quiet response.

Belle suddenly recoiled. "We shouldn't be touching the paper . . . It probably has traceable fingerprints . . . And if it truly reveals something about my father . . . Central America connections . . . or . . . or boats . . . or aliases, then we'll need to know who sent it."

Sara's hands also leapt off the page. "But we already have handled it. Numerous times."

Instead of replying, Belle picked up the phone and punched in Rosco's office number. When she reached his answering machine, the message she left was both oblique and businesslike. "Sara's with me. She has new information . . . I don't want to say more over the phone . . . Also, I received a very unsettling crossword. Sara and I started to fill it in. Now, we're worried we might have compromised evidence. Give me a call. A-S-A-P." Belle began to replace the receiver, then lifted it again and added a wistful: "I love you."

While Sara, no more relaxed than Belle, announced, "But if we deliver the cryptic to the police, we won't be able finish it."

"No . . . No, we won't. Well, I mean we could finish it . . . And then . . . No, there's no point."

The women looked at each other. This time Belle took the pen. "Do you mind putting your gloves back on, Sara? Although they might get ink-stained—"

"A drop or two of hydrogen peroxide will set them right as rain in no time, my dear." When Belle began to smile at this old-fashioned-sounding remedy, Sara continued with a lofty, "Those who manage homes for as many decades as I have develop certain housekeeping 'recipes': cigar ash and rubbing alcohol mixed in a paste and applied to wood that's been water-damaged; tea leaves rolled in stored woolen carpets; and so forth . . . Even my great-grandmother had her share of homey remedies—one of which was to clean silk ribbons with a mixture of gin and honey."

Belle smiled in earnest. "You're a wonder."

"It never seemed like a wise combination—particularly for the bibulous," was the old lady's doughty reply. Then she pulled on her gloves. "I'll hold the paper. You write. Are you ready, my dear?"

By the time Rosco's Jeep pulled into the drive, the cross-word was complete. The message glared from the paper as though it had been formed of neon tubing.

"Are you thinking what I'm thinking?" Belle asked after a stunned pause.

"Your father *and* Deborah Hurley?" was Sara's steady reply. "Yes. Yes, I am . . . But her husband stated that she'd died as a result of a hit-and-run accident—"

"Just as my father succumbed to what appeared to be a heart attack."

Rosco walked into the office at that moment, followed by Kit, who nearly tripped him in her hopes of inspiring a game of chase. "I decided not to call. Your message sounded a little too urgent . . ." He walked to the desk. Belle turned the puzzle toward him. "I'm afraid we left some fingerprints on it."

Rosco glanced at the crossword as he spoke. "I'm sure they can be separated out, Belle . . . On the other hand, since this came from someone in Belize, it's unlikely any prints of the constructor would be available." He gave Sara a distracted kiss and clasped his wife's hand.

"I think it's the other way around, Rosco, dear," was Sara's bemused response.

"What?"

"The other way around. You kiss your wife, and shake my hand.

Rosco stared in confusion.

"Never mind." Belle smiled up at him, then returned her total concentration to the crossword. "There are a number of clues that indicate the constructor was aware of my father's interest in Central America . . . For instance, his name appears at 63-Across; 61-Across is *January, south of the border,* which may reference a journey my father took . . . But more importantly, look at the answers to 18, 33, and 52-Across."

"*Wise man's tip, part 1, 2, and 3,*" Rosco read aloud, then whistled under his breath. "Holy smoke!" He looked at Belle. "THREE MAY KEEP A SECRET IF TWO OF THEM ARE DEAD." Finally, he added a quiet, "Debbie . . ."

"That was the connection Sara and I made, too . . . And Father . . . making the third person—"

"I'm going to call Al," Rosco said. "Get this puzzle over to him . . . I don't know what he'll suggest in terms of Deborah Hurley, since her death occurred in New Jersey, but I'm pretty sure he'll recommend having your father's body exhumed for a full investigation into homicide . . . If Carlyle's suggestion was correct, and poison was used, the lab will need to provide specifics to strengthen any potential criminal case Al might decide to open. The situation involving Debbie is different—and definitely beyond his jurisdiction—but we'll cross that bridge when we come to it."

Belle bit her lip. "I wish there were some other way of determining if Father—"

Sara interrupted. "But, Rosco, if my brother's hints and warnings are true, and it was some type of drug cartel that was responsible for killing Belle's father, wouldn't their activities be well-nigh impossible to trace? Foreign nationals drifting in and out of the country. No American police files, et cetera—"

"Unless they contracted a local to do the work," he said. Then he also paused in thought. "Before we address the issue of exhuming the body, maybe we need to examine Dr. Graham's final days . . . We know he took the train from Florida, made a private stop in Princeton . . . Marie-Claude Araignée told me it was your father's idea to attend the talk given by the CEO of Savante—meaning that he'd clearly scheduled his entire trip north around that event—"

"And then argued publicly with the man," Belle added in some excitement before her shoulders slumped again. "But Father was apparently only concerned about drilling practices in the regions where the Olmec culture existed—something

Savante obviously wasn't involved in because of Mexico's government-run monopoly."

"That's where you may be wrong," said Sara. "The potentates who preside over international businesses either intentionally—or not—share a great deal of information about each other's practices, be they industrial or fiscal. Conspiracy isn't the sole purview of government agencies."

All three considered their pronouncements. Finally, Belle posed another question. "The cocaine intercepted by the Coast Guard was hidden on a boat, wasn't it?"

"A Belizean fishing trawler, according to Hal," was Sara's swift reply.

"And crude oil from the Gulf of Mexico travels to refineries in North America via ship, doesn't it—with the participation of U.S. companies?"

Rosco stared at his wife. "Are you honestly thinking—?"

Sara finished the sentence for him. "That Savante's tankers may be involved in drug smuggling?"

"It's conceivable, isn't it?" was Belle's quick reply. "Because if we take Senator Crane's warning to heart, then my mind jumps to the fact that Father's research on the Olmecs accidentally uncovered a linkage between oil drilled in Latin America—"

"And millions of dollars of illegally imported drugs," Sara said.

It was Rosco who spoke next. "I think it's time I set up a visit to the Savante Group."

New York, New York. Rosco hadn't visited the Big Apple in over six years. Back then his attention had been focused on discerning the whereabouts of a runaway teenager—a boy who'd been missing from Newcastle for three months. Rosco had eventually traced him to the campus of Columbia University on Manhattan's Upper West Side. The kid had settled in fairly well there; he was working for a bicycle messenger service on Times Square, pulling down a decent income, and wasn't too keen on the idea of being dragged back to Newcastle, Massachusetts, to finish high school.

But Rosco had talked to him; then talked and listened some more—the result being that the former truant had returned home, where he'd quickly applied the lessons on competition and ambition he'd learned in New York. At the age of twenty-two, he was currently the manager of Global

Delivery's Newcastle office—the same people who'd just delivered the crossword puzzle Belle had received from Belize.

All these memories flooded into Rosco's brain as he passed the university and continued down Broadway toward lower Manhattan. Since his 2:00 P.M. meeting with Carl Oclen, Savante's CEO, was scheduled for the company's corporate headquarters on Exchange Place, the easier and quicker route would have been for him to take the West Side Highway straight to the city's Wall Street area. But Rosco actually enjoyed riding down the length of Manhattan Island on Broadway. In his opinion, New Yorkers were always good for a show; nothing slowed them down, and nothing ever would. The drive would probably provide as much entertainment as going to a movie. Anything, and everything, could, and would, happen in New York.

The day had reached ninety degrees and Rosco had removed the canvas top to his Jeep, making it, quite possibly, the only *convertible* in the city. Open-air automobiles were not a New York thing; who knew what you might find in your lap? And overnight parking with a cloth roof? Forget about it. Or as they like to say in the city's outlying boroughs: *Fuggedaboutit.*

"Hey, fella," Rosco remembered hearing a thick Bronx accent warn him on his last trip. "Youse knows what's gonna happen to yo' rag-top afta da sun goes down? Heh, ya don't wanna know. Betta look for a garage, pal." The fact that Rosco left no valuables in the Jeep, and never locked it, seemed to make the New Yorker laugh harder. "Hey, ya think anyone's gonna bodda to see if da door's unlocked? Where's da fun in dat?"

Rosco continued down Broadway, through the Upper West Side, past Columbus Circle, and into the Theatre District. The Broadway show marquees hung out over the sidewalks blaring the names of the various "hot" musicals and "brilliant" stars. He began to notice a strange phenomenon whenever he was halted by a traffic light. As soon as a pedestrian would espy the Red Sox license plate on his front bumper, an immediate scowl would form on his or her face. A couple of men even felt obliged to spit into the crosswalk ahead of the Jeep's grill. Rosco gathered that it was just a gutsy response to the fact that the Red Sox were four games out in front of the Yankees in the AL East. One pedestrian, who seemed to take particular offense, actually walked up to him, looked him in the eye, and said, "It ain't over till it's over, buddy boy," then marched off toward Radio City.

After the Theatre District came Times Square, then the huge Macy's building, the Garment District, Madison Square, Union Square, and eventually Greenwich Village—where Broadway was considered the western fringe of the famed East Village. The city was so massive, each block so crammed with buildings, and so packed with businesses and residences, that the streets continuously teemed with men and women. Everyone was moving fast; everyone was on a mission; trucks double-parked to discharge goods; dollies rolled along sidewalks; pedestrians dodged out of the way, then sprinted into traffic; car horns blared; and drivers yelled obscenities that were lobbed back at them like tennis balls by those on foot.

Rosco pushed farther south, across Houston Street and into Soho. It was at this point that a parking place appeared directly in front of a deli, and he decided it would be a good idea to get a bite to eat before meeting with Carl Oclen. He snagged the place, dropped two quarters into the meter, and scanned the street, taking in the sights.

"You're not going to leave your car like that, are you?" The words came from a young woman dressed in business clothes and carrying a stainless-steel attaché case.

Rosco glanced at her in surprise. "What? The Jeep? There's nothing in it worth taking."

She laughed; it was a quick, no-nonsense, I'm-too-busy-to-be-talking-to-this-yokel sound. "What about the seats? You don't think they'll take the seats?" She marched to the rear of the Jeep, glanced at his tags, said, "Massachusetts! Ho-ho-ho. Figures," and walked off.

Rosco watched her leave. Out of either stubbornness or pride, he opted not to heed her warning; instead, he stepped into the deli and ordered a pastrami sandwich from the take-out window. Then caution got the better of him, and he brought the sandwich back outside, sat on his front fender, and enjoyed his lunch—al fresco.

After he finished with his sandwich and pickle, he walked to the corner and tossed his paper wrapper into a trash can. When he returned, a man was sitting in the passenger's side of the Jeep, pawing through the glove compartment.

"Something I can help you with?" was all Rosco could think to say.

"This your car?"

"Yep."

"Jeep, huh?"

"Sure is."

The man stepped back onto the sidewalk, gave Rosco the once-over, and said, "Just lookin' for some change, man. Got any you can spare?"

Nonplussed at the reply, Rosco forked over a dollar, then climbed into the Jeep and continued down Broadway toward the Wall Street area. Street parking was nonexistent so he pulled into an underground garage that advertised a rate of six dollars.

"How long ya gonna be?" the attendant drawled.

"About an hour. Six bucks, right?"

The attendant merely grunted. "Nah, man, six is for the first twenty minutes. An hour'll be closer to twenty, twenty-five. Longer's more . . . Leave the keys."

Rosco opened his mouth in protest, then thought better of it. "Leave the keys . . . Right."

The Savante offices were on the thirty-third floor of a gray granite building on the corner of Broadway and Exchange Place. Rosco entered through a revolving door and moved over to a bank of elevators marked FLOORS 30–40. He stepped into a car as the door slid open and pressed 33. The car shot upward, and he walked out into an expansive waiting area only seconds later.

Savante appeared to take up the entire thirty-third floor. A chrome and teak reception desk sat in the center of a waiting area furnished with minimalist pieces crafted from similar materials. Rosco approached the receptionist and said, "I have a two o'clock appointment with Mr. Oclen. I'm Chuck Balboa . . . With the Back Bay Film Project?"

"One minute, please." The receptionist tapped an intercom button. "Candie, Mr. Oclen's two o'clock is here. The gentleman with the Boston film company . . . and accent."

The voice on the other end came back with, "Ask him to have a seat. We'll be with him in a moment."

The receptionist pointed to a couch on the assumption Rosco had overheard Candie. When he sat, his exposed ankles were given a sour and unapproving glance.

He shrugged, said, "Hey, I spend too much time on 'the Coast'—what can I say?" then picked up a copy of *Crude*, a trade publication dedicated to the oil business. The magazine was five months old, leading Rosco to wonder why it hadn't been replaced with a newer issue. But upon closer examination, he realized the man on the cover was no other than Carl Oclen himself. He was standing on the bow of a supertanker in a pose that surreally appeared to mimic the movie *Titanic*. Behind Oclen stretched a long and lusciously verdant coastline that Rosco guessed to be in the Gulf of Mexico while inside the magazine was a lengthy article entitled "The Midas Touch: Swimming in Liquid Gold," profiling the Savante Group and Oclen.

According to the article, Savante's CEO had been born in rural Texas, dropped out of high school, and had worked as a wildcatter in the Iranian, Saudi, and Southern California oil fields. He'd moved up industry ranks and was one of the premier explorers and developers of the offshore drilling in California's Santa Barbara area before cutting out on his own to create the Savante Group, Inc. Over the years the company had branched out, and now had controlling interests in supermarkets, banana imports, Florida citrus groves, a fast-food chain, a popular breakfast cereal, and infant and toddler foods, formula, and "hygienic supplies." Oclen, himself, also owned a minor league baseball team in Texas.

"Mr. Oclen will see you now," a young woman said as she approached. She looked more like a Dallas Cowboys cheerleader than a secretary, and her heavy Texas accent only seemed to cement that image.

"You must be Candie," Rosco said as they walked down the hallway, wondering what had happened to the snooty assistant who'd arranged today's meeting.

"Why, yes. I am." *Am* came out like *aay-em*.

"You're not the person I spoke with when I made the appointment."

"You mean Jules?" The name sounded as if it would go a long way in a jewelry store.

"I'm afraid I didn't get the man's—"

"I'm sure it was Jules. He handles all Mr. Oclen's appointments . . . Jules and I perform very different duties for Mr. Oclen. Mr. Oclen believes 'the staff should suit the task'—or is it the other way around?"

"I guess it depends on whose staff you're talking about."

Candie continued in her molasses-sweet drawl. "I understand you-all are in the film business?"

"That's right. We're shooting a little thriller up in Boston right now."

"I used to do some acting in Houston . . . But nothing you might have seen . . . The films were more of the adult variety." Candie appeared to think for a moment. "I'd be happy to audition for you—if that might be of interest. I can read from a play . . . or, you know . . . extemporize?"

"I'd hate to take you away from your duties here at Savante, Candie, but when we reach that point in production, I'll be sure to have the casting people get in touch."

She gave Rosco a sugary smile and opened a mahogany door that led to Carl Oclen's inner sanctum. "Mr. Balboa's here, Mr. O. The movie director . . ."

Oclen's three-sided office faced south, west, and north and consumed nearly fifteen hundred square feet, its windows affording a sweeping view that included the Statue of Liberty, the Hudson River, and nearly all of lower Manhattan. The CEO's desk was almost as large as Rosco's entire office while the man sitting behind it was clearly the same person who'd graced the copy of *Crude* in the waiting area.

Impeccably sculpted hair that had probably been *enhanced* into a lustrous chestnut color, a physique that cried out *per-*

sonal trainer, and a suit that looked as if it would cost more to replace than Rosco's aging Jeep, Carl Oclen was the picture of wealth. He was on the phone and waved for his guest to take a seat. Instead, Rosco walked to the window and looked out over the tip of Manhattan. Thirty-three stories below sat Trinity Church. The church was illuminated by a single ray of sunlight; an untouchable beacon of peace in a cavern of vast skyscrapers.

Oclen dropped the telephone receiver into its cradle, stood, and moved alongside Rosco. "Hell of a view, isn't it? I was at this very desk when those vermin took out the towers. What did they think? They'd break New York? Break New Yorkers? Break America? Not in a million years, pardner." The Texas drawl had been smoothed into an all-purpose good-ole-boy twang, but Rosco guessed the accent could just as easily vanish—or thicken—depending on the circumstances, or the guest.

"As a film person I'm always looking at the visual; camera angles, interesting locations, et cetera." Rosco extended his hand. "I appreciate you taking the time to meet with me on such short notice. I had a meeting set with Exxon, but they canceled out on me at the last minute."

"Happy to do it. Especially when it means beating out the competition." Oclen smiled. It was not a warm and fuzzy expression.

"I have a good notion to dump their credit card as a result of the mix-up . . . Unfortunately we get caught up in a film slate, and any little thing can throw us off schedule."

"I've always been a bit of a movie buff, Mr. Balboa, so, like I said, I'm happy to help out."

"Please . . . Call me Chuck."

"All right."

Rosco noted that the first-name-basis invitation wasn't reciprocated as Oclen walked back to his desk and sat. "What can I do you for, Chuck? I believe Jules mentioned that the picture you're making is an action-adventure . . . something to do with oil imports?"

Rosco sat in a brown leather chair opposite Oclen. He also smiled. "Well, let's start with this: Is it possible that a company like Savante could smuggle cocaine into the United States on its oil tankers?"

Oclen's face turned to stone.

CHAPTER

26

R osco remained focused on Carl Oclen's hard, unwavering stare, hoping to garner information, but the eyes revealed nothing.

"Sorry," Rosco finally said, "that was just a little ploy we directors like to use—Actors' Studio stuff; mention something deeply personal, something shocking, and then gauge the reaction. It helps me with my actors . . . I learn what's real and what isn't—emotionally speaking . . . I get to know what I want to use down the road. I get to learn what buttons to push . . ." Rosco was weaving his story from whole cloth, but it was sounding pretty good to him—pretty believable, too. Or so he hoped.

Oclen's expression softened slightly, but only slightly.

"Anyway," Rosco continued with another sunny, L.A.-type grin, "I'm getting ahead of myself here. The screenplay—as Jules correctly inferred—is an action-adventure tale about a

DEA agent on the trail of drug smugglers: i.e. *The Bad Guys*. My writer has the cocaine shipments entering the U.S. on fishing boats . . . I'm sure you heard about that load the Coast Guard pulled off a Belizian boat a while back . . . ? Our timing is perfect on this."

"I . . . did read something on that, yes. It was in *Daily Finance* . . ." Oclen's tone remained cautious.

"Right. I guess everyone did . . . Anyway, that's my point; fishing boats have been done to death. You got storms—been done; whales—been done; old ships; new ships . . . You heard of *Moby Dick*, right? *The Old Man and the Sea*? I mean, who hasn't? Classics, both of them . . . Apparently they were books first. Anyway, what I'm thinking is this: Everyone's got storms; everyone's got fish. What I need is a fresh angle . . . So, here's the deal: We give this script a quick rewrite and change the venue to an oil tanker. Plus, we get all that testosterone stuff—guys on a mother of a boat, polished steel, uniforms, a bow slicing through the sea . . . And I mean a *big* bow. I saw that picture of you on the cover of *Crude*, out in the lobby"—Rosco cocked his thumb over his shoulder—"and I'm thinking: Is this a dynamite setup or what? I mean, like that's the money shot right there—"

"And what is it exactly you want from me . . . Chuck?" The tone was still frosty although Rosco sensed he was making headway. Everyone liked to imagine they had movie star potential.

"Just a little background, really, so that the *color* rings true for the audience. I'm placing my action down in the Gulf of Mexico . . . pretty places, fab food—the crew has to eat, know what I mean? So I'd like to stay with those locations . . . And I've booked gear for December . . ." On the assumption that all film directors behaved like Woody Allen, Rosco moved his hands in jerky motions as he talked. The nervous movements, as well as what his attempt at Hollywood-speak were clearly beginning to win Oclen over. "I figure we can have an American oil company drilling off the Mexican coast—"

"Whoa, hold up there, Chuck." Oclen's small smile had turned decidedly smug. "Let me tell you how things work down in the Gulf. First of all, once you get south of Texas, I hate to break it to you, pal, but it ain't America no more. *Enchiladas* or no *enchiladas* . . . The rules change. Big time. The oil and natural gas industry in Mexico is one hundred percent government controlled. You've got to be solidly outside of Mexico's territorial waters if you want to start sinking wells. And if the water's too deep, you're talking a floating rig . . . first tropical storm that rips up the coast is going to take your rig straight to New Orleans to join the Mardi Gras parade." The CEO chuckled at his own witticism. "Look what happened to that baby off of Brazil. *Adios, amigo.* Davy Jones's locker for everyone on that baby."

"Is that the same with the other countries down there? Belize? Guatemala? Nicaragua? All government controlled?"

"Look, Chuck, each nation sets different policies; and any oil company—be it owned by the Brits or the Dutch or whoever—has to obey local government regulations. Look at Alaska. And that's the U.S. of A., for pete's sake . . . You've got to pick up a few politicians along the way. It's not like the old days when you could just buy a tract of mineral-rich land, cross your fingers, and pray for the mother lode . . . Latin America's different, sure. None of the owl-huggers we have up here. The rules are more *flexible,* but you still have to deal with governments—"

Rosco interrupted. He tried to look crestfallen. "Damn . . . That's bad news for me . . . So we don't get any Mexican oil here in the States?"

"I didn't say that. But what you're talking about there is transportation. That's another ball of wax all together . . . Now, I deal with Pemex. We all do. The company's the government monopoly south of the border. We transport Mexican product up to New Jersey all the time. It's contract work. Subcontract, actually . . . But to be honest: Most of our imports are coming from Venezuela now. And I'm working on some Cuba stuff—but that's off the record."

"But you do have tankers coming from the Gulf?"

"Absolutely."

"Okay," Rosco said, watching Oclen's reaction closely, "this is only hypothetical . . . the hypothetical back-story to my plot—that's the . . . um . . . that's the reason for making the film . . . Now, suppose someone—like yourself—owned an oil tanker, and wanted to smuggle drugs into the country. It would be pretty easy, right?"

Oclen's expression again darkened. "Look, Chuck, I'm trying to help you here . . . I don't know what it's like in the fishing business; I don't know what the boat owners are into, but I can tell you one thing: They don't have the kind of money invested in their vessels that I have. A shrimp captain goes out into the Gulf . . . ? Hey, one quick cocaine drop can make his day. He can pay off his boat's mortgage in a weekend, so maybe it's worth the gamble for him. But Savante? I have millions tied up in a single tanker. You think I'd risk letting the DEA impound one of my ships, all of my ships, just to pick up what amounts to little more than pocket change for me? Not on your life."

Oclen's point made a lot of sense. Rosco was about to try a

different tack when Savante's CEO opened his desk drawer, removed a baseball, and flipped it toward his guest. Rosco caught it instinctively. It was signed by Babe Ruth.

"Is . . . this . . . real?" Rosco stammered.

"See, that's my point exactly, Chuck. That ball's worth about twenty thousand dollars, maybe more. I should have it in a glass case somewhere, right? But I don't because I can afford to hold it. I can afford to roll it in my hand and enjoy it. If I ruin it someday . . . ? Well, hell, that's my business, and nobody else's. Once I buy something, it's mine—I do with it as I please."

Rosco set the ball on the desk—reluctantly.

"Now," Oclen continued, "if you want to make a movie about someone smuggling drugs on an oil tanker, you have to look at the little guy. You can't make your bad guy the CEO of a multinational petroleum company." Oclen chuckled again. "It makes no sense. Hell, I make too much money off the damn oil to worry about a sideline as picayune as drug smuggling . . . No, you've got to make your smuggler one of the crew."

"Like the captain?"

Oclen shook his head. "No . . . And the more I think about it, it's too implausible. On a tanker, nothing's loaded or unloaded like it is on a freighter. The cargo's pumped; tankers don't require cranes and they don't even berth at loading facilities that use cranes . . . Oh, sure, one of the crew could bring on a small package; maybe ten or fifteen pounds, and no one would notice . . . but if you're thinking a big-time smuggling operation . . . No, I'm sorry to say, Chuck, I think you have to stay with the fishing boat angle. They're the only ones with the loading equipment. And they can off-load in smaller facilities." Oclen shrugged slightly. "What did you say the title of this flick was again?"

Rosco sidestepped the question with a facsimile of a long and frustrated sigh. "I see your point . . . Damn. I thought I was really on to something . . . Sort of a *Top Gun* meets *Raiders of the Lost Ark* . . . Well, you never know until you ask—"

"What do you mean: '*Top Gun* meets *Raiders of the Lost Ark*'?"

"Oh, sorry . . . that's Hollywood talk. What it means is a combination of two films. You take strong elements from a couple of flicks . . . In this case, macho guys . . . huge boats . . . And you spell Adventure with a capital A, and profit with a capital P—"

"*Raiders of the Lost Ark* didn't have any boats in it."

Rosco stared. He'd never been good at remembering movie plots, and he'd pulled the title out of some long-retired memory bank assuming the ark meant—well, an ark. "Right . . ." he now said. "Of course not . . . I was just using it as an example of the way things work out on the Coast." He picked up the baseball once more and turned it over in his hand. "You're sharp, Mr. O. Real sharp. But I guess you don't get to be CEO or a multinational without serious smarts . . . No ark in the *Raiders* movie . . . Boy, are you ever right about that!" Rosco's eyes wandered back to the windows and the view of the Statue of Liberty sitting serenely in the wide, blue bay. "There's one other little thing I wanted to ask you. I sent my screenwriter down to Princeton a few weeks ago to sit in on your speech . . . I was hoping he might get a few ideas by listening to you—"

Oclen stiffened immediately. "That talk was closed to the public."

"I know that. The guy couldn't get in. And man, was he steamed about going all the way down there and coming back empty-handed . . . It's a boring drive from Boston to Princeton. Anyway, after your presentation ended, he heard that some old coot really laid into you, and that you two shared some pretty fiery words—"

Oclen leaned across the table. "What's that got to do with your movie?"

Rosco grinned apologetically. "Oh, nothing . . . Just backstory . . . *color*, like I said. You know how these screenwriters are. Their imaginations go crazy. He came back saying he had a great concept for a new screenplay, but wouldn't tell me what it was . . . I just wondered what the heck the blowup was all about?"

Oclen gritted his teeth. His eyes were as unforgiving as granite. "What went on at that speech, and after it, is confidential information. You tell this writer of yours that if he's considering using one particle of the information—or misinformation—he gleaned from *not* being present, he's a dead duck. The Savante Group is a responsible organization. It's important for us that the public understand that fact. I'm sure you get my drift. All of our operations remain well within the limit of the law."

Rosco nodded, his face wreathed in a bland smile. "Not to worry, Mr. O. I'll pass along your . . . suggestion. Even screenwriters aren't dumb enough to want to risk lawsuits. And like I said, he didn't tell me anything . . . Except, well, one thing: He said the old guy who yelled at you turned up dead the next day. Weird, huh? And then his secretary turned up dead a couple days ago."

Oclen's head jerked up. "You're going to have to leave now. I have another appointment."

Rosco stood. "Hey, *no problemo*. And I really appreciate your time, Mr. O. Too bad this oil tanker thing didn't fly . . . I mean that *Crude* pix . . . All I can say is: Wow." He turned and walked toward the door, but Oclen stopped him.

"Chuck?"

"Yes?"

"Leave the baseball here."

"Right."

CHAPTER

27

Belle couldn't sit still, couldn't remain fixed in one place when she was standing, couldn't keep her brain focused on a single issue for more than a few seconds. *Rosco's attempting to pry incriminating information about drug smuggling from the CEO of a multinational oil company,* was one thought; *Deborah Hurley died in a supposed hit-and-run in New Jersey,* was another. *My father visited the same state the day before he passed away. It was there that he decided to argue with the head honcho of the Savante Group. Is there a connection? And if there is, how on earth do I find it?*

To say that Belle felt like jumping out of her skin would be an understatement. *And what about Woody? Where does he fit in? Or Franklin Mossback? And who has been "borrowing" my father's identity?* Here her intellectual skills took another swift leap. *The constructor who sent the* Words to the Wise *puzzle needs to remain anonymous, because he—or she—is also in danger. And*

*the reason that person's in trouble is that whoever murdered my
father—and may also have arranged Debbie's death—is still at
large. And still searching for a vital piece of dangerous information.
Such as my father's missing notebook.*

Without a second to pause and collect herself, she picked
up the phone and punched in the number to Deborah Hurley's aunt, Rachel Volsay.

A youngish child answered, which was fortunate because
the little girl's need to "hunt down Great-Aunt Rach" gave
Belle the moments necessary to formulate her speech.

"Yes?" an adult voice finally said into the phone. The
sound was empty with grief.

"Is this Mrs. Volsay?"

A long sigh served as response, then the tone became even
more subdued. "Who is this?"

"I'm Annabella Graham . . . Belle . . . My father was Professor Theodore Graham. Deborah was doing research for him."

The voice collected itself. "I'm sorry for your loss, Miss
Graham. Deb was so shaken by it . . . She was very fond of
your dad. He was 'a great boss,' she told me over and over. 'A
great man.'"

"And my father was equally fond of Deborah, Mrs. Volsay."
Belle could think of nothing more to add. She had no specifics
to substantiate the statement. Instead, she took a breath. *How
does someone suggest to a family member that a relative might have
been murdered?* "Mrs. Volsay, I'm sorry to intrude at a difficult
time like this—"

"Oh, it's no intrusion . . ." Again, the sad, wispy voice.
"Besides, with Deb gone, there's so little for me to . . . to . . ."
She stopped herself, and continued in a steadier tone. "Mike's
here now, and he's contacted the friends they had who'd
remained nearby . . ."

Belle took another long gulp of air. "Mrs. Volsay, this may
ound unbelievable . . . but is it possible that Debbie's death
asn't accidental?"

The silence of confusion and disbelief echoed through the
one. "You mean: Could someone have wanted to kill my
ttle girl . . . ? Whyever for?"

"I don't know, Mrs. Volsay."

A sob caught in Debbie's aunt's throat. "But that's . . .
at's an abominable suggestion, Miss Graham . . . My Debo-
h wouldn't have hurt a fly—"

"I didn't mean to imply—"

"You ask any of her friends. Everyone loved that girl.
veryone!"

Belle paused. The conversation was proving even more dif-
cult than she'd imagined. "I realize that, Mrs. Volsay. Of
urse, I do . . . I didn't mean to infer that an acquaintance
ight have wished Deborah dead . . . I was thinking of a
ranger—"

"You mean like a random act? By a crazed person?"

"That's not precisely what I meant, Mrs. Volsay . . ." Belle
eared her throat. "I . . . well, the police here in Newcastle
ave reason to suspect that my father did not die of natural
uses—"

Anger blazed through the receiver. "Oh, right! I remember
ow! Debbie told me about you . . . Married to some private
vestigator . . . and you've both tracked down criminals up
Massachusetts! Well, that's not the way things work in a
ommunity like ours, Miss Graham. We don't need private
vestigators and their ilk skulking around. We don't tolerate
nlawful behavior: gangs and kids who disrespect their eld-
s. Thieves, and all that . . . We know each other down here.
Ve respect each other. When someone dies, we gather

around. We show our love . . . And we don't invent evil where none exists!"

Belle resisted pointing out the obvious: that the driver of the vehicle that struck down Deborah Hurley hadn't played by those same cozy rules of small-town living. "But that's precisely what I'm getting at, Mrs. Volsay. Maybe the driver of the car wasn't from the environs of Kings Creek or even from New Jersey—"

An abrupt and irritable sigh interrupted Belle's speech. She decided to backtrack. "I'm sorry. I didn't mean to upset you."

"Well, you did! And if I were you, Miss Graham, I wouldn't be so quick to suspect that your father didn't simply have a heart attack and drop off to sleep. Good people like your dad don't get murdered. And it won't do your brain any good searching for devils when none exist."

"I apologize again, Mrs. Volsay . . . I didn't intend to suggest that Debbie had personal enemies—"

"She certainly didn't! Everyone around here adored her. When her mother passed on—my sister, that was—and then Deb's own little sister, why, the whole town was just that upset . . ." Again, the aunt's tone took on a muffled, exhausted sound. "Cancer's a terrible thing," she finally added.

"Yes," Belle managed to murmur. She felt like a criminal making this poor, bereft woman recall other times of loss.

"Well," Rachel Volsay at last concluded, "there's none of us on this earth who hasn't been touched by sorrow. It's the way of the world . . . It always has been . . ." Then she seemed to shake herself back to the present. Belle's thorny question seemed forgotten. "The funeral's the day after tomorrow, Miss Graham . . . as I'm sure you know. I'd best be getting to my chores if I want the house to do honor to Deb's memory . . .

I'll tell Mike you called, shall I? He's been such a comfort, that young man—although, how he continues to bear up, I'll never know."

Belle found herself gulping back tears of both sympathy and empathy. "Yes, please, Mrs. Volsay. Please tell him I called."

"He's away down at the police station or I'd put him on for a moment."

Belle's ears perked up, but Deborah's aunt continued with a wistful: "Such good friends all those boys are . . . That's what comes from living in a community like ours."

"I'm so sorry, Mrs. Volsay."

"Deb worshipped your father, you know?"

"Yes. Yes, I do know."

With the phone replaced in its cradle, Belle could only stare disconsolately at it. *Poor Mike,* she thought. *Poor Rachel Volsay . . . Poor Debbie. Shattered lives, and so much pain . . .* Belle sighed. *And Father, too . . .* But even as she considered those intertwined existences, she realized she'd reached another impasse in her search. *If Debbie Hurley's "accident" had been staged to resemble a hit-and-run, there was obviously no one in the small New Jersey town who would believe it. And certainly no one who would even remotely consider an underworld connection. Drug lords and shipments of cocaine belonged to a different universe than the loving sphere of Kings Creek.*

And maybe that's the better way, Belle thought. *Because where's the good in conjuring up paid assassins or international cartels harboring dirty secrets? Isn't it easier to assume my father succumbed to heart failure? And Debbie to the injustice of picking the wrong moment to cross the street? Isn't there enough sorrow in death without adding the element of human cruelty?*

Belle rose slowly from her chair. The fax was busy spitting out a message, and she glanced idly toward the machine, realizing she'd been so deep in contemplation she hadn't even heard the phone ring.

It took her less than a heartbeat to recognize the design on the flimsy paper, another second to detach what was obviously an additional clue to the mystery—in the form of another crossword puzzle. Her eyes raced over the Across and Down columns. "Skulls," she gasped. "They're all skulls."

She grabbed the phone, punched in the number to Rosco's cell phone, and left a rapid message. "Don't come home. Meet me in Princeton. I'm taking the train. I'll phone again with my arrival time . . . That's all I want to say for now . . ." She broke the connection and immediately called Sara, who answered on the second ring. Belle hardly waited for the old lady to speak.

"Can you keep Kit at your house for the night? I think I've discovered who killed my father."

Across

1. Bit of info
4. Neg. opp.
7. __Martin
12. The__on drugs
13. Like some tires
15. __Fulci, Italian horror director
16. With 1-Down, a punch
17. Some woodwinds
18. Radio station sign
19. Frenchman Flat overlook
22. St. Francis's birthplace
24. Pretoria's land; abbr.
25. Yarmulke
28. Soho's locale
32. "Je__Français."
33. Argentine aunts
35. Chemical suffix
36. Obsession, suffix
37. Computer scanner; abbr.
38. On the briny
39. To endure in China
40. Museum on S. Michigan Ave.; abbr.
41. Acquire
42. Fringe
45. Cushing and Lee classic
47. Neither's partner
48. Debbie's aunt
49. Jolly Roger
55. Guff, var.
56. Erected
57. Bull or bear ending
60. Savante CEO
61. From the beginning, Lat.
62. Grampus
63. Jacob's twin's
64. Compass reading
65. Skid or stick lead-in

Down

1. See 16-Across
2. Writer Fleming
3. Squeezing
4. John Q.__
5. Sixth of a drachma
6. Appear
7. Poet, Dámaso__
8. Vacationer's goal
9. Tile worker's org.
10. Four for Caesar
11. Scandinavian goddess of past, present, or future
13. Dishevel
14. Brit. Mil. award
20. Eliminates
21. Dot-com addresses; abbr.
22. Seek
23. Played hockey
26. Yours on the Yon
27. Lace loop
29. Debate
30. __Beach, Oahu
31. Almost
34. St. Louis sight
38. Talus
40. Taj Mahal site
41. Knows
43. Instead
44. Like a pinhole camera?
46. Grow
49. "If the __fits"
50. Some lodges; abbr.
51. __Road, Truk Island
52. Celtic's org.
53. Voices over
54. C.V.s
58. Angel's favorite letters
59. Chemical symbol for prussic acid

USE YOUR HEAD!

CHAPTER

28

During the train ride south, Belle's confidence in the crossword's message began to waver. *Use Your Head!* She read the title over and over again, then returned to the answers that had propelled her onto an Amtrak car and a journey to Princeton. 19-Across: SKULL MOUNTAIN; 25-Across: SKULL CAP; 45-Across: THE SKULL; and the most lethal at 49-Across: SKULL AND BONES. But there the hints—if they were indeed hints—disappeared. And if anything, SKULL AND BONES was a secret *Yale* society and had nothing to do with a university in Princeton, New Jersey.

She stared and stared at the page while the train hurtled through the green and varied scenery of Rhode Island's farmland and oceanside, then down past New London, Connecticut, with its commanding sea view. Use Your Head! she thought, Use Your Head! *The title obviously refers to the skull theme, but it probably also indicates that I'm supposed to make some sort of cerebral—and lexical—leap.*

She reexamined the clues. They were quirky and erudite—some almost overly so. After all, how many people could readily fill in the answer to 7-Down: *Poet, Dámaso* ALONSO; or NORN as the solution to 11-Down: *Scandinavian goddess of past, present, or future?* And there was the Chinese word REN at 39-Across; the Latin AB OVO at 61-Across or LUCIO *Fulci* at 15-Across: *Italian horror director.* Whoever had constructed the crossword possessed a wide-ranging body of knowledge.

Like my father, Belle thought with a grim smile, then her brain jumped beyond Theodore Graham to Franklin Mossback and his widowed wife, the keeper of an unusual collections of skulls. Marie-Claude . . . *Can she really be a murderer? Perhaps even a serial criminal who likes to keep mementos of her victims in the forms of their skulls? There are such people, after all . . . Could it be that she really is a spider lady, killing the men she mates with?*

Belle stared out the window at the scenery rushing past: a curving, sandy beach replete with families enjoying an August outing, a pasture inhabited by a contented horse, woods speckled with the furtive early beginnings of yellow, autumnal leaves. It was a pretty ride and surprisingly bucolic—especially given the population living in the area Amtrak referred to as its "northeast corridor."

She purposely brought her glance back into the train carriage, then picked up the puzzle again. 32-Across: *Je* PARLE *Français* . . . 26-Down: *Yours on the Yon* . . . A TOI . . . Belle shook her head in frustration. *Am I supposed to believe that the perpetrator is French?* But there was *Debbie's aunt* at 48-Across; and *Savante CEO* at 60-Across. And the clincher: *The* WAR *on drugs* at 12-Across. *What's going on here?* Belle's brain demanded. *Who is the constructor? And why does this person know these names?*

Bridgeport, Connecticut, hove into view at that moment, and the scenery changed drastically, becoming gritty and gray and unwelcomingly citified. Abandoned tires, an occasional rusting bed frame, and other detritus littered the tracks and adjacent weed-choked dirt. Plastic bags in various states of decay either blew along the roadbed or hung from the limbs of malnourished sumac trees. Belle made a face of disgust and dismay. She decided to avoid looking out the window.

Okay, let's examine the previous crossword I received: Words to the Wise. *Let's see what similarities I can find.* She pulled the puzzle from an overstuffed manila envelope in her canvas book bag. Stuck to it were two of the cleverer submissions she'd decided to use in her collection. "Work comes later," Belle muttered. She returned both crosswords to her satchel, and concentrated on *Words to the Wise.*

"*Wise man's tip, part 1, 2, 3 . . .* hmmm . . . that could well refer to a professor . . . and here we have the French words ETE at 19-Down and PEU at 37-Down . . . *Monsieur Gide* at 46-Down . . ." Belle gasped and sat bolt upright; a new sequence of theories whipped around in her brain. *What if Franklin Mossback isn't dead? What if his wife tried to kill him . . . but he escaped . . . What if she's unaware that he survived . . . And what if her "friendship" with my father was heating up before Franklin "disappeared in Guatemala," causing him to believe my father was in collusion with his wife: lover and wicked female plot plodding mate's death, etc.? What if . . . ? And here's* FRANKLIN *as the answer to 50-Across . . . Right in the puzzle . . . What if the reference is to Mossback and not the illustrious Ben?*

Belle gasped louder. The person in the seat across the aisle scowled in response, but she was unaware of the censorious glance. Instead, another pair of startled questions leapt forward. *What if Franklin Mossback killed my father—and then borrowed his identity? What if Mossback is the person Hal Crane's 'contacts' 'researched' . . . ?* But even as those queries formed, Belle found herself demanding an equally perplexed: *But why did Mossback wait so long to take his revenge? And where does Debbie Hurley fit in? Or the Savante Group? And who constructed these crosswords and sent them to me?*

At that exact minute, train number 85, the Northeast Direct, whooshed into the tunnel that would bear it under the East River and into Manhattan. The car was plunged into darkness, the overhead lights only flickering at rare intervals like sparks from a dying fire.

"New York," Belle heard a conductor announce. "New York's Penn Station . . . All doors out . . . We'll have a twenty-minute layover for those remaining on board . . . no reading lights; the café car will be closed until we depart the station . . . All doors out, folks. New York's Penn Station. Use all doors. Check luggage areas for any personal possessions . . . And take your time detraining."

Despite this reasonable injunction, most of the other passengers immediately began grabbing carry-ons from the overhead racks, and clambering into the still-jostling aisles. By the time the train had actually stopped, they were anxiously pushing their way toward every available door. Belle suspected this was typical Big Apple behavior: No one appreciated being told what to do—especially if the suggestion was "take your time."

As the train's exterior doors slid open, the hot smell of the crowded platform blew in. In the dusty whirls produced by thousands of moving feet, sandwich wrappers and pizza-stained lengths of waxy paper danced in the air. Every trash bin was full to overflowing with empty soda cans and discarded newspapers. *What a wasteful nation we are,* Belle thought. She closed her eyes against the sight; she tried to close off her sense of smell, as well.

Okay, she thought, *what have I got? Rosco's going to be meeting me in less than an hour and a half. What am I going to tell him? That Mossback has the goods on his wife? That he also killed my dad—and that somehow he's involved with this Oclen guy and Debbie's aunt?* Belle stifled the desire to growl aloud. "What a mess," she said instead.

Rosco met her—as she'd all but ordered him to do—with a mock salute. "I take it you've solved all our problems." He held her and kissed her. She kissed him back, lost for a blissful moment in their happy proximity, the pleasant lure of the future. "I've missed you," she said.

"I only left this morning."

"Well, I missed you anyway . . ."

Rosco kissed her again. "So what's the emergency?"

In response, Belle retrieved the latest crossword. "I think Marie-Claude is guilty of something big . . . I just don't know what . . ."

"And for that, you came all the way down here?"

"I—"

"Wait. I know . . . You had a brainstorm, but on the trip down you began to have second thoughts."

Belle stared at her husband in amazement. "How did you know that?"

"It happens to everyone investigating a baffling case. You

get a sudden flash of insight . . . Then the lightbulb goes out, leaving your brain darker than it was before."

"What do you do when that happens?"

"I go with my instinct. You know . . . where there's smoke, there's fire."

Belle nodded. "Or where there are skulls . . . there are bound to be dead people."

CHAPTER
29

Rosco pulled into a parking space on Nassau Street and stepped out of the Jeep. Before he could cross over to the sidewalk, Belle had jumped from the car and pumped four quarters into the meter.

"How appropriate that we're off to Aaron Burr Hall," he observed with a wry smile. "You look like you're ready for pistols at twenty paces."

"She's guilty as sin, Rosco."

"She *may* be."

"Well, she's guilty of *something,* because someone is clearly directing us back to Marie-Claude."

Rosco studied his wife, then hesitated for a moment before speaking. "That may well be . . . But let's not charge into the arena without a battle plan. We have no hard evidence—only a crossword full of SKULL references. If we're too aggressive, if we play the wrong cards, she'll clam up and we'll have nothing. So . . . what is it we're after? A confession?"

"That would be nice."

He nodded. "Right. But we're not likely to get that. *Madame* Araignée's not stupid . . . And another thing . . ." He placed his hands on Belle's shoulders. "If this woman killed your father . . . And if we become convinced of that, are you ready to look her in the eye? Personally, I would have some trouble with that."

Belle thought. "I can control myself. I have to control myself."

"Okay . . ." Rosco finally said. "Given the fact that she's probably not about to confess, we have to find a hole in her story and exploit it. Keep your ears open for any contradictory statements—that's when we push."

Belle took Rosco's hand and squeezed it.

Marie-Claude could not have been more accommodating and gracious when Rosco had phoned her from the train station. *"Bien sur,"* she'd laughed in her husky voice. "Of course, I will meet with you both . . . I shall greet darling Teddy's daughter at long last. I will clear the decks . . . That is the American expression for 'to begin again'—*n'est-ce pas?*"

Now, face to face, she made every effort to appear as hospitable and helpful as her telephone persona. "I cannot express the *plaisir* of finally seeing the daughter . . . *la fille de* my dear friend . . ." She took Belle's hand and held it, even though Belle instinctively flinched.

SKULLS, she thought, *a crossword full of* SKULLS. Belle remained in this outlandish position of guest and hostess only because she told herself that she was here to catch a murderer. A *murderess*.

Rosco noted that, in person, Marie-Claude had chosen to drop the intimate term "Teddy." Belle only noted that the French woman wouldn't release her hand. *Franklin Moss-back—and my father,* she silently recited. *What is this lady hiding?* Then those queries led immediately to: *How could Father have tolerated this phony and fawning behavior? What on earth was the attraction?*

But two could play at this game. Belle kept her many objections in sight even as she turned an enigmatic smile upon her father's paramour.

The ruse worked; Marie-Claude completely misread Belle's seemingly benign expression. "So lovely," she said. "So much like your dear *papa.* The family resemblance is undeniable." A small tear slid down her perfectly made-up face.

Belle stifled a grimace and finally pulled her hand free. She looked at Rosco, who shrugged his shoulders in an attitude that said: *She's a pro, what can I say? You were warned ahead of time.* Belle tightened her lips and decided to take charge of the situation. This wasn't a Parisian *salon,* after all—or a time to share loving reminiscences. "Professor Araignée, my husband and I have reason to believe that my father did not die of natural causes." She watched for a reaction, saw nothing, then continued, "We believe, in fact, that he was murdered."

"*Ah, mon Dieu.*" Marie-Claude raised her eyes heavenward. She looked as though she were about to swoon. "But *non* . . . He . . . He . . . suffered from the *coeur* . . . from the heart attack, *n'est-ce pas?*" With her well-honed instincts for female competition, she'd already deduced that Belle wasn't going to be as soft-hearted—or as malleable—as she'd hoped. Instead, Marie-Claude looked toward Rosco, hoping his reaction would be more indulgent. "But surely it was a heart attack, *non?*"

"That was the police's initial—" he began.

"But the failure of the heart is not a gunshot wound, *monsieur* . . . or the stabbing with the knife."

As Belle opened her mouth to speak, Rosco noted how dark her gray eyes had become, and decided to intervene. "You are absolutely correct, Professor Araignée. There is some thought that . . . Well, perhaps a sophisticated poison—"

"*Ah, mon Dieu! Mon Dieu! Mon cher* Teddy . . . How he must have suffered . . ."

Rosco watched Belle's expression grow more and more irate while Marie-Claude uttered a plaintive:

"What *terrible* fiend would do such a—?"

This time it was Belle who answered. Her voice had turned measured and hard. "We have reason to suspect that someone—possibly a person with whom you are well acquainted—believes that you are either directly involved in my father's death or know who is."

Marie-Claude gasped, her eyes grown wide with horror. "*Moi?* How can that be? Who is this person? Why would I have wished . . . ? But no, *c'est impossible*—"

"Impossible or not," Belle continued in a sterner tone, "there is someone who strongly suspects your collusion."

"Collusion?" Marie-Claude looked to Rosco to rescue her from this attack. "What is this word 'collusion'? But, of course, I must know who my accuser is!"

Belle all but growled; Rosco reached out a hand to calm her, but she only frowned in response. *Why did Rosco mention the possibility of poison?* her brain demanded. *Aren't we here to interrogate Marie-Claude—instead of playing into her hands?*

"I understand, dear girl," Marie-Claude finally began, "dear *belle fille,* that you are—how you say in English?—discomfited at meeting me, perhaps, even of discovering my existence in your father's—"

"These charges have nothing to do with my personal feelings, Professor—"

"Non?" Marie-Claude allowed herself a tragic smile. "Then you are a better woman than I."

Again, Rosco stepped into the breech. "Professor Araignée, in light of what we now suspect regarding Dr. Graham's death—"

"The case of poison, yes?"

"Yes," Rosco answered while Belle remained ominously quiet. "In light of that situation—as well as other potentially criminal issues—I'd like to question you again in regard to your husband's disappearance. My wife and I have reason to suspect that the two deaths may be linked."

"Franklin and Teddy?"

Rosco nodded.

"As I said, *monsieur,* we were in Guatemala . . . François went away in an *aeroplane*—"

"Where was he going?" Belle interjected.

Marie-Claude affected an innocent shrug. "François was a man given to privacy. He liked being *privé* with his work. I assumed he was doing some piece of field research—"

"Assumed," Belle said. "You use the word in the past tense. Do you no longer believe that was the case? Or are you convinced that his body will never be found?"

Marie-Claude looked from Belle to Rosco. Her eyelashes appeared to tremble. "You must forgive my English," she said to Rosco. Belle, she ignored.

The subject of this snub deepened her scowl, but continued her interrogation. "Were you there, Professor? With your husband in Guatemala when his plane departed?"

"We had traveled to the airport together . . . However, I boarded a commercial jetliner for the States. François had leased a small, single-engine plane. So very *petit,* so very *dangereux.* His disappearance was not noticed for more than a week, and only then because I had not heard from him. Although, such instances were—how shall I put it?—not uncommon in our . . . our *marriage.*" She paused, looking again at Rosco, who nodded once but didn't say more.

Marie-Claude continued. "The American Consul did what he could . . . The local police sent out a photograph of François, contacted other airports and so forth, but I do not believe they took my husband's disappearance seriously . . ." Her voice began to crack; she heaved a heartfelt sigh, then resumed her tale while Belle continued to sit in stony silence. "François's body was never found—"

"And that's when my father became such a *comfort* to you? I believe that's the term you used when my husband initially spoke to you?"

Marie-Claude turned to Belle. Her eyes were full of sorrow. "You are angry with me, I know. *Je comprends tous* . . . And maybe you are also a little jealous, *non?* But you have no cause to suspect me of evil, *mademoiselle . . . madame,* I should say." Marie-Claude tried for a conciliatory smile; Belle didn't reciprocate. "I was exceedingly fond of your father, and he was—"

This time it was Rosco who interrupted. "I realize I've asked this before, Professor, but at the risk of repeating myself, I'd like to try and clarify a few additional issues . . . My wife's father arrived in New Jersey at around noon on the twelfth. That leaves six hours before he met you. Originally, you said you didn't know where he spent the time. I ask you to think back . . . Are there any hints he might have dropped—?"

"*Non.*"

Belle stifled a frustrated groan. "Perhaps you'd like to hazard a guess, *madame*? I find it very hard to believe you have no idea whatsoever."

"But he did not speak of such things! And I did not ask. Why would I? I assumed that he had only just arrived by train that evening, and then come directly to see me. At any rate, it did not matter. He was here to see me. That is all I needed to know. You find it puzzling, *non*?"

"Did you discuss his argument with the CEO of Savante?" Rosco asked.

Marie-Claude gazed at Belle, and then at Rosco; her lips twitched. "I told you, *monsieur*, when you originally posed the same question . . . I told you what Theodore's reaction to his . . . his *confrontation* had been . . . Now I will say only that Teddy talked of his strong dislike of makers of pollution . . . You know how firm was his passion in his research project, and his deep desire to protect the ancient sites in Mexico . . ."

Belle looked away. She didn't believe a word this woman was saying. And the more she listened, the more impossible it was to imagine her father in the thrall of someone so obviously conniving. For a moment, she considered getting up and walking out of the room and away from this exercise in futility. Belle sighed aloud. *There had to be some trick she could employ, some means of tripping up this devious woman.* "You obviously knew my father very well, *madame*. So you would have recognized a notebook he always carried with him——"

"*Mais, oui!* Black with funny white markings . . . Like the ones schoolboys carry——"

"And he had it with him when he left here?"

"But of course, *ma chère* Annabella. But then, you must know how much he loved to watch the birds!" Marie-Claude smiled and continued with a blithe: "And he also had with him his very proper blue box."

Belle looked in Rosco's direction. "What blue box?" he asked, although it was to Belle that Marie-Claude directed her response:

"Your *cher papa* did not not tell you about this most *important valise?*" She held out her hands to indicate a rectangular object fourteen or so inches long. "A shiny lock and a small, precise handle? Very *dangereuse,* he said. 'It contains blood, sweat, and tears.' An absurd concept, no?"

CHAPTER

30

"'Blood, sweat, and tears'... and a specious 'blue box'! Why did we let that hideous woman get away with making such absurd statements, Rosco? I thought we were going to ask tough questions—not let her do her how-you-say-in-English-French-flirt bit!"

"Something was way off in there. The way she was talking in circles made me feel as if there was someone in the next room, listening in."

Evening had darkened into night, but she and Rosco continued to sit in the Jeep's front seats, a host of unanswerable and rancorous questions wedged between them. After another few minutes of embattled silence, Belle spotted a weary meter reader approaching, a ticket at the ready for their long-expired slot. She dragged herself from the car, removed a quarter from her pocket, and said, "I have that, sir, we just pulled up a moment ago."

He replied, "Not a problem, miss," and moved to the next meter.

"You're becoming a pretty good liar . . ." Rosco offered as she slid back into the car.

"I've been taught by the best."

"And I've had better compliments," was Rosco's brief response.

They remained speechless for several additional minutes. Finally Rosco placed his hand on Belle's leg and said, "I shouldn't have let you meet that woman . . . The emotions were running too high—"

"We were supposed to get Marie-Claude to trip herself up," was Belle's irritable reply, "not play into her hands—"

"We weren't playing into her hands—"

"It sure felt as if *you* were—"

"You know that's not the case—"

"But that's what it felt like!"

"It wouldn't have helped if we'd both chosen the confrontational route, Belle. One of us had to be the 'good cop.' And you know it could never have been you."

"But you told her we suspected Father had been poisoned, Rosco!"

"Yes. Yes, I did."

"But for all we know, she's the one who did it!"

"True."

Belle grumbled a disgruntled: "Well? What now?"

Rosco remained silent a moment. "What if the 'blue box' isn't an invention?"

"A valise containing 'blood, sweat, and tears,' Rosco? Come on! That's the name of an old rock group. My father wouldn't have known them from Adam!"

"We can't deny the *possibility* of a box matching that description—"

"Oh, baloney! What Marie-Claude described sounded like a fancy makeup case . . . And judging from the incredible care—and time—she obviously devotes to her appearance, my guess is she was giving us a perfect example of one of her dearest possessions."

"Okay . . . You may be correct there . . . But bear with me a minute . . . What if this valise exists?"

"With a bunch of blood and tears sloshing around inside?"

"I'm being serious, Belle. Bear with me, please . . . And what if your father, in fact, *was* involved in a covert activity, and therefore acting as a courier—"

"You mean running drugs?"

"No. That's not what I mean at all . . . What if the valise contained incriminating evidence of some sort—"

"Like what?"

"I don't know . . . photographs . . . records . . . No, it would need to be something physical . . . something that needed to be given to another person . . . someone in law enforcement . . . FBI . . ."

"Which would mean that whoever killed Father needed to steal the case, and that's why it never appeared with his other luggage . . ." Belle groaned aloud. "But your supposition is based on the hypothesis that the spider lady was telling the truth."

Rosco didn't answer for a moment. "I shouldn't have let you meet her," he finally said.

"That's not the point. The point is that you were playing into her hands. You still are." Belle's words caught in her throat. "Just like my father." Then tears filled her eyes while her chest shook with a stifled sob. "Why do women like Marie-Claude exist? Why does anyone trust them?"

Rosco made no move to assuage Belle's sorrow. Instead, he let her give vent to her outrage and indignation, finally producing a folded handkerchief from his jacket pocket. She sniffled into it, dabbed at her eyes, and at last drew out a lengthy sigh. "Promise me you'll never take up with a witch like *Madame* Araignée."

"I promise."

Belle looked at him, her mouth still tight.

"I won't, Belle . . . And I haven't a clue why your father was involved with her . . . But then . . ." His words trickled off as he thought. "You know, we have only Marie-Claude's word on it that she and your dad *were* involved . . ."

Belle nodded slowly. "What's your point?"

"Well, maybe the entire focus of our investigation is wrong . . . We've been going under the assumption that your dad stayed with *Madame* Araignée, that they had a long-term relationship—"

"But she and Father had to be connected in *some* fashion. Otherwise how would she have known about his confrontation with Oclen?"

"I don't know . . ." Rosco admitted. "But I suggest we reexamine your hunches again . . . skulls in one crossword and another stating a definitive THREE MAY KEEP A SECRET IF TWO OF THEM ARE DEAD—"

"But that's the problem! My hunches keep disappearing on me!"

Rosco leaned across the Jeep and took his wife's face in his hands. "What do you say we shelve this discussion for tonight? I'll treat you to a night in a local inn . . . a romantic dinner . . . candlelight . . . We'll call Sara. I'm sure she'll be happy to keep Kit for an extra day."

Belle gazed at him. "Okay . . ." Then she added a soft and conciliatory. "You're a good person, Rosco."

"It helps to hear you say it."

The bedroom in the country inn in neighboring Lawrenceville was awash in chintzes and pastel-hued stripes and plaids: blues and lilac pinks and daffodil yellows. Belle was delighted at the welcoming scene. Rosco was happy she was pleased. "And lavender soap," she murmured. "I love the smell of lavender."

"I didn't know that."

"Well, I'd forgotten until this very minute . . . You know, when we get home, I'm going to get a book on home decorating, and start from scratch. No more crossword-themed rooms—"

"But your office is where I fell in love with you . . . Anyway, I'm not sure all this—" Rosco indicated the floral drapes, the pillow-laden chairs, the bed's fluffy quilt and matching dust ruffle, but words seemed to fail him.

"You're right," Belle interjected. "It is a bit over the top . . . definitely not a 'guy look.' "

"Al wouldn't go for it, that's certain."

Belle smiled at the notion, then the expression vanished.

"I shouldn't have mentioned Al, Belle. Forget what I said. Let's just have a nice night; we can get back to business in the morning."

"No," was her pensive reply. "We came to Princeton for a reason . . ." She paused in thought. "I want you to look at these two puzzles with me, Rosco. Maybe I missed something."

"How about we wait till tomorrow?"

"How about we give them a half an hour—max? Then I'm all yours."

Rosco chuckled. "Half an hour . . . Promise?"

"Scout's honor. Besides, when have you known me to lose track of time?"

Sitting side by side on the bed, Rosco scanned the printout at the top of the crossword. "Faxed from Belize," he mused.

"I gather the sender's number belongs to a Central American version of an office superstore," Belle answered. "At least that's how I interpreted the logo . . . Which means that the puzzle could have been transmitted by someone using a phony name."

Rosco nodded as he scanned the SKULL clues. "But why wouldn't this person simply contact us by telephone if he or she has information to share?"

"Well, here's what I'm beginning to wonder . . ." Belle began. "It might seem far-fetched initially . . . When my father and mother lived in Princeton, I remember them talking about Woody Woo—"

"Who's Woody Woo?"

"It's not a who. It's a place . . . an institution . . . the nickname for the foreign affairs school at Princeton—the Woodrow Wilson School. It used to funnel a lot of people into the State Department back when my father was here; maybe it still does. Anyway, my mother used to joke that it was a 'Spy School—'"

Rosco cleared his throat; he seemed about to speak.

"Wait," Belle said, "let me finish . . . Now, we've got Woody in Florida—"

"And the boat, *Wooden Shoe*—"

"Yes . . . and the boat . . . But what I'm wondering is this: If my father were part of a covert operation—is it possible that Horace Llewellen was his contact? And the name 'Woody' was an inside joke—a reference to Father's Princeton days? Or maybe Llewellen graduated from the Wilson School?"

"And therefore, Woody would have known what was in the blue box?"

"I'm not addressing that issue yet . . . I'm only talking about the possibility of Llewellen/Woody being an under-cover operator . . . Maybe he can't contact us without blow-ing his cover . . . Thus the clues in the form of crosswords."

Rosco was quiet for a moment. "Interesting theory. But how could Woody/Llewellen send the puzzles? There's no way he could have motored that Hatteras from Sanibel to Belize in time. He'd have to cruise down the Keys and gas up in Key West before shooting across the Gulf. I imagine a trip like that would take over a week. At the minimum."

"Couldn't he have just sailed up the coast to the next marina and taken a flight out of Tampa?"

Rosco considered this suggestion for a moment, then said, "Okay . . . I agree, it's a possibility, but right now you and I aren't jumping on a plane to Belize to hunt down a mystery crossword constructor . . . Whoever sent these puzzles, sent them . . . and the one with the SKULL theme was intended to get us down to New Jersey and Marie-Claude . . . which, I'm sorry to say, brings us right back to our questionable *valise*." Rosco pulled out his notebook as he reached for his cell phone.

"Who are you calling?"

"John Markoe, the Amtrak conductor who discovered your

father . . . Al gave me his number. I'd like to see if he remembers an unusual-looking piece of luggage. He seems to have remembered everything else."

Rosco punched in numbers, and waited. Eventually he mouthed, "No answer, just a machine . . ." Then he left a message asking Markoe to return the call.

"What about Shawn at the rental car company? Would he have noticed if my father were carrying anything out of the ordinary?"

Rosco thought for a second. "It's pretty late, but I'll give it a try . . ." He punched in the listing, and was more than a little surprised when Shawn answered. The question he'd put to John Markoe was repeated. Then Rosco clicked off. "Strikeout," he said. "But that kid sure puts in some long hours . . ."

Belle sighed. "There must be something we haven't explored yet . . . or something we're ignoring . . ." She studied the crossword puzzles again. "The only other New Jersey reference I can find is at 48-Across: *Debbie's aunt.*"

Rosco raised an eyebrow. "In Kings Creek . . . which might very well put us in range of the unaccounted miles your father racked up. You didn't bring the address, by any chance?"

Belle grabbed her book bag. "It's 127 Oak Lane—"

"That could well be where your dad went . . ." Rosco reached across the bed, took the file folder from Belle's hand, and dropped it on the nightstand. "How about a drive to Kings Creek first thing tomorrow?"

"As opposed to tonight?"

"If you look at your watch, you'll notice your half hour is up. And I doubt anyone in Kings Creek would appreciate a midnight visit."

* * *

Rosco turned the key in the Jeep's ignition. "The Jersey map's in the glove compartment."

Belle opened it. "Okay . . . first, we need to get onto Route 206 and head north. It's back that way." She pointed; and Rosco made a quick U-turn, narrowly missing a pedestrian with an ankle cast who was hobbling along the crosswalk on crutches.

"I can't believe you just did that! You almost hit that poor kid." Belle shook her head from side to side.

"I saw him."

"Right . . . And I'll bet there isn't a cop for twenty miles. I'd be in jail right now if I tried a stunt like that."

"There aren't any cops around. I looked."

"That still doesn't make it legal, you know?"

Rosco only grumbled as he headed in the direction of Route 206. Finally, Belle spoke again. "This isn't going to be easy . . . seeing Debbie's aunt . . . and Mike . . ."

When Rosco didn't answer, Belle looked over at him. "What are you thinking?"

"I'd be devastated if anything happened to you. I've never met Mike Hurley . . . I don't know what I'm going to say."

Belle placed her hand on Rosco's. "I guess, just that you're sorry . . . All we really have to offer is our sympathy." She also fell silent. "I'm going to make a suggestion . . . With the funeral tomorrow, why don't we just wait a few days and then phone Rachel and ask her if Father went to Kings Creek?"

"My instincts tell me it's a good time to stop by, Belle. Number One: It'll look more polite. We can offer our condolences in person, bring flowers or something . . . Number

Two: If there's anything fishy about the situation—or even an inkling that Mrs. Volsay knows more than she's telling—it'll be easier to detect the lies in person."

Belle's shoulders tensed. "I don't like this," she said at last.

"And I don't like the fact that your dad may have been murdered."

They drove on in silence, the heavy greenery of a New Jersey summer making the air feel thick and wet and slumberous. Belle yawned once, then twice.

"Not enough sleep last night?" Rosco smiled.

Belle grinned in reply. "Not hardly." Then she pulled the *Use Your Head!* crossword from her book bag. "There are some far-fetched answers in this puzzle," she mused aloud. "U-O-L-A." She spelled it out. "As in UOLA Road, *Truk Island* . . . U-C-L-A would have made a lot more more sense, besides being an answer any crossword aficionado would recognize—"

Rosco chuckled. "You're sounding a trifle fanatical—"

"I *am* fanatical . . . A person who creates a word game should use language that's in common usage—unless, if you will, he's extremely short on imagination . . . I mean, look at the entire lower-left corner here . . . UOLA instead of UCLA . . . The same thing's true with the bottom right corner . . . 59-Down: *Chemical symbol for prussic acid* . . . I only got that one by completing the other words—"

"You mean HCN, as in hydrocyanic acid?"

Belle glanced up abruptly. "Don't tell me you once considered a career in chemical engineering?"

"High school science, actually. Mr. Manzo, the teacher, mixed up a batch of hydrocyanic acid one day and had us all take a whiff. HCN's one of the deadliest poisons around, and you know what? It smells like peaches—or peach nectar, to be more precise." Rosco chuckled. "Nobody went within ten feet of a peach or a peach product for the rest of the academic year." He laughed again, but quickly noticed that Belle found nothing humorous about his story. "What's wrong?" he asked.

"My father was addicted to peach nectar."

"Peach nectar . . ." Belle repeated while Rosco grabbed his cell phone and placed another call to John Markoe's home number. As it had the previous night, the Amtrak conductor's answering machine picked up.

"This is Rosco Polycrates calling again, John . . . I have another question regarding Professor Graham. Do you have any recollection of whether or not there was a beverage container on the tray table when you found the body: coffee, milk, beer, soda, whatever . . . ? I realize you've supplied the police with a good deal of useful information, but there's one further lead we need to follow . . . Please give me a call at your earliest convenience. I appreciate it." Rosco reiterated his thanks, repeated his contact numbers, and rang off.

"Why didn't you just ask him if Father had a can of peach nectar?" Belle asked while Rosco switched off the phone.

"I don't want to put words in his mouth. Either he remembers seeing a fruit juice container, or he doesn't. And trust

me, Belle, if there's *any* piece of information—large or
small—that's connected to this case, Markoe's the guy to drag
it out of his memory bank."

They reached Kings Creek at that moment, and began
driving slowly along Main Street, which then bisected Central Avenue. Belle saw what she assumed was the library in
the distance, shuddered, and averted her gaze. Instead, she
studied the other buildings as they cruised by, noting with
dismay that a number of the town's commercial sites were
vacant—victims to glossier chains or plain, old hard times.
No more *Edie's Dresser Drawers;* no more *Tots 'n Teens;* no more
Knittin' Bag: The locally owned retail shops that had once
supported Kings Creek's economy had seen better days.

Rosco angled the Jeep into one of many available parking
spaces while Belle willed herself not to look in the direction
of the library.

"You know," she said after a troubled moment, "if my
father *was* poisoned with this prussic acid, and if the substance was added to a can of peach nectar, it would have to
have been done by someone who knew he loved the stuff."
She frowned in concentration. "Besides which, the person
must have been traveling with Father—and carrying a vial of
HCN."

Rosco set the parking brake and turned to face her. "Not
necessarily, Belle . . . Those individual fruit juice cans are
very easy to tamper with. They have a foil tab on top; it
wouldn't take a rocket scientist to peel back the tab, add a
drop of poison, and reglue the foil . . . However you're on the
money in assuming that someone knew he was fond of peach
nectar . . . But that *someone* could have supplied him with an
entire six-pack as far back as Florida—and your father didn't

consume the lethal can until he was nearing Newcastle . . . On the other hand, Marie-Claude could have given it to him the night before . . . *Bon voyage!* Have a nice trip!"

Belle nodded, then cocked her head to one side. "Marie-Claude, again. . . . But Father was robbed, Rosco—"

"I hate to say this . . . but for the sake of playing devil's advocate, it *is* possible that the culprit *was* simply a thief—stealing from a man he assumed was asleep."

"Arrrgh," Belle groaned. "I hate this. The closer we get, the farther away we seem to be."

Rosco shook his head. "No, we're closer than we think. We just haven't put the pieces together properly." He looked around the town. "I wonder where Oak Lane is?"

Belle stepped out of the Jeep.

"Where are you going?"

She laughed. "Into that dry-cleaning establishment across the street. I'm going to ask them where Oak Lane is . . . But don't worry; I won't let on I'm with you. Heaven forbid you should get caught driving around with someone who asks for directions."

Belle stepped along the sidewalk and disappeared into the dry cleaners, while Rosco reached for the *Use Your Head!* crossword and stared at the answers she'd filled in. For all her complaining about the peculiar choice of words, she hadn't made a single mistake. Her red ballpoint pen marched confidently over the paper. Rosco glanced at the two corners that had so irritated her. UOLA," he mumbled, "UOLA . . ."

Belle returned a minute later. "Oak Lane is about a half a mile further down the road over the bridge. We make a right at a You Save and Tell All gas station, and it's the next street."

Belle noticed that Rosco had a smug smile on his face. "What . . . ? What are you thinking about?" she asked.

"I just figured why the puzzle constructor put UOLA in the puzzle instead of U-C-L-A. He *couldn't* put U-C-L-A in."

"Why? What do you mean?"

Rosco handed Belle the crossword. "Look at that corner. 49-Down . . . The answer is SHOE, and the last letter is an E, right?"

"Yes."

"Okay, next word over, 50-Down: *Some lodges; abbr.* . . . Knights of Columbus . . . Focus on the C."

"Right."

"Keep going on the diagonal." Rosco pointed his finger at the lower-left-hand corner of the puzzle and moved it on an angle up to the upper-right corner. "The O in UOLA *has* to be there to spell out the message. The constructor couldn't use UCLA, because he—or she—needed that O."

Belle silently mouthed the letters that ran from corner to corner. When she'd finished she read the message aloud. "ECOLOGICAL STAIN . . . But what do you think it means?"

"My initial guess is that this may come full circle back to Carl Oclen . . . Maybe your father—and possibly Debbie— stumbled on to something big while researching your dad's paper on the Olmec people. For instance, maybe one of Oclen's offshore rigs has been secretly leaking oil into the Gulf of Mexico, and your father was going to blow the whistle on the whole thing."

Belle stared at Rosco. "And Oclen killed Deborah Hurley and my father?"

Rosco thought for a long moment. "Probably not Oclen, himself . . . He's not the kind of guy who'd get his own hands dirty . . . But money talks, Belle; and he could have hired someone to take care of business for him . . . Which also means that even if we'd gotten a better description of the guy who accompanied your dad to the Jarvis counter—well, it might not mean much."

"A hit man with peach nectar," Belle said quietly.

"That's *if* your father was poisoned with prussic acid." Rosco grew silent; his brow furrowed. "However, the only way that situation would play out successfully is if Oclen had prior knowledge of your father's fondness for peach nectar . . . Then there's also the matter of finding and hiring an assassin and bringing that person to Trenton in less than twelve hours' time." Rosco sighed. "We're talking a lot of lucky coincidences." He put the Jeep in gear and began driving toward Rachel Volsay's house.

"A lot of ifs." Belle agreed. As she spoke, she pointed through the windshield. "There's the bridge. And that must be Kings Creek below it . . . The gas station should be on the other side. You Save and Tell All, the lady at the dry cleaners said."

Rosco angled the Jeep onto the narrow steel-decked bridge. The creek was withered and parched from the summer's heat. On the other side sat the USAv•AN•TELL•ALL gas station.

"I see they like cute names around here," Belle said.

"The USA part is a nice touch."

"It must be a local brand. . . . Okay, now a right on Tucker." Belle pointed to the sign at the far side of the service station.

Rosco did as he was told, then made another quick right into Oak Lane, before proceeding down the shady street until he was abreast of Number 127. It was a small, wood-frame house, the last in a block of modest, but well-maintained, single-family dwellings. White vinyl siding and a side-facing screened-in porch completed the picture. The porch fronted what Belle assumed was a continuation of Kings Creek. Two young boys in the yard across the street tossed a baseball back and forth as a spaniel-type dog dashed between them, hoping for an error.

"Small-town America . . . It has a beauty all its own . . ." Belle murmured as Rosco parked near Rachel Volsay's mailbox. "Picture perfect . . . I think we're barking up the wrong tree here—excuse the pun. No one living in a setting as serene as this conspires with criminals. And they don't want to hear about *possible* corporate crimes, either . . ." She hesitated, her hands on her knees, her neck suddenly bent in discouraged frustration. "I think we should turn around and go home, Rosco. I have a feeling we're making a big mistake, and that this is probably going to be a horribly awkward and painful situation."

Rosco took her hand. "Belle, we have to find out what your father did—and who he saw—before he arrived at Marie-Claude's. If Rachel Volsay can't help us, and if it's obvious she's sharing everything she knows, then we'll make our apologies, repeat our condolences, and leave."

"But why not simply pursue the hired murderer scenario you started spinning? ECOLOGICAL STAIN and Carl Oclen's possible connection . . . That seems a lot more logical than this." She gestured, the motion taking in the pretty lane, the tidy houses, the kids, their pets: the total harmony and tranquillity of the scene.

"One step at a time." Rosco stepped from the Jeep, walked around to the other side, and opened the passenger door. "Just look at this initial stage as a trip to the dentist. It'll be over before you know it."

Belle attempted a brave smile. "Where's my novocaine?"

CHAPTER

32

When Rachel Volsay opened the front door, Belle was surprised to find someone so apparently calm and composed. A woman in her late fifties, Deborah Hurley's aunt wore a tailored charcoal-gray suit and low-heeled black pumps; her wavy auburn hair had just been "done," and gold-and-silver-toned earrings complemented her suit. However, two red and puffy eyes belied her outward ease, and the powder and rouge on her cheeks couldn't disguise the fact that she'd been crying.

"Yes?" Rachel Volsay looked from Belle to Rosco, visibly drawing back as she scanned his face. "I've already told the police everything I know . . . So has Mike. Mike Hurley. Deborah's husband. I guess you two are from out of town . . . big-city homicide—"

Belle interrupted with an apologetic: "I'm Belle Graham . . . And this is my husband, Rosco Polycrates. We were nearby and thought we should pay our respects . . ."

Rachel fixed Rosco with a disapproving glare; Belle, she treated with a little more warmth. "Come in," she finally said.

"I . . . I know this is a difficult time for you, Mrs. Volsay, and we don't wish to intrude—"

"She was so young . . ." Debbie's aunt choked back a sob.

"Yes," Belle answered, "yes, she was."

"I don't want to hear any more of that murder talk you were spouting about the other day. It's hard enough . . ." Rachel Volsay pulled a tissue from a box and dabbed at her eyes. "I have an appointment shortly—down at the funeral parlor . . ." Again, tears threatened to overwhelm her. "I don't know what's wrong with me . . . I'm like a leaky bucket, but I've lost so many loved ones . . ."

Rosco cleared his throat, and Rachel regarded him sharply. She then focused on Belle. "I'm sure your husband was close to your father, Miss Graham, and this isn't an easy time for him either, but I'd be less than candid if I told you I liked private investigators. My late husband was a state trooper. He didn't trust them, and neither do I."

Belle glanced in Rosco's direction. "Would you be more comfortable if my husband waited in the car? Because I'd like to talk with you for a moment—if that's agreeable."

In answer, Debbie's aunt merely nodded. Then she sat stiffly in a rocking chair and indicated that Belle was also free to take a seat. A sky blue couch devoid of throw pillows or any other signs of comfort faced an equally austere coffee table. Belle chose the couch's far corner while Rosco walked to the door:

"My wife and I wish to intrude as little as possible, Mrs. Volsay. I have no problem waiting outside."

After the front door closed, Belle turned toward her

unwilling hostess. "He's a good person. He only came along as a way of comforting and supporting me."

"I'm sure he is." The words were toneless. Rachel sighed and reached for another tissue. "You'll have to forgive me . . . In the last few days, I've been just at sixes and sevens—"

"Of course you have," was Belle's soft reply. She paused and took a long and steadying breath. "Mrs. Volsay . . . when we spoke the other day—"

"I told you I don't want to hear about that murder stuff again, Miss Graham. Whatever happened to your father and my Deb are two different—"

"Belle." She tried for an encouraging smile.

"Belle." Rachel Volsay used her visitor's first name, although her demeanor didn't mellow. "Your dad seemed like a nice enough man when I met him, and everyone knows my Deb was a pure angel—"

Belle sat forward on the couch. "So, you did meet my father?"

"Yes. I thought I told you that when we talked on the phone." Deborah's aunt's swollen eyes narrowed with increasing mistrust. "He dropped by . . . Told me he was passing through, and wanted to meet 'the lady Debbie thought so highly of' . . . It would have been the day before he died . . ."

"The day before he died." Belle repeated the phrase.

"That's what I said."

Belle nodded slowly. "So . . . So, Father came here before he was scheduled to visit me in Newcastle . . . But I guess it wasn't like having a total stranger visit, because Deborah must have spoken of him."

"Deb and Mike, both. They were very fond of him."

Belle took another breath and tried for a brighter smile. "Did my father seem distracted, or upset about anything? Or did he mention if he was paying other calls nearby?"

"If he had other people to see, he kept it to himself," was the starchy answer. "As to his being upset: He wasn't in the least. In fact, he couldn't have been more pleasant or charming. But you must know that."

"Yes," was all Belle could think to respond. Everyone in the universe, it seemed, knew a different Ted Graham than she. "What did you talk about—if you don't mind my asking?"

"Nothing much . . ." Rachel Volsay allowed herself to lean slightly back in the rocker. "He brought me up-to-date on how Deb and Mike were doing in Florida. Commented on how pretty the creek must be when it's full. I told him he couldn't imagine how nice . . . And you can't, either. When the butterflies come—or in daffodil season—why, it's just like a picture book. When Deb was a kid, she and all her friends used to fish in it, and build dams in the spring. Regular little beavers, they were . . . Oh, and we talked some about my sister, and of course, Deb's sister—my other niece . . ." Rachel Volsay's face creased with sudden fury. "That damn disease! The doctors tell you it's a family thing—a 'predisposition' . . . like the Tollivers—"

Belle interrupted what she intuited was going to be another lengthy aside. "Mrs. Volsay, I know how much my father relied on Deborah—"

"And he should have done. She was a wonderful girl. Real steady—"

"And how much she helped him with all his research—"

"He told me that. As I said, he was real nice."

Belle straightened her spine. It was now or never if she was going to start tackling the serious questions. She tried for a third and even more engaging smile. "Debbie said that my father had started carrying a notebook with him. One of those composition books with the black and white covers. When his body was found, it wasn't among his effects . . . Do you happen to remember if he had it with him when he stopped by?"

"The one he drew pictures in?"

"Yes," Belle said although this was a new piece of information: her father as a budding artist—as well as a naturalist.

"Sure, I remember it. He sketched the house and the street . . . No offense, but they weren't very good . . . And he went down to do a drawing of the creek—and the birds . . . Deb told me he was a birder." Rachel paused to think. "She was real concerned about what happened to that notebook, too . . . Looked all over the house for it when I told her he'd dropped by for a visit."

Belle felt her shoulders tense up. "But she didn't find it?"

Rachel shook her head. "If it had been anywhere in this home, Deb would have unearthed it. Like a terrier, she could be—"

"So my father must have taken it with him when he left you?"

"Must have." Rachel shrugged. "I told her that, too. I don't mean to be impertinent, but I don't see why you're so interested in a cardboard book with some not very good pictures in it. Unless it's sentimental?"

Belle nodded, and manufactured what she hoped was a decent lie. "Yes, it was sentimental. I'm trying to locate everything he owned." Then she considered the fragments of information Rachel Volsay had supplied; *the only possible conclusion seemed to be that Theodore Graham had recorded important and potentially incriminating data in his notebook, that Deborah*

Hurley knew this, and that when she'd learned it was missing, she'd immediately flown north to her aunt's home in the hopes it had been inadvertently left there.

"Did Debbie get a chance to visit with you often? Or was last week's trip a surprise?" Belle's tone was conversational.

"A surprise. A nice surprise . . . Mike could get her cheap standby tickets on account of she was a military dependent. He comes up a lot, too; technically he's still stationed in Bayonne. Florida's just temporary duty for him . . ." Rachel's mouth tightened, and her voice wavered. "Like I said, it was a nice surprise . . . But I wish . . . I wish . . . Well, if she hadn't come up here when she did . . ." The words trailed off. Rachel hung her head.

They sat quietly for several moments, Debbie Hurley's aunt staring down at the soggy tissues clutched in her lap, and Belle looking around the immaculate, if strangely impersonal, room. Eventually her eyes settled on a table beneath the window, and its sole decoration: a small box inlaid with mother-of-pearl.

"I don't want to take any more of your time, Mrs. Volsay. And again, I apologize for the intrusion . . . But there's one more item I can't account for—a box my father may have brought with him. It was blue—"

Rachel Volsay didn't hesitate a second. "Bright blue. I thought it was an odd color for a man . . . He seemed quite worried about it."

"Worried? What do you mean?"

"Well, he wouldn't let it out of his sight. Even took it with him when he went to the bathroom."

* * *

Rather than sit in his Jeep, Rosco had walked the thirty feet to the end of Oak Lane. There was a large yellow street sign surrounded with a dozen red reflectors reading DEAD END, and he found himself wondering how many unsuspecting motorists had ended up plunging their cars into the creek before the New Jersey Highway Department had deemed it necessary to post the warning. Next to the sign was a park bench. It had a bronze placard indicating that it had been placed there by the residents of Oak Lane in 1998 in memory of Rosa Tolliver. Rosco sat on the bench and began tossing pebbles into the creek bed. Several small birds started up out of the undergrowth surrounding the stream's far side while in the treetops an eruption of noisy cawing was followed by the swooping flight of one and then two argumentative crows. Rosco looked up and followed their movement as they disappeared from sight.

A voice startled him out of his reverie. "I don't think I know you."

Rosco turned around and saw a man standing about fifteen feet away on the road. He wore a dark suit that seemed out of place on a sunny summer morning on a tree-lined lane.

"Are you talking to me?"

"Sure am."

"Well, I'm not from around here . . ."

"That much I figured. I don't mean to seem rude, mister, but there are a lot of children in this neighborhood . . . We try to keep an eye out for strangers." The term "unwelcome and possibly predatory strangers" remained unspoken but very much present.

"A good policy," Rosco replied with an affable nod. He

stood. "I'm visiting Mrs. Volsay . . . Or I should say, my wife is visiting Mrs. Volsay. I'm just waiting for her to finish up."

The man smiled for the first time. The smile dropped years from his face, placing him in his early thirties. "You're not Rosco, are you?"

"Yes. Yes, I am." Rosco stepped forward.

The man extended his hand. "Mike Hurley here."

"Of course. Sorry, I guess I expected you to be in uniform."

They shook hands. Rosco looked away briefly, then brought his eyes back to meet Mike's. "I'm sorry about Debbie. That's got to be . . . That's got to be devastating . . . I'd be a wreck if anything happened to my wife."

Mike didn't answer for a moment. His young face creased in pain. "Yeah . . . Yeah, thanks. You're right . . . It hasn't been easy."

"Do the police have any clues—a description of the car or any idea who was driving it?"

"Nothing yet. But two of the officers went to high school with me—they've got everyone in the department on the case. I'm sure they'll come up with something."

"I don't know if I can be of any help, Mike, but I'm happy to stop in and talk to them. I used to be with a metro force up in Massachusetts."

"That's what I'd heard . . . I appreciate the offer, but that car will turn up. This is a small burg. Everyone knows everyone's business."

"Well, the offer's out there." Rosco looked toward the Volsay house while he searched for words. "Belle was really grateful for your help down in Florida."

Mike shrugged. "All in the line of duty."

"Have you met her yet? In Mrs. Volsay's home?"

Mike shook his head. "I saw you down here, and I—"

"Right . . . It makes sense to be careful—even in a quiet place like this. Well, Belle will be really glad to meet you . . . I was waiting for her down here. Apparently Mrs. Volsay doesn't like PIs."

Another smile briefly transformed Mike's somber face. "Deb's aunt can be a tough one. She has her favorites. I'm military, so in her book, I'm the golden boy . . ."

Rosco and Mike both dropped their hands into their pockets and began walking back to the house. Mike was the first to resume the conversation, although his friendly tone had vanished.

"Rachel said that Belle had some crazy idea that Deb's accident might be connected to her father's death . . . that it might not have been an accident."

Rosco paused before speaking. "I know this is hard for you to consider, Mike, but yes, Belle and I—as well as the Newcastle Police Department—are considering homicide in the case of Professor Graham."

Mike didn't speak for a long moment. When he did, his words sounded forced and jerky. "But why would anyone want to kill him? Or Deb?"

"That's what we're trying to find out."

"I don't know everything Professor Graham was into. I didn't know him all that well. But I did know my wife. And I'll tell you, Rosco, she wasn't a secretive person. Not in the least. If she learned something—even a little thing like how a flower got its name, or when whales calf—I'd have to learn it, too . . . If Deb was worried over something, she would have told me."

By now the two men had reached the Volsay yard. Rosco

hung back, remaining at the curb near his car. "I'll wait for Belle out here. She shouldn't be much longer. Mrs. Volsay has an appointment."

"Yes. We're due at the funeral home in a couple of minutes." Mike glanced at the fender of Rosco's Jeep; another gently smile appeared on his face. "So you're a Sox fan, huh?"

Rosco also attempted a light approach, "Sort of."

"You know, it ain't over till it's over."

"I've been hearing a lot of that lately."

The front door of the Volsay house opened, and Belle and Rachel stepped out. "Good," Rachel said. "Right on time." Her glance swept past Rosco and returned to Mike while Belle walked toward him and extended her hand.

"All our deepest sympathy . . . to you and Debbie's aunt . . . To all your family."

Mike took Belle's hand and held it. Tears had welled up in his eyes. "Thanks," he managed. "Thanks." Then he dropped his hands to his sides, and looked at Rachel. "I guess we'd better get going."

Rachel nodded, then turned back to Belle, squaring her shoulders as if making a momentous decision. "You're welcome to attend Deb's service tomorrow. You and your husband—"

Belle's posture went through the same seismic shift as Rachel's. "Thank you, Mrs. Volsay. Thank you . . . Of course, we'll be there . . . And thank you for speaking with me this morning." Then she walked toward Rosco in order to give Mike Hurley and his wife's aunt some private time before facing the ordeal of the funeral home.

*　*　*

Rosco began retracing the route back toward the town of Kings Creek. Belle sat beside him as the Jeep rolled up Oak Lane, turned left, then left again. "Where to?" he finally asked.

"The hospital."

CHAPTER

33

"The hospital should be about two miles past the gas station." Belle looked intently through the Jeep's windshield as she spoke.

Rosco glanced at his wife. "Mind telling me what this is all about?"

"I don't know for sure. Mrs. Volsay finally admitted that my father went to Mercy Hospital after he visited her home. He wanted to meet with a Dr. Edwards. Apparently, he knew Debbie very well; he's the physician who first treated her sister. I called the hospital. He's in. He's expecting us."

"Let it not be said that you're not a woman of action." Rosco smiled while Belle turned to face him. Her eyes were animated and bright.

"Debbie's aunt also confirmed the existence of the blue box."

"That's important news . . . Did she have any idea what it contained?"

"No." Belle thought for a moment. "But she did tell me my father seemed 'quite worried about it.'"

"So, are you thinking Edwards was your dad's contact? The person he was supposed to deliver the *valise* to . . . i.e., he came up here on the pretext of visiting Rachel Volsay when in fact—?"

"I'm not sure what to think. All I know is that Debbie Hurley must have been very deeply involved in all of this. What her role entailed, I can't even guess—"

Rosco interrupted. "Do I have time to tank up before we see Dr. Edwards? We're riding on fumes here."

Belle glanced at her watch. "Well, we certainly don't want to be stranded in the wilds of New Jersey."

Rosco angled into the USAv•AN•TELL•ALL gas station, pulled up to a pump, got out, and removed the Jeep's gas cap.

"Sir," the attendant said as he trotted over, "you can't pump your own."

"You're kidding?"

"Not in this state, it's against the law. I'll get it."

"Fine . . . Go for it—all the same price."

The attendant perused Rosco's front bumper as he attached the nozzle to the Jeep. "Sox fan, huh?"

Rosco smiled. "I know: It ain't over till it's over."

"You said it, buddy, not me."

Belle was so engrossed in staring at the gas station sign that she didn't stir when Rosco climbed back into the driver's seat. "Look over there." She pointed to the large red and blue plastic billboard that hung out over Route 206. "What do you see?"

"Other than a garish blight on the landscape?"

"Well, there is that . . . but what else do you notice?"

"That gas is a lot cheaper in New Jersey than it is in Massachusetts?"

Belle shook her head. "I'm being serious."

"So am I."

"Just study the sign for a minute, and tell me if you make any unusual connections."

Rosco did as he was directed while Belle continued to speak:

"Take the four Ls and the A off the end of "USAv•AN•TELL•ALL, and the—"

"—U off of the front."

"Exactly."

Rosco spelled it out. "S-A-V-A-N-T-E. Savante." He cocked his head, stepped from the Jeep, and looked closely at the fine print on the gas pump. "*Owned and operated by the Savante Group, Inc.*," he read aloud. "Well, what do you know? One big happy family."

"It looks like Carl Oclen has some business interests right here in Debbie Hurley's backyard."

Rosco handed his credit card to the attendant, waited for the transaction to be completed, pocketed his receipt, and returned to the Jeep. His face was creased in a frown. He looked at Belle, noting the sudden change in her expression.

"Wait a minute!" she burst out. "I figured it out! Debbie's sister died of cancer . . . Rachel mentioned the Tolliver family had been hit, too . . . supposedly a genetic 'predisposition' to the disease . . . OCLEN in the crossword . . . ECOLOGICAL STAIN running across the puzzle's diagonal . . ." Belle paused, her absolute focus making her sit taller and straighter. "Is it possible my father's death had nothing to do with covert operations or international intrigue?" She turned toward Rosco. "He confronted Oclen, right? Our assumption was that he was concerned about pollution in the Gulf of Mexico . . . But is it possible that it's right here in Kings Creek? Is it possible we're sitting on top of it?"

"A gas station?" Rosco passed his hand over his brow, then slowly shook his head from side to side. "But what about the skulls and Marie-Claude—?"

"And her missing husband, and the entire Central American connection . . . Yes, I know . . . But someone sent us *to* her, Rosco . . . Someone is guiding—almost masterminding—our investigation."

"Unless coming to Kings Creek is a wild-goose chase."

"Then what was my father doing here?"

Rosco put the Jeep in gear. "Dr. Edwards?"

"Dr. Edwards," was Belle determined response.

M ercy Hospital was small, the size of a large clinic rather than a suburban hospital. There was an ambulance entrance, but the parking lot was large enough for only fifteen or twenty vehicles, and Rosco guessed that the ten or so cars in the lot probably belonged to employees rather than patients. They pulled in beside a late-model Ford, strolled across the lot, and entered the hospital's main entrance, where an admission nurse directed them down a well-lit corridor with an efficient: "Dr. Edwards's office is on the last door on the left. He'll be right with you." The statement was correct. Edwards stepped into the room a scant two minutes later.

He was in his forties with jet black hair and a meticulously trimmed mustache. He wore a pressed white hospital jacket with his name clearly embroidered in red on the left-hand pocket. However, despite the clinical garb and rather fussy appearance, he exuded the air of an attentive and sympathetic listener, a conscientious healer. After introductions, Belle said, "It was good of you to take the time to meet with us, Doctor."

"As I told you on the phone, I enjoyed talking with your father . . . I've got to admit that the news of his passing comes as a shock. He appeared to be a very healthy individual . . . But heart disease is an insidious enemy—"

"A heart attack was the medical examiner's *original* assumption," was Belle's careful reply.

Edwards studied her, then he looked at Rosco. He seemed to be entering into some private and complex inner dialogue. Finally he redirected his attention to Belle. "Do you, or the examiner, have cause to believe your father did not suffer from a heart condition?"

Belle nodded.

Again, Edwards paused. When he spoke again, his tone was as cautious as Belle's. "Are we talking about a possible homicide?"

It was Rosco who answered. "What makes you ask that?"

In answer, the physician tapped the tips of his fingers together and stared up at the ceiling. "Whew . . . That's very . . . that's very disturbing . . . Especially given the nature of the conversation I had with him . . ." He tapped his fingers together again, then drew in a long and steadying breath. "I'd better start at the beginning," he said at length. "I'll lead you through what I know—"

Belle touched Edwards's sleeve. "You may be putting yourself at risk, Doctor."

"Yes . . . Yes, I realize that. And I won't say it doesn't worry me . . . But I will tell you that in the brief hour I spent with your dad, I was inspired by his compassion, his sense of justice. He seemed on a mission to right the wrongs of the world . . . We'd be a different place if we had more committed people like him on this planet . . . As his daughter, you're undoubtedly well acquainted with those traits . . ."

Belle lowered her gaze. Despite the warmth of the room, she felt utterly chilled—and utterly worthless.

"You're aware, I assume, that both Debbie Hurley's mother and sister died of cancer?"

Belle nodded.

"When your dad came to see me, he was attempting to discover a connection between the deaths of *four* women who lived in the Oak Lane area of Kings Creek. All four had succumbed to cancer, and the timing of their illnesses was, well, let us say: curious."

"Was one of them Rosa Tolliver?" Rosco asked.

Dr. Edwards looked at him. "As a matter of fact, yes. Did you know her?"

"I saw her name on a bench at the foot of the street."

Edwards nodded gravely, and resumed his story. "According to Professor Graham, he'd begun to suspect the existence of some type of contaminant—a carcinogen—in the Oak Lane region. Of course, he requested that I keep our discussion in the strictest confidence. He didn't want to alarm Debbie or her aunt until he had some hard evidence."

"The four women in question, were they your patients?" Rosco asked.

"I'm a general practitioner here in Kings Creek, but yes, they were my patients. Initially. Once I determined the seriousness of their conditions, I referred them to an oncology team in Trenton."

"But what kind of 'hard evidence' did my father hope to find?"

Edwards took a breath. "He'd become convinced that the tanks at a USAv•AN•TELL•ALL gas station in the proximity of Oak Lane were leaching gasoline into the ground . . . He'd collected tap water from the Volsay house as well as random samples from the stream. Those findings were kept in sterilized bottles—"

Rosco interrupted. "That he carried in a blue case?"

Edwards nodded agreement. "I believe that would describe the equipment he brought with him."

"We stopped at the service station in question," Rosco interjected. "It's fairly new, from the looks of it . . . Did Belle's dad think those tanks were already having problems?"

"I've lived in this area for fifteen years now, and I think that's the fifth time that particular station has changed hands. Prior to Savante, the present owner, the operators were smaller independents. As soon as one company failed, a new one moved in. They'd spiff up the building's exterior, put in new pumps, glossy signage, et cetera, but who knows whether appropriate maintenance checks were made on the underground tanks."

"So my father was hoping to find the presence of gasoline in—?"

"Not gasoline itself, but an element known as MTBE."

"MTBE?"

"Methyl tertiary butyl ether. The oil companies have been using it as an additive since the 1970s. Theoretically, it makes unleaded gasoline burn cleaner—as well as increasing the octane rating. However, some states are beginning to outlaw the use of MTBE. It's a known animal carcinogen, although tests on humans have been inconclusive."

Belle considered the statement. "The assumption would be

that humans and animals don't share similar physical traits? Or that humans don't matter? Aren't we all animals?"

Edwards raised an eyebrow. "Your father had the same reaction, Belle . . . At any rate, MTBE is water soluble and moves very quickly underground."

"Meaning it can enter the water table and contaminate private wells?" Belle asked.

"Exactly . . . After my conversation with your dad, I did some sleuthing on my own and discovered a similar situation—also in New Jersey, also involving a service station, and a report that was 'misplaced' for well over a year. In that instance the tested wells showed levels of MTBE that were between 180 and 545 parts per billion. In one case the level was 940 PPB . . . According to the state's Department of Environmental Protection, the safe drinking level is 20 PPB. New York State has also has problems, one in particular involves an elementary and middle school—"

"Wow," Belle murmured while Rosco posed another question:

"And what did Professor Graham's samples show?"

"That's what I meant when I said I wasn't much help. I told him our lab wasn't equipped for that type of testing, and that he needed to seek the services of a specialized facility."

"And?" Belle asked.

Edwards looked at Rosco. "He'd told me he planned to take them to you."

"Me?"

"He said, 'My new son-in-law is a private detective. He'll know exactly how to handle this.' He seemed very impressed with you."

"But . . . He never met me," Rosco stammered while

Belle's face crinkled in sorrow. After a long moment, she said:
"Those water samples have disappeared."

"Collect some more," was Edwards's decisive reply. "It's easy enough to do . . . I'll help in any way I can, because I think your dad was on to something. And if your suspicion of homicide proves correct, it may be something very big."

"Five hundred and forty-five parts per billion of water . . . nine hundred and forty . . . I can't believe those numbers, Rosco . . ."

They'd left Mercy Hospital, and were returning to the Volsay home. Beyond them the countryside looked radiant and green—and exuberantly healthy.

"And private wells again, how many did Dr. Edwards say were involved?" Rosco asked.

"Two hundred and seventy-seven in one New Jersey county alone—with another fifty-five cases of leaked diesel fuel." Belle shook her head from side to side as she perused the notes Edwards had lent her. "What's scary is the level of secrecy . . . leaks from old tanks that could have been prevented with appropriate monitoring . . . filtration systems that were never installed . . . bureaucratic delays in obtaining scientific testing—"

"Especially when you consider this one report Edwards quotes—the one where New York State residents were warned not to drink from their wells—or even cook or shower at home. That tells me the DEP's really concerned."

She remained quiet for several moments. "I think we've opened a very unwholesome can of worms, Rosco."

"It was your dad who wielded the opener, Belle."

"Yes," she finally added. "Yes. He did." Her voice contained more than a little pride. And a good measure of awe.

Rosco squeezed her hand. "I'm sorry I never met him," he finally said.

"So am I."

After another few minutes of silence, Rosco spoke again. "Okay . . . Given the seriousness of what we've picked up—as well as a *strong* probability of major criminal activity in repressing your father's concerns, I think we need to again address this issue of exhuming his body."

Belle reached over and touched Rosco's arm. "I know what you're going to say . . . If we can make a link between Father's death and the deaths on Oak Lane—" She stopped speaking and shut her eyes. "Murder," she eventually murmured. "I know we've been using that word . . . but I wasn't fully aware of the implications until this minute . . . It's a bizarre notion, Rosco . . . to think of someone plotting to kill my father . . ."

They drove on without talking. At length Belle resumed the discussion. "So . . . So, I guess I should call Al and give my approval for an autopsy . . ." Again, she paused. "But what about looking into Debbie's death, too?"

"Let's start with your dad. If Carlyle discovers traces of any toxic substances, it won't be difficult to get the Kings Creek Police to cooperate." He paused. "But let's not mention our concerns to Mike or Rachel yet. They've got enough on their plates at the moment."

R osco and Belle made a brief detour, stopping at a convenience store to purchase two liter-sized bottles of drinking water. They dumped the contents onto a nearby pot of geraniums, and continued to the Volsay home. Rosco angled the Jeep into the same spot he'd previously used. Rachel's car was parked in front. "That's a lucky break," he said, "They're back from the funeral home."

In the distance they could see Mike Hurley seated on the bench at the end of the street. His slumped position indicated a state of intense depression.

"I feel so sorry for him," Belle said as they stepped from the Jeep. "Perhaps I should go talk with him."

"I'll do it. I think Mike needs a pal more than anything right now. I don't know if I'm the right person, but I'll give it a shot . . . Why don't you try to get a tap water sample from Rachel's house; I'll work on the creek."

"Without Mike noticing?"

"I'll think of something."

Belle tried for a lighthearted smile. "Should we coordinate our watches?"

In answer, Rosco gave her a kiss. Then he stuffed an empty water bottle into a canvas satchel while Belle hid hers in her purse.

She walked to the house. Rachel Volsay opened the door before she had time to knock.

"I heard you pull up . . ." Rachel's eyes pooled with tears as she spoke. "Deb looked wonderful . . . They did a good job. She looked, well, almost . . ."

Belle stepped into the entryway and attempted to place an arm around Mrs. Volsay, but the gesture only served to increase the older woman's bitter unhappiness.

"I'm so sorry," was all Belle could say.

Rachel pressed a tissue against her eyes. "What brings you back here?"

"We weren't sure where the cemetery was," Belle lied. "We didn't want to be late tomorrow and I thought a phone call seemed too impersonal."

"Won't you come in for a moment? I'll make us some tea."

As Belle entered the living room, the front door swung shut, then Rachel Volsay disappeared in the direction of the kitchen. "I'll only be a minute," she called out. "Make yourself comfortable."

"I wonder if I might use your powder room first?"

A disembodied voice provided directions. "Down the hall . . . first door on the right . . ."

Belle found it, and closed and locked the door. She was surprised at her own nervousness. *There's nothing illegal in asking to use the rest room,* she told herself. *Why should Rachel Volsay suspect me of doing anything underhanded?*

Belle examined the room: a petite avocado-colored sink, a narrow shower stall hidden by a striped green and white curtain, a plush "commode cover" on the toilet seat. Pulling the empty bottle from her purse, she tried to place it under the sink tap but found the container too large. She moved to the shower stall, attempting to fill it there, but only about seventy percent of the water entered the bottle's neck while the rest ran down her arms or misted against her dress. "Darn it!" she groused under her breath as she reached for a paper hand towel, found it inadequate, then turned the hem of her skirt inside out, sopping up additional beads of water—all the while growing more and more apprehensive and agitated. Beads of sweat started up on her forehead; the minutes seemed to stretch into a good half hour. Finally, she jammed the bottle back into her purse, flushed the toilet for effect, and reentered the living room. Rachel was waiting there with a plate of cookies and a tray containing sugar and milk. She pointed to an object on the floor near her feet. It was a small squarish valise covered in blue Naugahyde. "I assume this is what you've been hunting for."

"W hy did you come back?" Mike almost glared at Rosco as he spoke. "We didn't expect to see you again until tomorrow." Then his shoulders sagged deeper, and his spine curved forward. "Sorry . . . That's rude of me. But I just . . . I just . . ."

Rosco touched his shoulder. "Belle forgot something in Rachel's house. And I spotted you sitting down here . . . and, well, you looked like you could use a friend."

Mike didn't answer. Instead he stared at the creek's far bank.

After an uncomfortable silence, Rosco tried again. "So . . . I guess you'll be heading back to Florida when . . . this is all over?"

"My emergency leave's up on Thursday . . ." The words were a monotone mumble.

"Right . . ." Rosco struggled for words. "I, uh, really admire you guys . . . You give up a lot. I hope you're aware of how much your work is appreciated by people."

Mike drew in a tortured breath. "To be honest, it'll be good to get out of New Jersey—and back on the water. I need to air out my brain . . . Decide where I go from here . . ."

"You're lucky you like being on the water," Rosco said

after another weighty pause. "But I guess that's what attracted you to the Guard in the first place, huh?"

Mike nodded once, but didn't offer a more detailed response.

"Florida," Rosco mused. "Most of your operations must be INS related? Illegal aliens, that sort of thing?"

Mike shook his head. "Not me . . . I'm drug interdiction. We try to get the stuff before it hits the States. Fishing boats, small pleasure craft: They're the usual means of transport . . . Texas used to be the main place of entry, but Florida's catching up."

A ping went off in Rosco's brain: *Drug interdiction, fishing boats, pleasure craft,* but he ignored the warning, instead, continuing with an affable: "That's a lot of coastline to cover."

"More than any state in the Union."

"But you're only down there temporarily, right?"

"Yup . . . My home base is in Bayonne. We run the same type of ops in New York Harbor. And on the Hudson River . . ." He sighed again.

"Dangerous job," Rosco finally said.

"If there are drugs aboard . . . sure, it can be . . ." Then Mike changed the subject, gazing wistfully down into the creek. "Deb used to catch sunnies here when she was a kid . . ."

"Is that so?"

"No fish in it now, though."

"I wonder why?" Rosco said. "The water's clear as glass." He climbed down the slope to the water's edge, crouched and placed his hand into the flowing stream. "You're right," he called back, "there doesn't seem to be much in the way of marine life." He glanced over his shoulder; the bench and Mike were completely hidden from view.

Rosco pulled the empty bottle from his sack, twisted off the cap, and plunged the bottle under the surface. The gurgling sound disappeared beneath the noise of shallow water rushing over the rocks. Nonetheless the bottle seemed to take forever to fill. He tilted it from side to side in an effort to expedite the process.

"Picking up where Ted left off?"

Rosco jerked upward to find Mike staring down at him. "Ahh . . . As a matter of fact, yes . . . Yes, I am . . . So . . . You were aware of what Ted was doing?"

In answer, Mike turned and stalked back to the bench. Rosco capped off the bottle and climbed back up the creek bank, repeating his question. "Did Ted tell you why he was taking water samples? Because I was under the impression that he wasn't discussing—"

"Yes. Yes. He told me." The words were bitten and hard.

"Ah . . ." Rosco again fumbled for words. *If Mike was aware of Ted Graham's efforts, then Debbie should have known also, meaning the possibility that the hit-and-run was more than accidental was now even stronger.*

But before Rosco could pose another question, Mike added a subdued: "Deb . . . She didn't know anything about what Ted was doing . . ."

Rosco continued to stare. "Meaning that you . . . that you and Professor Graham kept his research on MTBE contamination a secret? Meaning that Rachel's also in the dark."

"Right . . . He didn't want to scare them before he had better data."

Rosco could only shake his head. "How could you not talk to your wife?"

"I don't want to discuss this, okay?" Mike almost yelled. "I mean, maybe I did the wrong thing. Maybe Ted did the wrong thing. But it's too late now, isn't it? Nothing's going to bring my Debbie back. It's over."

The fierceness in the tone told Rosco to back off. He took a deep breath. "You're right. Nothing will change what happened. But Ted was trying to help Debbie . . . help her family—"

"I don't want to talk about her, *okay?*"

Rosco moved to sit next to him, but stopped. Instead he placed the water bottle on the bench and crossed his arms over his chest.

"Mike, I know how broken up you're feeling. I do . . . But don't you see, the companies that cause this type of pollution—in this case, Savante—have an enormous amount to lose. If they need to keep a secret, keep people quiet, what does it matter if innocent people—"

Mike jumped up. "I told you, I don't want to listen to this! And I wish Ted had never stuck his nose in here where it didn't belong. All this hero stuff. Change the world? That's not me. That's never going to be me. Besides, what difference does it make anymore?"

"I understand your feelings, Mike. Believe me . . . But it *does* make a difference . . . You can't bring Debbie back. But you can help other people. You especially . . . Coast Guard personnel. A good-looking guy facing a terrible loss . . . You have a level of credibility, of trust and honesty, that isn't afforded to most people . . . If you don't want to talk about it now, fine. But don't turn your back on this one, Mike. There's too much at stake . . . Besides, you know how much the media loves those DEA ops you guys do . . . criminals brought to justice? This is just another battle front—"

"DEA? DEA? Where do you get that? I'm not some . . .

some agent. I run drug *tests*. I test bags of white powder to determine if they're cocaine, heroin . . . whatever. That's what I do. I told you I'm not a hero, and I'm not some secret agent waving a gun. I'm a chemical engineer."

CHAPTER

35

"You're a chemical engineer?" Rosco made no attempt to hide his surprise. His brain jumped to his discussion with Belle: *The obscure crossword puzzle answers, the HCN/prussic acid/hydrocyanic acid debate—and her insistence that only a chemical engineer would be familiar with those terms.*

"Then it was *you* who constructed the puzzles." Rosco stared dumbfounded at Mike. "And sent them to Belle . . ."

Mike remained silent, so Rosco continued, "But how were you able to transmit them from Belize?"

"I don't know what you're talking about—"

"THREE MAY KEEP A SECRET IF TWO OF THEM—" Rosco was interrupted by the ringing of the cell phone clipped to his waist. "Arrrgh," he groaned. "I have to take this . . ." He paced rapidly along the creek bank until he was out of earshot, then flipped open his phone. "Rosco Polycrates."

"This is John Markoe, Mr. Polycrates. I apologize for not

getting back to you sooner, but my Amtrak schedule can be erratic—"

"Yes . . . John . . . Thanks for returning my call." Rosco spoke slowly and carefully, using the time to refocus. "There are a couple of points I hope you can clear up."

"Shoot."

"This is back on August thirteenth, the day you discovered Dr. Graham's body—?"

"Yes, sir. I'm not likely to forget that one. No, siree-bob—"

"My wife and I believe he was in possession of a blue box— or an unusual type of suitcase. Does that ring a bell?"

There was a pause, then Markoe said, "That's a tough one; I'm not sure I can recall exactly . . ."

"We're fairly certain he had it when he boarded the train, but it didn't appear among the effects forwarded from Boston."

"No . . . Sorry . . . I can't say I remember seeing anything like that. That doesn't mean he *didn't* have luggage matching that description, but you'd think I would have seen it if he had it—"

"I see. Well, thank you—"

"Now, that other message you left: wanting to know what the gentleman was drinking? That I can tell you."

"And . . . ?"

"It was peach nectar."

Rosco glanced back at the bench and Mike Hurley. "You're sure of that?"

"Absolutely. See, I thought it was a little odd, because we don't sell that type of fruit juice on board. I mean, well, maybe it's not so odd . . . Now, obviously the professor could have brought it with him . . . Myself, I'm a peach nectar junkie. That's why I remember it."

"Is there a possibility the empty container might still be around?"

"I'd sincerely doubt it. The police left it on the train when they removed the body, so I tossed it."

Rosco thought for a second. "You don't recall anyone sitting with my wife's father, do you?"

"The train was fairly crowded that day. I'm sure someone occupied the seat—at least for part of the ride . . . But to be honest, I couldn't provide any type of description—"

"Could it have been a man wearing a Yankees hat?"

Another hearty chuckle. "Those hats are all over the train this time of year! Everyone in the world's a Yankees fan by the time Labor Day rolls around."

Rosco resisted the temptation to say, *Don't count on it,* instead closing with, "I appreciate your help, John."

He snapped the phone shut and clipped it back onto his belt on the right side. *Prussic acid smells like peach nectar,* he thought as his brain leapt to the crosswords and Mike. *A chemical engineer* . . . Instinctively Rosco tapped the left side of his belt, expecting to find a .32 caliber pistol, but he found nothing. He wasn't licensed to carry a gun in New Jersey; he'd left it in Massachusetts. He squared his shoulders and walked back along the creek.

"That was an interesting call," he said as he approached. "John Markoe, an Amtrak conductor . . . his memory's sharp as a tack. He was aboard when Professor Graham died . . . It seems he recalls a strong odor of something that smells like peach nectar."

Mike brought his eyes up to meet Rosco's. "Look, I already told you: I don't want to discuss this subject anymore. What happened to Ted Graham has nothing to do with me."

Rosco nodded. "Well, all I'm asking for is a little help here . . . You just told me that you're a chemical engineer. Now, in a discussion with the Medical Examiner up in New-castle, he ran through a number of poisons that could have been used to . . . Well, substances that might produce an *appearance* of heart failure. One of them was hydrocyanic acid, also known as prussic acid or hydrogen cyanide . . . Seems like it smells a lot like peach nectar."

"What are you getting at?"

"In your estimation, is that a substance that can kill peo-ple?"

"I suppose."

"A good chance, would you say? I mean, given a large dosage, easy to camouflage, and all that?"

"I'd have to look it up."

Rosco nodded thoughtfully. "All right . . . Well, let me ask you something else. When Ted died, you and Deb . . . you were in Florida, right? Eh, it's a matter of record."

Mike remained icily still for a moment, then finally said, "No. I was up here. I told you, my work brings me up North a lot." His voice grew softer. "Debbie was in Sanibel."

"But she flew up to see her aunt right after Belle left Florida?"

"That's right."

"Because she wanted to find Ted's missing notebook."

Mike started visibly. "What do you mean?"

"Rachel told Belle that Deb looked high and low for it . . . turned the house upside down—"

"But that doesn't make any sense . . . I mean, she told me . . . she said it was his bird-watching book. Why would she need to get it back?"

"Maybe because she knew all about Ted's research into

MTBE contamination. Maybe because she knew how crucial his discoveries were. Maybe she believed there was a case against Savante."

Mike didn't reply. He shut his eyes. A long sigh seemed to shake his frame.

"So, here we have a peculiar situation," Rosco continued. "A husband whose wife's boss shared potentially dangerous data with him—with the stipulation that the data be kept secret. And a wife who was keeping the *same* information hidden from her husband. Doesn't that seem foolish to you? Two people who 'told each other everything,' according to you?"

Again, Mike made no reply.

"Now, my guess is that Debbie was *deeply* involved with Ted's efforts regarding her family and the Tollivers—"

"But she never . . . She never—"

"She never confided those concerns to you?"

Mike's head sank lower. "No."

Rosco remained silent a moment. "You may be interested to know that John Markoe just told me he remembered a guy sitting next to Ted—a guy wearing a Yankees cap . . . He said he can provide a description. I told him to contact the Boston Police." Rosco paused, waiting for a reaction that didn't come. "He also said that the police in Boston are holding several items in sealed evidence bags. One of which is an empty individual-sized can of peach nectar—which is a fruit juice Amtrak doesn't sell in its café car."

"Why didn't she tell me?" was all Mike said in response.

"You mean about the data Ted was collecting on the MTBE situation?"

Mike nodded. Once.

"The data you discovered when you took that same notebook from Ted on August thirteenth?" Rosco continued to gaze down at Mike's bent form. "How much did Carl Oclen pay you to kill Ted Graham?"

Mike didn't make a move.

"Dr. Graham was trying to help you, Mike. You and Debbie and Rachel—"

"Help us?" Mike's neck snapped upward. "Help us? Since when does stealing a man's wife away from him constitute help? *Oh, Ted's so smart, Mike . . . He's so clever . . . He's like a genius . . . blah, blah, blah . . .* She never stopped talking about him. Not once."

Rosco could do nothing but stare in disbelief. "Wait a minute," he said. "You mean Oclen—?"

"I don't know any damn Oclen."

"So, Oclen had nothing to do with—?"

Mike's face had turned an ugly red. He glared up at Rosco, who was left stammering a dumbfounded:

"You mean *you* murdered Theodore Graham because you thought that he and Debbie . . . ? But he was close to forty years older than she was—"

"Since when doesn't that happen? Old guys preying on younger—"

"No. Not in this case. I'd put money on it."

"I know . . . I know that now . . ."

Rosco shook his head while Mike's voice exploded:

"The damn notebook! I thought it contained . . . I don't know . . . something incriminating . . . love notes or something . . . but all I found were references to contaminated wells, diesel leaks, people getting sick, people dying—" Mike's voice broke; his chest shook with a soundless sob. "I thought he was taking my wife away from me . . . But Debbie . . . Why didn't she tell me what they were up to?"

Rosco waited a long moment before speaking again. "What about the train tickets? The rental car agreement?"

"I didn't want anyone snooping around New Jersey—"

"So you stole the blue box, too?"

"It's in the house."

"And the peach nectar?"

"Deb told me about that . . . when she first started working there . . . *Ted's favorite beverage. Oh, he can't get enough,* she used to say . . . It wasn't hard to add the HCN." Mike put his fists against his head. His grief was so absolute, he seemed incapable of thought or action.

Finally, Rosco said, "I've got to take you in, Mike. You know that, don't you?"

Mike stood, his body hunched and hopeless. "I know."

Rosco stepped up behind him, placing a hand on his shoulder.

Without warning, Mike whipped his left elbow skyward, slamming it into Rosco's ribcage, then plowed into him shoulder to shoulder. Rosco pitched backward toward the creek, regained his balance at the edge of the embankment, but Mike was already on him. He landed a hard right to Rosco's jaw, and sent him sprawling down the bank into the shallow water.

It took Rosco a good thirty seconds to lift his head from the rocky stream bed, then he half crawled, half stumbled up to dry land. When he got there, Mike was already opening the driver's side door to Rachel's car. By the time Rosco pulled his cell phone from his belt, Mike was gone.

Rosco punched in 9-1-1 and provided a description of the car and driver to the dispatcher—along with Mike's name. His friends on the police force would have to confront their own sense of duty—and allegiance. Rosco trusted they were professionals. He then knelt to wipe the mud from his soaking trousers and walked toward the Volsay house . . . And Belle.

CHAPTER

36

Rosco's cell phone beeped with a tone that sent shivers down the spines of every customer seated in the subterranean cocktail lounge of Princeton's Nassau Inn. Those perched at the horseshoe-shaped bar turned and shot contemptuous stares toward the corner table where he sat with Belle and Marie-Claude, while the muted conversations of other patrons ceased altogether as they swung in their padded leather chairs to ascertain the identity of the low-class individual who'd broken one of the cardinal—but unspoken—rules of their private domain. Cell phones, beepers, and other outward manifestations of the "information age" were not welcome in this firmly antediluvian haunt.

Rosco stood and whispered. "I think I'll take this one elsewhere."

Belle watched him cross the oak-beamed tavern room and slip upstairs to the hotel's lobby while Marie-Claude leaned toward her and uttered a sotto-voce: "Your husband is a wise man, *ma chère* . . . Sometimes, the walls, they have very sharp ears. Perhaps you can understand why I appear to speak in non sequiturs when in my office at the university." Then she sat back and smiled for all the world to see. She was the picture of an academic entertaining out-of-town guests. "You know, this building dates to 1756 . . . Many *clandestin* gatherings must have occurred here since that time, wouldn't you agree? In fact, I read of one such *conversation* in December of 1776—shortly before your General Washington crossed the Delaware River . . . I believe we French were involved in some *petit* fashion . . ."

Belle nodded although she felt trapped in Marie-Claude's typically circuitous conversation. *Let's cut to the chase!* her brain railed, but her companion merely perused her glass of white wine. "So, you see, *chérie,* we inhabit a secretive *région* . . . Life and death: always a *balance* . . ."

Belle also stared at her glass. The questions she most yearned to ask concerned her father, but what she chose to say next was an oblique: "Is this Woody's life you're speaking of?"

Marie-Claude nodded almost imperceptibly. "And François."

"You suggested that he's still alive?"

Marie-Claude tossed her hair. "For your—shall we say—well-being, these are issues better left unclarified. Franklin Mossback is dead . . . but a name is merely *un nom* . . . What did Shakespeare say? 'A rose by any other name'?"

Belle gazed at her searchingly while Marie-Claude lowered her eyes. When she resumed speaking, her voice was the merest whisper.

"Do not think of me as a *horrible* person; do not assume that your father and I were carrying on *une affair de coeur.* The picture we presented was only that—a picture . . . *Theodore* was a friend only . . . and a sometime . . . well, a transporter of information—as we all are in our own way. You bring me news today of a man named Mike Hurley. I tell you . . . other things . . ." Then the whisper grew even fainter. "Make no mistake, *chère belle,* in this war on drugs, government officials on all sides are involved . . . Some of these persons are good; some are not." She looked up. "Ahh, yes. You assume that all secret agents are virile young men equipped with numerous stealthy weapons. You are wrong . . . The most effective operative may be a dottering old lady in a bookstore."

Belle's gray eyes grew thoughtful. *What to believe of Marie-Claude's fantastic tale of secret informants and government agents? What not to believe?* "So, you're telling me that my father never boarded an airplane for Belize?"

Marie-Claude laughed. "*Sacré-Cœur!* Not our Teddy. He purchased the tickets . . . Nothing more need be said."

"And *Wooden Shoe?* The boat Father purchased?"

Marie-Claude gazed across the room. "A paper trail—"

Belle sighed in baffled frustration. "I can't fathom the idea of my father being some type of operative."

Marie-Claude placed her hand on Belle's wrist, but Belle pulled her arm away. "Ah, *ma belle,* your *cher papa*'s involvement was the barest minimum . . . A name on a ticket and on an ownership document, an infrequent visit to see the wife of a friend . . . With that, we end our discussion. Your *papa* would not wish to place you in peril." Marie-Claude Araignée suddenly glanced across the tavern. "So! *Bon!* Here is your dashing husband returning."

The two women remained silent as Rosco approached and dropped into his chair.

"That was the Kings Creek Police Department. They've

arrested Mike Hurley. Al Lever and the FBI have been notified."

No one spoke for several minutes. Finally Belle said, "I had
assumed that apprehending my father's killer would please
me. I guess the illusion was that it would bring him back—
that he and I could make amends . . . A fairy-tale ending."

Rosco took her hand. "The police in Kings Creek also
informed me they found the car that struck Debbie Hurley.
It's owned by a local with a history of DUI convictions; he
claims he doesn't remember anything, but witnesses at a bar
he frequented have confirmed the time he lit out—"

"So, it was an accident?" Marie-Claude asked.

Rosco's answer was stony. "If you call drinking until your
brain is too impaired to function, and then driving an automobile, an *accident* . . . From my point of view, the only accident is that Deborah Hurley happened to be crossing the
street when this idiot careened around the corner—"

"At least her death wasn't orchestrated by Carl Oclen,"
Belle interjected.

"She's still pretty damn dead," was Rosco's bitter reply.

"Ah, yes . . . Savante," Marie-Claude added slowly. "We
were so certain this Oclen was *responsable* for your father's
murder—"

"We?"

Marie-Claude stared enigmatically at Belle. She said
nothing.

"Was it Woody who constructed the puzzles?" Belle asked
after another edgy moment.

"No. I cannot answer that."

"Was it Franklin?"

"Please . . ."

"Was it you?"

"I am not at liberty to discuss this."

"But the reference to hydrocyanic acid?"

Marie-Claude laughed. "A guess . . . But perhaps not an uneducated one. Adding the substance to a container of peach nectar would not be an insurmountable task . . . Surely everyone knew of his foolish addiction."

Belle closed her eyes. Marie-Claude continued:

"This is a type of crime not uncommon in countries where the drinking of sweetened fruit juices is an everyday practice."

It was Rosco who spoke after another moment of silence. "Well, whatever the mistaken assumptions as to who murdered Professor Graham, the final result is that the Savante Group has a lot of answering to do—to Rachel, the Tolliver family, and all the residents in the Oak Lane region."

"Ahhh," Marie-Claude said with true sadness. "But if only you had been able to connect this *Monsieur* Oclen to the first two word games you received . . . Perhaps events would have turned out differently."

Belle shook her head. "Even if we'd noticed SAVANTE GROUP INC running on the diagonal of the *"It Hurts So . . ."* crossword, it wouldn't have helped. Debbie Hurley would still have been in the wrong place at the wrong time."

Marie-Claude stood. "I am afraid I must leave you now. I have a lecture to prepare." She placed her purse on the table, opened it, removed a folded piece of paper, and handed it to Belle. "Perhaps this will explain the larger picture, *un philosophie, peut-être . . .*" Her smile turned serious. "*Ma chère,* always remember that your father was a remarkable man." She lifted her purse and draped the strap over her shoulder. "*Au revoir.*

We shall meet again, *non?*" Then she strolled upstairs and out of sight.

Rosco turned to Belle. "Did she just wink at the bartender, or was that my imagination?"

"It wasn't your imagination."

Belle lifted the piece of paper from the table, and unfolded it.

"What is it?" Rosco asked.

"Another puzzle . . . *Once the Game Is Over . . .*"

Across

1. Despots
6. Throughout, in music
12. Boat in Bayonne
14. Time immemorial
15. Serve a soda; Midwest style
16. Least strict
17. Wardrobe
18. Certain Middle Easterner
20. End of quip, part 1
22. Ms. Charisse
25. Dry
26. Latin one
27. Pervasive quality
29. Defeat
32. 22-Across, e.g.
34. End of quip, part 2
38. Crib item
39. Gem state
40. Yen
41. Agcy. created in 1933
42. Weather__
46. "__Done Him Wrong"
47. End of quip, part 3
50. Strips
52. Certain salt or ester
53. Mysterious
56. Evicts
58. FBI datum
59. Thrive
60. Swaps
61. Water__

Down

1. More tense
2. Judy Garland film
3. Game maker
4. Write once more
5. __Paulo
6. Cheers!
7. Old oath
8. Some serapes
9. "The Raven" author
10. Literary monogram
11. N.J. time
12. Nobel winner of '54
13. Quits, Southern style
15. Butter portions
19. Collection of information
21. Craig:Peter—Stevens:__
23. Word of disgust
24. Eins und zwei
28. Scottish alder tree
30. Bud
31. Female sheep
32. AKA to the BBB
33. Sigh of relief
34. Cycle starter?
35. Boater and beanie
36. Engrave
37. Harem rooms
41. Common article
43. Humbles
44. Marker downer
45. Former husbands and wives
47. Lock
48. Detest
49. Bull__Party
51. Pot sweetener
53. Likely

ONCE THE GAME IS OVER . . .

54. Monopoly purchase; abbr.
55. Langley crew; abbr.
57. Agcy. created in 1975

The Answers

FATHER'S DAY

1 R	2 A	3 H	░	4 W	5 I	6 T	░	7 O	8 U	9 R	░	10 E	11 R	12 R
13 U	R	E	░	14 A	D	O	░	15 A	P	E	░	16 T	E	A
17 B	R	18 A	D	L	E	Y	░	19 K	E	20 N	N	E	D	Y
21 S	I	R	E	D	░	░	22 P	I	N	E	R	░	░	░
23 I	V	Y	C	24 O	25 V	E	R	E	D	W	A	L	L	26 S
29 N	E	E	░	30 A	M	O	R	░	░	░	░	31 E	E	L
░	░	░	32 C	33 A	L	I	F	░	34 E	35 S	36 P	A	N	A
37 T	38 H	39 E	O	D	O	R	E	40 A	G	R	A	H	A	M
41 R	O	T	T	E	R	░	42 S	T	E	A	L	░	░	░
43 A	A	U	░	░	44 S	S	T	S	░	░	░	45 J	46 A	47 I
48 P	R	I	49 N	50 C	E	T	O	N	52 T	53 I	G	E	R	S
░	░	░	54 E	L	G	A	R	░	░	55 M	A	R	I	O
56 S	57 T	58 E	W	A	R	T	░	59 M	60 A	D	I	S	O	N
61 L	O	T	░	62 S	E	E	░	63 S	T	U	░	64 E	S	T
65 Y	E	S	░	66 S	T	S	░	67 G	E	E	░	68 Y	O	O

SIGNS OF THE TIMES

1 A	2 S	3 P		4 F	5 A	6 T		7 P	8 T	9 A		10 O	11 S	12 S
13 B	A	G	14 P	I	P	E		15 A	Y	N	16 I	N	G	S
17 S	P	A	R	R	E	D		18 Y	I	G	L	E	T	S
		19 E	stop	S		20 B	E	stop	U	S				
21 K	22 E	23 M	P	T		24 A	D	E	S		25 L	26 A	27 G
28 U	R	I	stop	29 I	C	30 R	M	N		31 F	I	N	E
32 L	A	S	S	O	E	S	M	A		34 I	N	T	O
	35 H	O	N	E	stop	36 I	N	37 I	O	N	S		
38 A	39 L	A	I		40 E	X	E	S	N	E	E	41 D	42 S
43 D	I	P	L	44 D	R	E		45 L	A	stop	E	R	A
46 D	E	S		47 T	E	A	R		48 S	T	D	I	E
		49 P	E	A	T	S		50 A	L	I				
51 A	52 L	53 F	R	E	D	O		54 P	L	A	C	55 K	56 E	57 T
58 L	O	stop	E	N	E	R		59 C	O	N	S	U	M	E
60 E	T	S		61 S	R	S		62 S	E	T		63 R	S	T

IT HURTS SO . . .

¹C	²I	³R			⁴H	⁵A	⁶S	⁷H		⁸O	⁹C	¹⁰H	¹¹O	
¹²R	N	A	¹³S		¹⁴E	C	H	O		¹⁵R	E	E	S	¹⁶E
¹⁷A	G	I	O		¹⁸T	H	E	B	¹⁹A	D	S	E	E	D
²⁰B	A	D	P	²¹O	E	T	S		²²S	E	S	T	E	T
			²³P	U	R				²⁴I	A	N			
²⁵D	²⁶I	²⁷N	E	R	O		²⁸B	²⁹A	D	L	A	³⁰N	³¹D	³²S
³³W	O	O	D			³⁴R	O	L	E	S		³⁵O	W	E
³⁶E	N	E			³⁷D	O	G	E	S			³⁸T	E	L
³⁹E	I	N		⁴⁰B	U	L	G	E			⁴¹J	I	L	L
⁴²B	A	D	⁴³G	I	R	L	S		⁴⁴T	⁴⁵A	U	N	T	S
			⁴⁶U	G	H			⁴⁷I	N	D				
⁴⁸E	⁴⁹J	⁵⁰E	C	T	A		⁵¹B	⁵²A	D	T	A	⁵³S	⁵⁴T	⁵⁵E
⁵⁶B	A	D	C	O	M	⁵⁷P	A	N	Y		⁵⁸E	V	E	R
⁵⁹S	A	D	I	E		⁶⁰E	T	T	U		⁶¹A	G	A	R
	⁶²B	O	S	S		⁶³C	H	I	P		⁶⁴S	S	S	

WORDS TO THE WISE

Grid answers:

- GABS . . TAG . SMU
- SLATE / RACE / ALAS
- ALTAR / ATEE / PINE
- THREE MAY KEEP A
- BISECTOR / BRITS
- EMP / TEN / TAE / NEO
- NEON / GARROTED
- SECRET IF TWO
- PITHLESS / LAGS
- EGO / ODE / ERA / BLY
- UNFIT / FRANKLIN
- OF THE MARE DEAD
- ERIC / MAKO / RAZED
- TECH / ICER / ENERO
- ADE / TED / ERSE

Hidden quote: THREE MAY KEEP A SECRET IF TWO OF THEM ARE DEAD — FRANKLIN

USE YOUR HEAD!

¹T	²I	³P	█	⁴P	⁵O	⁶S	█	⁷A	⁸S	⁹T	¹⁰I	¹¹N
¹²W	A	R	█	¹³T	U	B	E	¹⁴D	█	¹⁵L	U	C	I	O
¹⁶O	N	E	█	¹⁷O	B	O	E	S	█	¹⁸O	N	A	I	R
█	¹⁹S	²⁰K	U	L	L	M	O	U	²¹N	T	A	I	N
²²A	²³S	S	I	S	I	█	²⁴R	S	A	█
²⁵S	K	U	L	L	C	²⁶A	²⁷P	²⁸L	O	N	²⁹D	³⁰O	³¹N
³²P	A	R	L	E	█	³³T	I	A	³⁴S	█	³⁵I	N	E
³⁶I	T	I	S	█	³⁷O	C	R	█	³⁸A	S	E	A
³⁹R	E	N	█	⁴⁰A	I	O	C	█	⁴¹I	N	C	U	R
⁴²E	D	G	⁴³I	⁴⁴N	G	█	⁴⁵T	⁴⁶H	E	S	K	U	L	L
█	⁴⁷N	O	R	█	⁴⁸V	O	L	S	A	Y
⁴⁹S	⁵⁰K	⁵¹U	L	L	A	⁵²N	⁵³D	⁵⁴B	O	N	E	S
⁵⁵H	O	O	I	E	█	⁵⁶B	U	I	L	T	█	⁵⁷I	⁵⁸S	⁵⁹H
⁶⁰O	C	L	E	N	█	⁶¹A	B	O	V	O	█	⁶²O	R	C
⁶³E	S	A	U	S	█	⁶⁴S	S	E	█	⁶⁵N	O	N

ONCE THE GAME IS OVER . . .

	¹T	²S	³A	⁴R	⁵S		⁶S	⁷E	⁸M	⁹P	¹⁰R	¹¹E
	¹²B	A	T	T	E	¹³A	U		¹⁴A	G	E	O	L	D
¹⁵P	O	U	R	A	P	O	P		¹⁶L	A	X	E	S	T
¹⁷A	T	T	I	R	E		¹⁸S	¹⁹A	U	D	I	
²⁰T	H	E	K	I	N	²¹G	A	N	D		²²C	²³Y	²⁴D
²⁵S	E	R	E		²⁶U	N	A		²⁷A	U	R	A	²⁸A
		²⁹U	³⁰P	³¹E	N	D		³²D	³³A	N	C	E	R
³⁴T	³⁵H	³⁶E	P	A	W	N	³⁷G	O	B	A	C	K	I	N
³⁸R	A	T	T	L	E		³⁹I	D	A	H	O	
⁴⁰I	T	C	H		⁴¹T	V	A		⁴²V	⁴³A	⁴⁴N	⁴⁵E
	⁴⁶S	H	E		⁴⁷T	H	E	S	A	M	E	B	O	X
		⁵⁰B	⁵¹A	R	E	S		⁵²B	O	R	A	T	E
⁵³A	⁵⁴R	⁵⁵C	A	N	E		⁵⁶U	⁵⁷N	H	O	U	S	E	S
⁵⁸P	R	I	N	T	S		⁵⁹P	R	O	S	P	E	R
⁶⁰T	R	A	D	E	S		⁶¹C	R	E	S	S	